The 117 American planes continued their flight. Luckily, they had not met any Jap fighters out of Lae, Madang, or Gasmata. And now it was 0745 hours and the US air formation was approaching the coast of Wewak.

Both fighter pilots and bomber crews grew uneasy. All of them knew that the Japanese had based more than 300 planes on their four Wewak airdromes. The skies over Wewak could be black with enemy fighters waiting for the Americans.

Col. Don Hall looked at his watch. Fifteen minutes from target. Hall stiffened and felt perspiration dampen his face. The colonel was a veteran pilot, yet he was obviously nervous, unsure of what lay ahead.

Other American airmen felt uneasy, too. Even veterans like Lt. Col. Meryl Smith, Capt. Tom McGuire, Capt. John Welch, and Maj. Jerry Johnson. Newer men to combat no doubt felt even more fear. They had heard enough about Wewak and just the number — 300 planes — had been sufficient to put the fear of God in their souls . . .

VALOR
IN THE SKY

BY LAWRENCE CORTESI

ZEBRA BOOKS
KENSINGTON PUBLISHING CORP.

ZEBRA BOOKS

are published by

Kensington Publishing Corp.
475 Park Avenue South
New York, NY 10016

First printing: April 1985

Printed in the United States of America

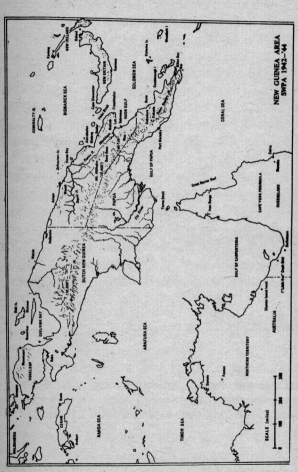

The New Guinea area battlefield just before the Wewak air offensives.

CHAPTER ONE

In the Southwest Pacific war, the six month Papuan Campaign between July of 1942 and February of 1943 had left both sides spent. Although Gen. Douglas MacArthur's Allied forces had finally wiped out the Japanese Nankai Shitai Force on Buna, the Americans and Australians had suffered miserably in the campaign. Besides battle casualties, the Allied troops had suffered from malaria, dysentery, and other jungle diseases. Thus MacArthur was in no position to take immediate advantage of his Buna victory.

During the next several months, the Japanese and Allies engaged in only minor skirmishes, while they rested and rebuilt their ground forces for a new major campaign in the Southwest Pacific. Both sides, however, had learned a valuable lesson in the Papuan Campaign—air power was vital to win battles in the hostile jungles of New Guinea.

The Japanese eyed the major Allied bases at Dobodura and Port Moresby: knock out these bases and the Allied troops could not make further advances in New Guinea. In fact, by reducing American and Australian air power, the Japanese themselves could launch a counteroffensive in New Guinea to retake Buna. In turn, the Allies looked at the major Japanese airbase in Wewak. If the US 5th Air Force could neutralize this stronghold, the Allies could begin a new offensive in New Guinea.

Both sides turned to air power to support a new operation in the Southwest Pacific war. The side which won control of the skies over the Bismarck Archipelago could win the next major battle in Papua, New Guinea.

Gen. Hitoshi Imamura, CinC of the Japanese 8th Area Forces with headquarters at Rabaul, had been massing thousands of troops, countless tons of supplies, and hordes of planes on that formidable Southwest Pacific stronghold in New Britain. By late June of 1943, he felt satisfied. He now had the means to chase the Allies out of northern Papua and recapture Buna.

Rabaul was a strategic base in the Southwest Pacific. Nippon troops had taken this excellent New Britain seaport from Australian troops in February of 1942 and since that time, they had continually worked to improve port and airfield facilities.

The two harbors, Simpson Harbor and Blanche Bay, could now hold an entire merchant and battle fleet, up to a hundred capital ships. The four airdromes could house up to 400 aircraft, while the oil storage tanks and warehouses could hold countless tons of fuel and supplies. The huge base generally housed up to 50,000 troops. Half of them were sailor, soldier, and airmen maintenance and supply personnel who tended to ships, planes, and combat units that passed through Rabaul. The others were transient infantrymen, airmen, or sailors who would move on to the fighting zones in New Guinea and the Solomons.

Rabaul had been the headquarters for the Japanese 8th Area Forces for more than a year, and cadre sailors and soldiers stationed here had grown accustomed to seeing VIPs move about the huge base. General Imamura as well as high ranking generals and admirals on the 8th Area Forces staff often moved about the Rabaul complex so that the common soldier and sailor hardly looked twice any more when they saw the shiny sedans of high rank with their insignia flags fluttering from vehicle fenders.

But if a high ranking officer who was not normally stationed here suddenly came to Rabaul, he aroused curiosity among the men. Such a visitor usually meant that a new operational plan was in the works.

On the sunny morning of 27 June 1943 two Betty bombers landed at Rapapo Drome, under escort from twelve Zeros. Japanese shore parties on the docks or soldiers in supply depots had begun the day's work. Service men on the airfield stopped their labors temporarily and stared at the group of officers who alighted from the planes. Some of the troops recognized Gen. Hatazo Adachi, the CinC of the 18th Army in New Guinea who had often visited Rabaul. Adachi's hard, sober face left a vivid impression on anyone who saw the general's countenance. Adachi rarely smiled, nor did he frequently display emotion: not pleasure, not satisfaction, not hate, not anything. A perpetual scowl had seemingly cemented itself on his round face, and his dark eyes always looked like two icy marbles.

The other two officers who alighted from the Betty, a brigadier general and a vice admiral, were not as well known, although a few of the men at Rapapo Drome recognized the army officer as Yamusi Arisue, commander of the Japanese 7th Air Division in New Guinea. As the trio of officers ducked inside two gleaming black sedans with aides, the men about the field conjectured about the identity of the third visitor, the admiral. Somebody finally remembered and gasped. This was Takeo Tanaka, the noted escort fleet commander of the old Tokyo Express fame in the Solomons — Tanaka the Tenacious. The admiral specialized in escorting troop and supply convoys as he had done for more than six months during the vicious Solomons battles.

Tanaka's appearance in Rabaul surely meant that a new invasion would soon be going on somewhere. No doubt the Imperial General Staff had some new war strategy in mind after several months of relative idleness. And this suspected operation would likely take place in New Guinea. Why else would Adachi and Arisue come here?

The troops and sailors of the Rabaul garrison knew well enough that all major activity in New Guinea had abated since the defeat at Buna in

February. Only minor skirmishes between Australian and Japanese troops in the jungles between Buna and Salamaua now prevailed on that island battlefield; or the Allied and Japanese air forces carried out routine air strikes against each other's New Guinea bases or each other's shipping in the waters of the Bismarck Archipelago. Apparently, Imamura had now decided to begin a new campaign. And why not? Rabaul was jammed with planes and crammed with combat troops. Warehouses and oil tanks bulged with countless tons of supplies, ammunition, and fuel.

The three officers and their aides who had just landed in the Bettys now rode leisurely in the pair of black limousines. The vehicles followed the Simpson Road that skirted the harbor and the vehicles soon arrived at the 8th Area Forces headquarters complex. The limousines drove up a long driveway and stopped before Imamura's bungalow. When the trio alighted from the cars and walked up to the front steps, they found Imamura standing rigidly on the porch in full dress uniform. The brass buttons, gold medals, and hilt of his sword glistened in the morning sun. On either side of Imamura two other officers stood rigidly: 8th Area Forces chief of staff Toshikaze Ohmae on the left and the 25th Naval Air Flotilla commander Junichi Kusaka on the right. Both army and navy units operated under the jurisdiction of the 8th Area Forces theatre of operations and Imamura, an army general, had assigned some navy men to high positions to balance the staff with both army and navy men.

The three visitors stood erect at the bottom of the porch steps and bowed before the CinC of the 8th Area Forces.

"Honorable Commander," General Adachi said, "we are grateful for this audience and it is our hope that this conference will nurture the seeds of victory."

Imamura nodded.

"I welcome the opportunity to challenge again our enemy in New Guinea," Adachi continued. "It is the hope of all of us in the 18th Army to strike a severe blow against these Yankee and Australian dogs."

"We will go inside," Imamura finally spoke.

In the conference room of Imamura's bungalow, other officers were already present: Adm. Kusa Morita of the 9th Fleet, Adm. Takeo Takagi of the 5th Transportation Fleet, Gen. Sadahiko Miyake of the Japanese 20th Infantry Division, Gen. Sata Nakano of the Japanese 51st Infantry Division, and Capt. Takashi Mino, the 25th Air Flotilla's chief of staff. An array of aides were also here, majors and captains who loitered in the room to serve the high brass when called upon. Atop the long oblong table in the center of the room was a huge map of New Guinea.

Imamura gathered the officers in an oval circle about the table before he took a pointer from an accommodating captain. Imamura then ran the tip of the pointer along the map.

"As you can see, two hundred miles of jungles separate our forces in Salamaua and Lae to the enemy's forces at Buna. In between are dense tropical forests with only a few native trails that cannot accommodate the movement of big guns or armored vehicles. Further, a mere handful of well entrenched soldiers can block any movement through these jungles. There is no doubt that the enemy would like to capture Lae but they could never move enough troops and equipment over these trails to do so. But the same thing may be said for us. We could never move a well armed army through this hostile terrain to wrest Buna from the enemy."

When Imamura paused, some of those at the table looked at Adachi who never altered the sober look on his face.

"Yes," the 8th Area Forces CinC continued, "it is our intent to recapture Buna. The 8th Area staff has drawn up Operation MO II for this major offensive. However," the general gestured, "we have learned a bitter truth in New Guinea: only the side with air superiority can hope to succeed. In the Papuan campaign, we saw the enemy snatch victory from certain defeat because they won control of the skies over New Guinea. Unless we reassert our domination of the air in the Bismarck Archipelago, we cannot possibly succeed in this proposed operation. We suffered horribly with the Lae resupply convoy in March because of enemy air power. Can you imagine what would happen to a similar or even larger convoy that sailed for the shores of Buna?"

"I can verify the Honorable Imamura's words," Admiral Tanaka suddenly spoke. "We lost Guadalcanal when we lost our air support in that area. We had no choice but to abandon that island."

"Honorable Commander," Admiral Takagi of the 5th Transportation Fleet spoke, "how soon do you intend to make this counteroffensive in Buna?"

Imamura looked at his chief of staff, Capt. Toshikazu Ohmae, who held several sheafs of paper in his hand. "Toshikazu?"

The chief of staff nodded and referred to his material for nearly a full minute. Captain Ohmae had been a naval officer for over 20 years, serving mostly in an administrative capacity, rather than as a combat commander. Ohmae had shown a remarkable ability in analyses, organization, and planning, so the Imperial Japanese Navy had considered him more vital to the war efforts as an operations officer.

For several years, Ohmae had worked at the Bureau of Military Affairs in the navy's Tokyo headquarters. He had done so well that the renowned Adm. Isoroku Yamamoto, the navy CinC who had planned the Pearl Harbor attacks, had selected Ohmae as his own chief of staff. In fact, Ohmae had helped to plan the Japanese surprise attack on Hawaii in 1941. In June of 1942, the IJN had transferred him to the Southwest Area Fleet at Truk, where he had again served under Yamamoto. He had planned the first Battle of Savo Island in the Solomons where, in August of 1942, a Japanese surface fleet had routed the American fleet and almost prompted the Americans to evacuate Guadalcanal.

After the death of Yamamoto, Imperial headquarters in Tokyo had assigned Ohmae to the 8th Area Forces where the perceptive Admiral Imamura had immediately made him the chief for operational planning in the 8th Area Forces. Since the 8th Area Forces included both army and navy units, Japanese naval officers were happy to see one of their own in such an influential position at Rabaul.

Ohmae looked at the officers about the table before he spoke. "None of us has yet forgotten the unfortunate tragedy of the Lae resupply convoy." He glanced at General Nakano of the 51st Infantry Division. "The Honorable Nakano recalls the incident all too well since most of his troops were lost with the convoy. He needed nearly two months to rebuild his combat division. Meanwhile, since March, we have been sending men, fuel, and supplies to New Guinea only at night in barges down the coast from Wewak, or we have been sending such provisions in submarines, also at night. We have, of course, sent supply vessels to Hollandia and Wewak, since these areas are out of range of the dreaded American skip bombers that destroyed the Lae convoy. But if we hope to retake Buna, a huge convoy even larger than the Lae resupply convoy must come down from Wewak with thousands of men and monumental tons of supplies to land on the Buna beaches. Our air forces must control the skies if we wish to succeed. Otherwise, such a Buna invasion fleet would suffer a terrible fate."

General Imamura looked at Admiral Kusaka.

"Junichi, since you are familiar with this proposed MO II operation, we ask if it is possible to have air superiority for this plan."

"I have read the invasion plans quite well," Kusaka said, "and we intend to make certain that we do control the air. We will send massive air reinforcements into Wewak, both fighters and bombers. Captain Mino has done an excellent job of planning and he will explain. Takashi?"

Mino nodded and rose from his chair. He had been a regular naval officer in the Japanese Naval Air Force since the 1920s. He had been one of Yamamoto's staunch supporters for air power, a philosophy that had no doubt cost him promotions because his arguments for air power had irritated the ultra-conservative navy brass who had still believed that battleships won naval battles. In fact, by the outbreak of World War II, Mino had only risen to the rank of lieutenant commander.

In December of 1941, Mino took command of the land based navy squadron in the Kasunugauta Air Force which defended the Japanese Ryukus Islands. In September of 1942, he assumed command of the 4th Air Squadron at Rabaul, but Admiral Kusaka soon discovered that Mino was more adept in formulating operational plans than he was at commanding combat squadrons. So in April of 1943 after the shake-up that followed the death of Yamamoto, Mino became the chief planner for the 25th Air Flotilla, just as Captain Ohmae had won an influential post on the 8th Area Forces staff.

Since April, Mino's main efforts had been confined to sending new allocations of planes to airbases in New Guinea and the Solomons because the war had settled to minor skirmishes and exchanges of air attacks. But now, with a new major campaign in the offing, Mino had drawn the important chore of planning their air support segment for the proposed MO II.

Mino looked directly at Gen. Hatazo Adachi, the CinC of the 8th Area Forces. "As you know, Honorable Adachi, for the past two or three weeks I have been making frequent flights between Rabaul and Wewak, and on three occasions I even flew to Lae. I could not fail to notice your eagerness to strike back at our enemies in New Guinea, and it is my personal hope that we can give you the kind of air support you need for such an endeavor. As you also know, I have worked closely with General Arisue to develop the airfields at Wewak, and I believe the 7th Air Division now has the capacity to house up to four hundred or even five hundred aircraft at these facilities. It is the intent of the 25th Air Flotilla to reinforce all four groups of the 7th Air Division at Wewak with new aircraft to bring these units up to full strength."

"I appreciate your efforts, Captain," Adachi said. "If the 18th Army has sufficient air power, we can succeed in this proposed operation."

Mino looked at a sheet in front of him before he continued. "My latest figures show that the four air groups of the 7th Air Division have about two hundred aircraft at the moment, with about fifty at Wewak, more than a hundred at Hollandia, and twenty-five or thirty at Lae. I must congratulate General Arisue and his men for their excellent work in developing four good airdromes at Wewak. While we cannot promise five hundred aircraft, we surely hope to bring at least four hundred new aircraft to New Guinea, of which one hundred seventy-five would be fighters."

"I might say," General Arisue suddenly spoke, "that Captain Mino's promised reinforcements in planes and airmen has delighted the 7th Air Division group and squadron commanders. They are eager to use such reinforcements in a new offensive against the enemy."

"But what of the American air force?" General Nakano of the 51st Infantry Division asked. "We would not want a repetition of the disaster that befell the Lae resupply convoy. As Captain Ohmae pointed out, we needed many weeks to rebuild the 51st Division, and we certainly would not want to see this combat unit destroyed during a sail to Buna."

"It will not happen this time, Honorable Nakano," General Arisue said. He tapped his fingers on two areas of the map. "It is true that the enemy has built a strong airbase at Dobodura on the Buna plains and it is also true that they may have as many as two hundred fighters and bombers at Dobodura, with perhaps three hundred more aircraft on the Port Moresby airdromes. But these hundreds of enemy aircraft will not be a problem for us."

"You must excuse my skepticism, General," Takagi said, "but if their air force is this strong and perhaps growing stronger, how can you say this is not a problem? You seem to be telling us that the enemy's forces are large. In that case, how can we possibly expect to send a huge invasion fleet to Buna without severe air attacks from the enemy?"

General Arisue grinned. "We find ourselves in a unique position, Admiral. We are building up Wewak and they are building up Dobodura. But we can strike them while they cannot strike us."

"I do not understand," Takagi frowned.

"It is our plan to destroy both the Dobodura and Port Moresby airbases so they cannot mount air strikes against our invasion convoy," Arisue said. "We have a tremendous advantage. While our aircraft at Wewak can stage at Lae or Finchhaven to attack the enemy, the enemy has no base north of Buna to stage aircraft for attacks on Wewak. Therefore, we can operate out of Wewak with near impunity because they can only make heavy bomber strikes at night against Wewak, and such attacks have been quite ineffective."

"The enemy can make no attacks on Wewak with their dreaded low level medium bombers, Admiral," Kusaka now spoke. "The American B-25s are within range of Wewak, but the enemy's fighter planes are not. The enemy would not dare to send these low level bombers to Wewak without fighter escorts. They tried this once but our fighters destroyed the B-25 formations and the Americans have not tried to do so again."

"Honorable Kusaka," Admiral Morita of the 9th Fleet said, "it is imperative that we have enough air strength to stop enemy air units before we send the 5th Transportation Fleet to Buna with these two fresh divisions of men and these countless tons of provisions."

"I can assure you, Kuso," Admiral Kusaka said, "that you will not get much opposition from their air units. Once we have fully strengthened the 7th Air Division at Wewak, we will begin massive raids against the enemy's bases at Dobodura and at Port Moresby. Not only will we destroy their airfields, but their aircraft as well. When this is done, the invasion convoy can sail to Buna and you will find the skies over the Bismarck Archipelago blackened only with our own fighters and bombers. Rest assured," he pointed to Morita, "there will be no repetition of the Lae resupply convoy disaster."

"Let us hope you are right," Morita answered.

Admiral Kusaka gestured to Captain Mino who once more addressed the officers. "We will begin next week to send new aircraft and crews to the 7th Air Division at Wewak and Hollandia. By early August, the air division should have five hundred aircraft, most of them at Wewak, where they will be in a good position to not only destroy the enemy's airbase but to furnish air support for the invasion fleet. If General Arisue uses these aircraft wisely, and I have no doubt that he will, there is no reason why the MO II operation should not succeed."

Admiral Morita nodded.

"It appears that Admiral Kusaka and his air commanders have planned well for the elimination of the enemy's air forces and for air support in this proposed invasion," General Imamura said. "Let us now turn to the operation itself." He looked at Admiral Morita. "Does the 9th Fleet have enough marus and warships to carry two divisions of troops and their supplies to Buna?"

"Yes, Honorable Imamura," the 9th Fleet CinC said. "We have been assured by Combined Fleet headquarters that we will receive a dozen transport marus and an equal number of cargo marus to carry these invasion forces."

"And what of the escort fleet?"

Now Admiral Tanaka spoke up. "We have now fourteen destroyers, four cruisers, and four submarines, and these should be enough to escort the marus to the landing sites. The 4th Air Group in Rabaul will furnish escort for much of the route before air units of the 7th Air Division assume the responsibility for air cover."

"Admiral," General Adachi said to Morita, "when will you begin moving the 51st and 20th Infantry Divisions to Wewak?"

"Within the next week," Morita answered. "Since the bulk of the enemy's air strength is not within range of Wewak, we can move these forces there before we have a large build up of aircraft at Wewak." He looked at a sheet of paper in his hand and then spoke again. "Two battalions of supply and shore troops have been allocated for the task of loading the troops and supplies on the marus. I am told that the men of the 51st and 20th Divisions are ready to move from their bivouac areas on a day's notice."

"That means they should be in Wewak by mid-

July," Imamura said. "And, since Admiral Kusaka will need several weeks to bring the 7th Air Division to full strength and to conduct his sustained air attacks on the enemy's airbases, we should set the tentative date for the Buna invasion as mid-August." He looked at Admiral Tanaka. "Will the 5th Escort Fleet be ready to accompany the marus to Buna by that date?"

"The warships will be ready," Tanaka answered. He looked at Kusaka. "I only hope that the 7th Air Division has indeed neutralized the enemy's airbases and air units before the invasion fleet sails."

"We will have the means to carry out these sustained raids quite soon," General Arisue said, "and I am sure that over a period of three or four weeks we will have accomplished the task of destroying the enemy air force in New Guinea. There is no doubt that by mid-August the invasion convoy can sail safely southward to its planned invasion sites."

"Admiral," General Adachi now spoke to Tanaka, "I would not ask the navy to transport a single soldier from my 18th Army to Buna before we are certain that the enemy cannot mount serious air attacks against such a convoy. I also recall too well the disaster of the Lae resupply convoy that forced us to cancel our first plan for a counteroffensive in Buna. It would be better to delay a new offensive even beyond mid-August than to imperil our ships, troops, and supplies. While I am quite eager to begin Operation MO II, I am not so rash as to do so without first taking every proper precaution to assure success."

"What of your intelligence reports?" Admiral Morita looked at Imamura. "Have we determined the strength of the enemy's ground forces in New Guinea?"

General Imamura looked at a sheet in front of him. "In combat strength, they have perhaps the equivalent of three Australian brigades and two American regiments. The other enemy forces in Papua are mostly airmen, engineers, and supply troops who work at the airfields, the port facilities, in quartermaster, or on road systems."

"Do you believe the enemy has any new plans for an operation of their own, Honorable Imamura?" Morita asked.

"Without doubt," the 8th Area Forces CinC said. "They are looking avidly at Lae which could furnish them excellent harbor facilities and areas to build airdromes. Lae would also put their air units within range of Wewak and Gasmata on New Britain. They would even be within heavy bomber range of Hollandia."

"Do they have enough ground strength to assault Lae?"

"Perhaps, but they would not do so without trying to knock out our own air power in New Guinea," Imamura said. "That is why they have made continual air assaults on Lae. But we do not keep many aircraft at Lae now and we are using this base primarily as a staging base for air units that fly out of Wewak and Hollandia to attack the enemy's airfields. Personally, I do not believe the enemy will plan any assault on Lae before the fall, by which time we hope to have recaptured Buna."

"Despite these frequent air attacks on Lae and sometimes on Finchhaven," General Arisue said, "our men at these bases usually have the runways back in condition within a few hours. So the airstrips are almost constantly available to stage aircraft."

"We have about five thousand troops in Lae at this time," General Adachi said, "and some of these units will drive down through Salamaua toward Buna over the jungle trails while the invasion fleet sails to Buna. The Lae forces will thus be a good diversion to keep the enemy off balance."

"Still," Morita frowned, "I must admit that I am fearful of the enemy's air power."

General Arisue grinned at Morita. "Admiral, your convoy will reach Buna in safety. As I said, Wewak is out of range and we can operate from there without interruptions from the enemy. They would not dare to send their B-25s into the Bismarck Sea without fighter escorts."

"General," Admiral Morita now pointed to the 7th Air Division commander, "the enemy is always full of surprises, so I take nothing for granted. We never expected the parachute bombs that thwarted the Port Moresby offensive, and we never expected the skip bombs that destroyed the Lae resupply convoy. They will soon enough become aware of the build-up in Wewak and they will guess that we plan to carry out a major operation. They might even use carrier planes to escort their medium bombers to Wewak. Suffice it to say that we must be certain that the 7th Air Division has neutralized the enemy's air forces. Only then will it be safe to send an invasion fleet from Wewak to Buna."

Those at the table did not respond to the 9th Fleet commander.

After a moment of silence, Gen. Hitoshi Imamura spoke again to his officers. "I believe we are now thoroughly familiar with Operation MO II. The first objective is to bring the 7th Air Division up to full strength. Then General Arisue's air units will commence a series of assaults to neutralize the enemy's air bases in New Guinea. Next, the convoy will sail from Wewak to the Buna landing sites. Let us hope that we can atone for the reverses we have suffered in the Solomons and in New Guinea. I need not tell you that we need a major victory to restore the morale of our people in Japan." He looked at his watch. "We will now retire to the dining room for tea and cakes."

Thus did the conference end. The Japanese had made their plans, hoping to recoup Buna. However, the Allies in New Guinea had grown restless and, as Admiral Morita suspected, MacArthur was indeed looking avidly northward to Lae.

CHAPTER TWO

The battle for Buna that ended in February of 1943 had been the most vicious fight of the Southwest Pacific War, all but wiping out the Japanese Nankai Shitai Force and leaving the American 32nd and Australian 9 Divisions totally spent, with most of the soldiers riddled with diseases if not killed or wounded. The capture of Buna had saved Papuan New Guinea while giving the Americans a forward base on this island battlefield. US 5th Air Force engineers had quickly developed a major airbase on the Dobodura Plain, some ten to fifteen miles inland from the Buna coastal area. Thus 5th Air Force had been able to mount B-25s to destroy the Lae resupply convoy in March of 1943.

The 871st Aviation Engineer Battalion under Lt. Col. Murray Woodbury had done an excellent job at Buna, building a 4,500 foot fighter strip (Horanda Drome) and a 5,000 foot bomber strip (Dobodura Drome), along with four taxiways and 200 hardstands or revetment areas. Engineers had also built several roads through the flat terrain between the beaches and the foot of the Owen Stanley Mountains for easy movement about the new American airbase.

Unfortunately the Buna shoreline ruled out its development into a good port facility, but Seabee engineers had built piers and breaker walls so the allies could bring in at least barges and small cargo luggers that came from Oro Bay with men and provisions. Air transport planes also brought men and supplies into the Buna area.

By the end of June, 1943, Dobodura housed three air groups: the 49th Fighter Group with P-40s, the 22nd Bomb Group with their B-26 medium bombers, and the 3rd Attack Group with the B-25 and A-20 bombers. Scheduled to arrive soon was the 475th Fighter Group with their long range P-38s. The 3rd Group's B-25 commerce destroyers, modified as skip bombers, had been the principal culprit in the destruction of the Lae resupply convoy during the Battle of the Bismarck Sea.

These three air groups at Dobodura made frequent air attacks on Lae and against Japanese shipping in the Solomon Sea between New Guinea and New Britain. The B-26s and B-25s had not attacked Wewak, however, because the P-40s and even the P-38s lacked the range to escort these bombers on a 1,000 mile round trip between Buna and the big Japanese base.

On the opposite side of the Owen Stanley Mountains in Papua, New Guinea to the south, was the sprawling allied base of Port Moresby that had been an invasion target for the Japanese since the earliest months of the war. By June of 1943, Moresby rivaled or even surpassed the big Japanese base of Rabaul in expanse and strength as a major military base. Six airdromes had been established in and about Port Moresby within an area 14 miles long and 7 miles wide. The thriving harbor could accommodate dozens of ships and its shore facilities were among the best in the Pacific for unloading men and supplies.

The US 5th Air Force maintained its ADVON headquarters here along with several Allied air groups: the 43rd B-17 Bomb Group, the 90th B-24 Bomb Group, the 38th medium B-25 Group that were also low level commerce destroyers, the 8th Fighter Group with its P-40s, the 35th Fighter Group with its P-38s and P-39s, the 9th Squadron of the 49th Fighter Group wiht its P-38s, and the Australian 9 Composite Group with its mixture of Beaufort light bombers and P-40 fighters. Also here were elements of the US 54th Troop Carrier Wing, whose C-47s and C-54s continually flew supplies and troops between Australia and Moresby or between Moresby and Buna.

Also stationed in Moresby were Allied ground troops of the New Guinea Force under the command of Australian Gen. Sir Thomas Blamey. The combat troops included the 7 and 9 Australian Divisions, the US 41st Infantry Division, and the US 503rd Parachute Regiment. The recent arrival of the paratroopers had left the personnel at Port Moresby filled with curiosity since nobody could understand why airborne troops would come into the dense New Guinea jungle where they were unlikely to find any clearing large enough in which to jump. However, Gen. Douglas MacArthur, CinC of the Allied SWPA forces, and Gen. Thomas Blamey, CinC of the New

Guinea Force, had a unique mission for these American paratroopers.

Totally, the allies had about 50,000 men in New Guinea, about the same number that the Japanese had in Rabaul and New Guinea.

While the Japanese planned a counteroffensive to retake Buna, the Allies had developed their own plan—Operation Eckton to capture Lae. General MacArthur and Gen. George Kenney, commander of the 5th Air Force, had seen Lae as an area where they could develop a huge airbase that could rival Moresby. The sprawling Markham Valley beyond Lae Harbor was big enough to build several airdromes. Lae Harbor itself was probably one of the best natural harbors in the Pacific, and MacArthur knew that if he occupied this port area on Huon Gulf he could move men, planes, and ships much further north to begin his obsessed plan to return to the Philippines.

MacArthur and his SWPA staff had been considering an invasion of Lae for the past three months, ever since the Battle of the Bismarck Sea. In March, however, the Japanese build-up at Wewak and Hollandia as major airbases and staging areas represented a serious threat to any invasion plan. Since April, Japanese air units continually flew down from Wewak, staged out of Lae or Finchhaven, and bombed Dobodura or Moresby.

MacArthur dared not launch Operation Eckton until something was done about Wewak. He could not afford to see hordes of Japanese bombers and fighters race down from this base to pelt his invasion fleets, a Lae beachhead, or a supply fleet. Further, although only 5,000 Japanese troops were in the Lae-Salamaua area at the moment, the enemy could swiftly send thousands of men southward to reinforce Lae.

In fact, on the afternoon of 29 June, the same day that General Imamura held his conference at Rabaul, the Allies at Buna got another taste of the Wewak thorn. At about 1400 hours, air raid sirens wailed about the Dobodura and Horanda strips in Buna. Japanese bombers were coming over again.

Lt. Tadashi Shizizui, commanding the 152nd Fighter Squadron of the Japanese 18th Sentai Group reached Buna with 24 Zeros that were escorting 22 Dinah dive bombers from the 18th Sentai's 151st Squadron, under Capt. Inada Tsukomoto. The aircraft had come down from Wewak and staged at Finchhaven and Lae before flying on to the Buna area.

Within ten miles of the allied airbase, Captain Tsukomoto cried into his radio. "All bomber pilots will attack in pairs. First Flight will attack Horanda Drome and Second Flight will attack Dobodura Drome."

"Yes, Honorable Captain," Lt. Sisai Anami answered.

Then Tsukomoto called Shizizui. "Lieutenant, you will keep your fighters well ahead of us to deal with interceptors."

"We will do so," Shizizui answered.

The cagey Japanese from the 7th Air Division had flown down from Lae at about treetop level to avoid radar in Buna. The Americans had found themselves with only moments to spare in mounting interceptors before the Japanese attacks. The 49th Fighter Group managed to get off only fourteen P-40s before the attack, while the ground crews of the 3rd Attack Group and 22nd Bomb Group, had been unable to get all of their B-25s and B-26s under cover before the Japanese aerial onslaught.

Within minutes, the 49th Fighter Group pilots tangled with the Japanese Zeros under Lt. Tadashi Shizizui. The rattle of machine gun fire and the whine of engines echoed across the sky, while American airmen in Buna quickly darted into foxhole shelters. The American Forty-Niner pilots knocked four Zeros out of the sky, while Shizizui's airmen from the Japanese 152nd Squadron shot down three P-40s. However, the Zero airmen had effectively occupied the American fighter pilots, while the Nippon bombers did their work.

In pairs, Dinah dive bombers swept over Dobodura Drome. Heavy ack ack fire knocked down three of the bombers and damaged three more, but Captain Tsukomoto and his fellow bomber crews did a creditable job with whistling 500 pound bombs and chattering strafing fire on the bomber strip that housed the planes and facilities of the 22nd Bomb and 3rd Attack Groups. Numbing explosions rocked the area as descending bombs shattered two B-26s and three B-25s, while damaging another four Marauders and two Mitchells. The same aerial assault punched several holes in the runway, damaged a service building, knocked down a control tower, and ignited several vehicles.

Over Horanda Drome, the Dinahs under Lieutenant Anami destroyed three P-40s, damaged three more, and flattened three service buildings. Fortunately US airmen had sheltered themselves quite well and the vicious Japanese air attack only wounded several men.

By 1420 hours, 20 minutes after the attack began, Captain Tsukomoto cried into his radio. "We have done all we can here; we will return to base."

"Yes, Captain," Lt. Tadashi Shizizui said.

Moments later, the Japanese planes were gone. US airmen cautiously left their shelters and stared at the blazing fires and dense smoke along the Dobodura and Horanda Dromes. The airmen would need to spend the rest of the day putting out fires, clearing away rubble, and repairing runways.

Sgt. Harry Kiser of the 3rd Group's 90th Squadron turned to a fellow gunner, Sgt. Woodrow Butler. "Son of a bitch; they hit us again. How come our fighters don't get the bastards?"

"They're too smart," Butler answered. "Those Nips come down from Wewak, stop and refuel in Lae, and then take off over the treetops to hit us. As long as Wewak is safe for them, they'll never let up on these air attacks."

"Bitch," Kiser cursed again. "I wish we could finish off that base."

Sergeant Butler shook his head. "We'll never get to Wewak until fighters can give us cover."

When the word of this latest Japanese air attack reached Port Moresby, Gen. Thomas Blamey of the New Guinea Force scowled in irritation. They would never take Lae if the Japanese could hit the allied bases in Buna and Moresby by flying out of Wewak with near impunity. He called General MacArthur in

Brisbane to report this latest Nippon raid and then asked about the conference to discuss the Eckton plan.

"We'll hold the meeting at your headquarters in Moresby in two days," the SWPA CinC said. "I'll fly up there with George Kenney. I want to complete this plan and maybe figure out some way to do something about Wewak."

"Yes sir," General Blamey said.

On 2 July 1943, the air service crews at Ward Drome in Port Moresby watched the two B-17s that landed on the runway, while six P-38 fighters hovered overhead. They knew instinctively that someone important had come to Port Moresby. They stared in awe when they saw General MacArthur alight from one of the planes with his SWPA chief of staff, Gen. Richard Sutherland.

The second plane landing at Ward Drome carried Gen. George Kenney, the CinC of 5th Air Force. Two staff members left the plane with him. When these VIPs from Australia got into a pair of staff cars and drove off, the airmen at the drome chattered furiously, conjecturing. Why had MacArthur and Kenney come to Moresby? No doubt, something big was up. By the time the men in Moresby filed into a dozen mess halls about the big allied base for their noon meals, rumors had become rampant. A new offensive was imminent and the target could only be Lae.

After a noon meal at the New Guinea Force officers mess in Moresby, the high brass retired to the operations room where Gen. Sir Thomas Blamey had posted a huge map of Papua, New Guinea on the wall behind the podium. He, MacArthur, and Kenney stood on the platform while other allied officers sat about the table. In attendance besides these men were Gen. Ennis Whitehead, of ADVON 5th Air Force, Gen. Paul Prentiss of the 54th Troop Carrier Wing, Gen. George Vasey of the Australian 9 Division, Adm. Daniel E. Barbey of the US 7th Amphibious Fleet, and Lt. Col. Murray Woodbury of the 871st Airborne Engineer Battalion. All of them knew that MacArthur was anxious to launch Operation Eckton, but they did not like the disturbing look on the face of the SWPA CinC.

When the officers had settled themselves at the table, General Blamey fingered some papers in his hand and then spoke. "All of you know that we've been planning Eckton for some time. We've certainly amassed enough air strength, combat troops, equipment, armament, and supplies to complete the operation. We'd like to occupy Lae as soon as possible. Admiral Barbey says that his amphibious fleet is ready to move. But," Blamey shrugged, "we still have the serious problem of Japanese air power at Wewak and Hollandia. Their air formations continue to hit Moresby and Buna with frequent regularity. We must find a way to neutralize Wewak before we launch Eckton."

"We've been hitting Wewak with heavy bomber night attacks," General Whitehead told Blamey, "but apparently these B-17 and B-24 assaults have not been as effective as we'd hoped."

"Wewak is a menace," General MacArthur now spoke. "We've seen the Japanese develop a base that nearly matches Port Moresby in its strength. Our intelligence and recon reports show that they've established four major airdromes in that area. Our intelligence also says that the Japanese have established several large camp areas. At the present time, the Japanese keep between one hundred and two hundred planes at Wewak and perhaps as many as thirty or forty thousand men. They have not built these airdromes and camp areas for nothing. I expect them to bring in hundreds more planes and perhaps thousands more troops. There isn't any doubt in my mind that the Japanese are planning something of their own."

No one answered and MacArthur continued. "They've also improved port facilities at Wewak Harbor and Hansa Bay and they've been sending ships in and out of there all the time."

"We've tried to hit the harbor, too, sir," Whitehead said to MacArthur, "but unfortunately we haven't been too successful there either."

"You need to get your low level strafer bombers in there to do a thorough job," MacArthur pointed at Whitehead. "You now have two full groups of these B-25s and you can even use the P-38s in low level fighter bomber attacks. That's the only way we'll take out Wewak."

"Sir," Whitehead said bitterly, "it's easy to make those suggestions, but it's something else to carry them out. We sent those B-25s up there once without escorts and Zeros mauled the bomber formations. Wewak is jammed with too many Japanese fighters, and they've got more fighters at Aitape, only one hundred miles or so to the north. Without fighter cover of our own, the Japanese would shoot down half of our B-25s before they even got near their Wewak airdromes. Our fighters can't make this five hundred mile trip from Dobo to Wewak, not even the new P-38."

"Can't you use some kind of auxiliary tanks on the fighters?"

"Even with a belly tank, Wewak is out of range," the ADVON commander said. "We need a fighter base at least two or three hundred miles north of Dobo, and that means Lae, the Markham Valley. We'd be able to hit Wewak from Lae."

"And we can't really get Lae until we've neutralized Wewak," General Sutherland suddenly spoke. "It's a vicious circle, isn't it?"

Whitehead did not answer, nor did any of the others. Then MacArthur spoke again. "Gentlemen," he shifted his glance among those present, "we're in a stalemate and we might as well admit it. It's a rather disturbing fact when we consider that our forces wiped out the Japanese at Buna after a terrible fight, and then we wiped out the major Japanese resupply convoy only a month later. Three months have passed since then and we still haven't initiated Operation Eckton. We simply cannot delay any longer. The enemy gets stronger with each passing day." He looked at Admiral Barbey. "I assume the amphibious fleet is ready?"

"Yes sir," Barbey answered. "We've got sixteen transports and twenty-two cargos set to go, with twenty cruisers, destroyers and submarines to act as escort. We might even get the 5th Fleet to release a couple of baby flattops to give us air cover during the operation. These jeep carriers can lie off the Lae coast while we land troops and equipment."

MacArthur nodded and then looked at Blamey. "Tom, what about the invasion troops?"

"They've been ready for weeks," Blamey said. "We've prepared the entire 7 Australian Division to land in Lae, while the 30 Australian Brigade and 162 American Regiment will go ashore in the Salamaua area. The parachute regiment will jump into the Markham Valley as soon as we give the word."

MacArthur looked at Kenney. "George, do you have enough troop carrier planes for these paratroopers and their supplies?"

The 5th Air Force commander looked at Gen. Paul Prentiss, the CO of the 54th Troop Carrier Wing. "Well, Paul?"

Prentiss nodded. "We've set aside four full squadrons of C-47s for Eckton. They'll easily carry the entire 506th Parachute Regiment and their equipment for the drop into the Markham Valley. We also have three other squadrons of transport ships for the invasions. I believe the 89th Squadron of the 3rd Attack Group is assigned to lay a smoke screen over the Markham Valley to cover the parachute jump. Is that right, Ennis?" he asked the 5th Air Force ADVON CO.

"Yes," Whitehead answered.

"However," Prentiss pointed, "I must tell you that Japanese air attacks on Moresby have destroyed about a dozen C-47 transport planes in the past month alone. We won't have enough aircraft for the Eckton operation if we don't start soon, or if we don't stop those bombing raids."

"What do you think, George?" MacArthur asked

Kenney. "Can we begin this operation despite the Japanese air threat in Wewak?"

"Probably," Kenney answered. "We do have five fighter groups and the Australian composite group to cover the amphibious force. That should suffice unless the enemy does indeed get five hundred planes into Wewak. However, we can't promise that the enemy won't hit the invasion fleet or the transport planes."

"I don't think you're sure," MacArthur frowned.

"Nothing is certain," Kenney said.

"Sir," Blamey said to MacArthur, "if what General Kenney says is true, I don't think it's a good idea to hit Lae at this time."

"We've delayed too long," MacArthur said. He scanned those around the table. "Has anyone got a suggestion?"

"Sir," Lieutenant Colonel Woodbury suddenly spoke. "I have a long shot idea that might work."

"Well?"

"We know that the Owen Stanley Mountains were once a mining area. Since the turn of the century, Australian prospectors came into those hills to mine for gold and silver. In many cases big mining companies were also involved. These activities continued in the rugged jungle mountains until they exhausted the mines. But," Woodbury continued, "during those operations in the 20s and 30s, the Australians often built airstrips to fly men, equipment, and ore in and out of the mountains. Wau is an example of where they left an abandoned airstrip behind, and we took advantage by turning Wau into an important highland base. Maybe we can find other abandoned airstrips a lot further north, somewhere much closer to Wewak, and we can set up a staging airbase similar to Wau."

The officers at the table frowned, but General MacArthur and General Blamey grinned. The New Guinea Force commander leaned forward and looked squarely at Woodbury. "There must be a dozen old airstrips in those Owen Stanley Mountains, Colonel. I'm surprised that my own lads didn't think of that. As you said, the old Wau strip was one of those bloody old runways that fell into disarray. There's got to be a lot more old airstrips in those hills. We can look at some old maps and maybe find out where some of those mining companies operated."

"Colonel," General MacArthur now spoke, "do you have some good men who could tell us if any of those old strips might be usable—assuming they find any?"

"Yes sir," Abbot said.

"How long would it take to turn one of those abandoned runways into a good fighter strip?"

"We can do it in a week," the 871st Battalion engineer officer said.

"But how will you get in there with men and equipment?" Admiral Barbey asked.

"We'll send in a C-47," Woodbury said.

General Vasey now grinned. "Even if you find an old air strip it'll probably be covered with kunai grass and brush. Are you sure you can land a C-47 in a place like that?"

"General," Paul Prentiss of the 5th Troop Carrier Wing now spoke, "all we need is a clearing that's a couple hundred feet in length, and my pilots will land Gooney Birds. Once we get one C-47 down with a small bulldozer, a couple of small trucks and a miniature scooper, we'll be on our way. They'll clear an area in a matter of hours so we can send in more C-47s. I guarantee that you'll be able to send a couple of full fighter squadrons into the area."

General Vasey nodded.

Gen. George Kenney turned and looked at the map on the wall. "We've got a base at Wau, but that's too far east. We'll need one around here," he tapped the map, "somewhere around the headwaters of the Watut River that flows down past Salamaua and into the Solomon Sea."

"That area you're talking about is populated by Chimbu natives, a rather primitive tribe," General Vasey said to Kenney. "However, those natives have been used rather extensively by old mining companies to help them dig for ore. Some of those old timers in that tribe probably remember where some of those old strips might be. I'd suggest that you fly to our small base at Bulolo and talk to some of the men in our Australian 3 Division detachment. They're on quite friendly terms with the Chimbus and our lads will be glad to help out. Lt. Col. Howard Morrison is in charge of the garrison there." He turned to Woodbury. "Colonel, would you want to fly some of your lads up there?"

"Fine," the lieutenant colonel nodded.

"How soon could you get them off?" MacArthur asked Woodbury.

"I'll fly a few men to Bulolo as soon as this conference is over," the aviation engineer officer said.

"Good," Kenney answered. He then looked at General Whitehead. "Ennis, do you think this can work? If we can develop a fighter base a couple hundred miles to the northwest, do you think you could base a couple of squadrons of fighters there to escort B-25s to Wewak?"

"I've got the 475th Group with its P-38s ready to move into Buna and the 35th Group is here in Moresby with a squadron of P-38s and two squadrons of P-40s," Whitehead said. "I'll talk to Colonel Moore of the 35th and tell him to ready all three of his squadrons for a quick transfer to a mountain airstrip. They'll be set to go as soon as Lieutenant Colonel Woodbury tells us it's okay to move."

"What about Japanese air units?" General Blamey asked Whitehead. "Could they interfere with this proposed construction of an airstrip in the highlands? They hit Wau often enough, and I understand they have continual air patrols over the Owen Stanley Mountains."

General Whitehead grinned. "We'll take one step at a time, sir. First, we'll have to find a place close enough to Wewak where we can build this airstrip. When we do that, then we'll worry about keeping the Nips in the dark."

"Fair enough," Blamey said.

General MacArthur looked at the map himself and then turned to his officers. "It looks like we'll have to keep Eckton on ice for the time being. I want air units hitting the Japanese wherever they can. We need to keep the enemy off balance so they can't mount any major operation of their own." He looked at Blamey. "Tom, keep those probing patrols in the Salamaua area. We don't want the enemy to think we've given up on them. And Dan," he turned to Admiral Barbey, "while we're waiting to shove off on Eckton, keep your destroyers on the prowl up and down the New Guinea coast to hit anything that moves."

"Yes sir," Admiral Barbey answered.

"I must tell you," MacArthur continued, "that I don't think the Japanese intend to stand still. They'll keep hitting Moresby and Buna and they'll continue their build-up at Wewak. It's my opinion that they still hope to recapture Buna. Despite their losses in the Bismarck Sea battle, they continue to send men and supplies into New Guinea in whatever way they can. Our own forces are now quite substantial, but we can't take anything for granted."

MacArthur paused and then looked at Ennis Whitehead. "General, the responsibility is in your hands. You've suffered severe damage at your Buna airfields from Japanese air raids, including the one today. Please make every effort to upgrade your early warning systems. Get some radar people in the hills north and northwest of Buna, so they can pick up oncoming aircraft soon enough to mount interceptors."

"Yes sir."

"Perhaps, Ennis," General Kenney now spoke to the ADVON 5th Air Force commander, "you should have at least two squadrons of fighters on alert at all times at both the Horanda Drome in Buna and the fighter dromes in Port Moresby. They should be in a position to get off in moments."

"I'll do that," Whitehead said.

Kenney nodded.

General MacArthur once more scanned the officers inside the New Guinea Force operations room. "I guess that covers everything. We'll keep Eckton on hold, but only as shortly as possible. General Blamey must continue to keep combat troops on alert for quick movement to Buna. Admiral Barbey must be ready to land amphibious forces and supplies on a two or three day's notice, while the paratroopers and transport planes must be ready. Meanwhile, let us hope that Colonel Woodbury can succeed in his mission to find a suitable site for a fighter base close to Wewak, and let's hope also that he can do it soon."

"We won't rest a single minute, sir," Woodbury assured the SWPA CinC. "If there are any old airstrips in those mountains, we'll find them. When we do, I can assure you that we'll have the place operating as a fighter base within a week."

"Good," General MacArthur nodded.

The allies left in a semi-limbo state the Eckton plan to capture Lae, while Lt. Col. Murray Woodbury assumed the most immediate responsibility. Could he find a suitable fighter base site in the Owen Stanley Mountains before the Japanese struck with their own MO II operation?

CHAPTER THREE

Lt. Everette E. Fraser, only 23 years old, probably knew as much about airfield construction as any man in New Guinea. In civilian life he had been a construction engineer, working on highways, bridges, and roads in his native Massachusetts after graduating from Boston University. Fraser had not been out of college for a year before he joined the United States Army Air Force with the hope of becoming a combat pilot. However, the air force had much better use for the young New Englander. They were short of aviation engineers, men who could lay out and build airfields on rugged landscapes in the Southwest Pacific.

At the air force training center in Houston, Texas, the air force commander had convinced Fraser that he could serve his country much better as an engineer than as a pilot, bombardier, or navigator. The air force had plenty of men to fill combat roles, but few men who could build and maintain airfields. Fraser then trained as an aviation engineer and by January of 1943 he found himself in New Guinea where he joined the 871st Airborne Engineer Battalion under Lt. Col. Murray Woodbury.

Fraser had aided the battalion in constructing the Durand Drome in Port Moresby to house the 38th Bomb Group and by February, he had reached the rugged terrain at Buna to help in the construction of the Dobodura and Horanda airfields. By late February the 3rd Attack Group and part of the 49th Fighter Group had arrived in Buna — just in time to maul the Japanese Lae resupply convoy in the famed Battle of the Bismarck Sea.

Fraser had won a Legion of Merit medal for his fine work on the Buna airfields, one of the highest awards for a man in a non-combat role. During his several months in New Guinea, he had established himself as an excellent engineer who had learned quickly and who had shown a good rapport with the men under him. Now the 5th Air Force called on him for a unique and exhausting job: beat the bush of New Guinea's hostile highland jungle to find a suitable place for an advanced fighter base.

On 3 July, the day after the conference at ADVON 5th Air Force, Lt. Col. Murray Woodbury called Fraser to the 871st Airborne Engineer Battalion headquarters at Port Moresby. The lieutenant colonel met the young lieutenant with a grin before he gestured.

"Sit down, Evie."

"Yes sir," Fraser answered.

Woodbury stared at his young engineer for a full 30 seconds before he leaned forward from behind his desk. "I've got a tough job for you, but it would need to be on a volunteer basis. If you don't think you can handle it, or if you don't want to do it, I'll understand."

"I'm listening," Fraser said.

"You're aware that we've got a problem with Wewak?" Woodbury asked. "The Nips have been hitting our bases from there because they've got Lae as a staging area. Meanwhile, we can't get up to Wewak since we don't have a similar staging base. At our ADVON conference yesterday, we discussed the idea of finding one of the old mining company airstrips in the mountain areas north of Wau. If we do locate such a place, we'll build a fighter base, so we can stage our own fighters to escort B-25s to Wewak. Such a base could also be used as an emergency landing field for any damaged B-25s coming back from Wewak."

"That sounds reasonable, sir," Fraser nodded.

"That's the assignment," the 871st Engineer Battalion CO said, "find a place where we can construct an airfield. Are you willing to take on that kind of assignment?"

"Why me, sir? You've got a lot of good engineers in this battalion, most of them with a lot more experience."

The lieutenant colonel grinned. "Two reasons. First, I think you're very smart. You know your business and you'd recognize a logical site if you found one. Secondly, and perhaps more important, you're young and strong; you've got a lot of stamina. This assignment calls for a man who can trek through the jungles for mile after mile and maybe for days at a time. But as I said," Woodbury nodded, "this job is strictly on a volunteer basis. If you don't want it, I'll

47

understand."

"I'm willing to try," Fraser said, "but I can't guarantee anything."

"That's all I'd expect, that you try. I have enough faith in you to know that if you find a place you say can be developed as a fighter strip, the place can be converted."

Lieutenant Fraser nodded. "When and how do I start?"

"You'll fly up to the Australian base at Bulolo in a C-47," Woodbury said. "There, you'll meet with Lt. Col. Robert Marston of the Aussie 60th Infantry Battalion garrison. He'll put you in touch with some Chimbu tribesmen who know the area quite well, and who supposedly know where some of these old airstrips are located. When or if you find any sites, you'll need to make your own evaluation as to whether or not the site can be converted into a fighter base. As I said, this assignment may entail plodding through harsh, dense jungles for many days,"

"I understand," Fraser said.

"As soon as you find a suitable site, contact me at once," Woodbury said, "and we'll get a C-47 Gooney Bird up there with mobile equipment and a crew of men to start building."

"Yes sir."

Woodbury rose from his desk, leaned forward, and gripped the lieutenant's hand. "Good luck, Evie."

"Yes sir," Fraser said again.

The very next day, Lt. Everette Fraser boarded a C-47 at Moresby's Ward Drome for the flight to Bulolo. He carried with him only a light bag with a single change of clothing, a sextant, a compass, some K-rations, salt tablets, medical kit, a .45 pistol, ample ammunition, and a full carton of atabrine tablets to take one daily for the prevention of malaria.

The young American officer stared from the window of the C-47 as the Gooney Bird transport plane droned over the Owen Stanleys. He felt somewhat uneasy when he saw the quartet of Australian P-40s hanging around the plane because he knew these escorts were keeping an eye out for possible Zeros that might come out of Lae. Japanese fighter pilots were always on the prowl over these New Guinea mountains and nothing suited them better than to shoot down fat, often heavily loaded transport planes.

But no Japanese Zeros molested the C-47 and after a two hour flight, the Gooney Bird touched down on the 4,000 foot Bulolo runway. When Fraser alighted from the plane, he gasped from the heat and humidity that prevailed even on this highland Allied base. He had only walked a dozen yards from the plane when an Australian corporal met him.

"Sir," the soldier said, "are you Lieutenant Fraser?"

Fraser nodded.

"Colonel Marston is expecting you, he is; says to bring you right to his hut as soon as you got 'ere."

Lt. Col. Robert Marston greeted Fraser with a wide grin and then offered the American a chair. "I've been apprised of your mission, Lieutenant, and I've already set up some people to work with you."

Marston, once he heard from New Guinea Force headquarters, had taken immediate action. The men of the 60th Battalion here at Bulolo had been on quite friendly terms with the Chimbu natives of nearby villages. The Aussies had often employed these natives at the base, furnished them tools and food, or helped the aborigines to upgrade their villages. The Bulolo village chief had always shown a willingness to help the Australians when the need arose.

The chief and several natives had come to Marston's hut, and when Marston explained the problem to the Chimbu chief and his men, they agreed to lead the American officer on a search expedition to find a good site for a fighter base. The Bulolo village chief had told Marston that some of his people knew of some old airstrips along the Watut River, some 50 miles northwest of Lae. The villagers would be happy to accommodate the American to search for these airstrips.

"Of course," Marston pointed to Fraser, "you'll need to trek through a lot of jungle once you leave our base here. You could be plodding through those bloody rain forests for days. Do you think you can do that?"

"I hope so, sir."

"A couple of my lads will go along with you. They understand the natives quite well and they'll be a good help."

"I appreciate that, sir," Fraser said.

Early the next morning, Lt. Everette Fraser, two Australians, and a dozen natives from the Bulolo village left the Australian base and began a harsh trek through the jungles northwest of Bulolo. The Aussie lieutenant, Ed Robinson, and the non-com, Sgt. Howard Lumb, had been part of the Bulolo garrison since the Australians first established this forward base. Lumb, a rugged, burly man from Yorks in Australia, was 40 years old, but he possessed the stamina of a man half his age. He had worked as a gold miner and prospector in Angua, New Guinea, in the 1930s, and when war broke out he had returned to New Guinea with the Australian army. Lumb had worked with natives for more than a year, building bridges over streams or clearing areas for campsites and airfields. He had won the total confidence of the Chimbus.

"We're 'eadin' for the Watut, sir," Lumb told Fraser. "It's about twenty-five miles from 'ere, and the trails through these bloody rain forests are not the best."

"How long will it take us to reach that river?" Fraser asked.

"Maybe three or four days if we're in luck," Lumb said. "Once you reach a possible site, you and Lieutenant Robinson will 'ave to make your maps in a hurry. There's a lot of Nip patrols in that area, there is."

"Are you sure we'll find some old airstrips?" Fraser asked.

"These natives say they know the location of a few old runways," the sergeant said. "We'll likely find them covered with brush, though."

"It won't matter, as long as we can get a C-47 in," Fraser said.

The party from Bulolo trekked through the dank jungle for three days. Fraser suffered continual perspiration from the harsh humidity, his face always covered with sweat which drew hordes of insects that constantly plagued him. The rash on his body worsened each day from the same perspiration, while his legs grew rubbery from heavy footsteps over tangled and matted brush. His face often burned from the searing sun that beat down on him; or his lean frame often felt leaden from a heavy rain squall that drenched him from head to foot.

At night, Fraser and the others slept on the damp ground, enclosed in mosquito netting to prevent the anopheles from transmitting malaria to them; or to prevent other insects from infecting them with dengue fever or skin diseases.

On the fourth day out of Bulolo, the party finally reached the Watut River and the native leader pointed northward. There was an old mining camp airstrip a few miles away. Fraser felt a surge of excitement and he urged the party to hurry on. They covered the six miles quickly and reached the site by late afternoon. However, when they arrived at the old camp, Fraser found the area too small. Lieutenant Robinson agreed. The old runway, covered with brush, only measured 2,500 feet in length, with high mountains all about the patch of flat kunai plain. While a C-47 could probably land here, the square of flat terrain was not long enough to build a minimum 4,000 foot runway; nor was there enough room to house many planes.

"It won't do, Sergeant," Robinson told his Australian companion. "We need an area at least twice as large."

Lumb turned to his native leader and explained, and the chief pointed to the east. "There was another old airstrip near the village of Marilinan," Lumb said, "about six miles away on the other side of the river." The party decided to camp here for the night and to leave for this new area the first thing in the morning.

At daylight, the party broke camp and trekked along a native trail that paralleled the Watut River, moving east by northeast until they found a shallow section of the river where they could ford across. On the opposite bank, the native leader pointed east again and the party continued on. By dusk they had reached the village of Marilinan where the Bulolo leader spoke to the chief. This second Chimbu native listened and then explained that an old airstrip lay a couple of miles to the north. They could visit the place in the morning.

The next day, several villagers from Marilinan accompanied the party from Bulolo and by mid-morning they emerged from the dense jungle to an expansive kunai field. Lieutenant Fraser grinned with excitement. The flat area was at least a couple of miles in length and nearly a mile wide. Within the next hours, the Chimbus found the old airstrip underneath thick brush.

However, as Fraser and Robinson cleared away some of the brush, they discovered a fault. There would be a serious drainage problem. Water coming down the surrounding slopes might inundate the airstrip after a heavy rain that often drenched these rain forests. Robinson turned again to Sergeant Lumb.

"I don't think this place will do. Is there another area around here?"

Lumb still again turned to the Chimbu natives

who now pointed to the north. There was a similar kunai plain on the other side of the mountain near the village of Tsili Tsili. The natives there were quite friendly and they would also cooperate with the Americans and Australians.

For the next two days the party trekked through more rain forests and finally emerged in another wide glade, also about two miles long and a mile wide. Within an hour, Fraser found another old runway that had been used by the Brisbane Mining Company in the 1930s. Although covered with brush, Fraser was certain that a bulldozer could clear the vegetation easily, leaving the strip as a basis for building a new runway.

"This site will do fine," Fraser told Sergeant Lumb.

"You're the expert, sir," Lumb answered.

Everette Fraser and Lt. Ed Robinson surveyed the site until dusk, studying the terrain, the soil, the brush, and the surrounding hills. Lieutenant Robinson meanwhile, drew maps and took photographs. He had also put many Tsili Tsili natives to work clearing brush and filling holes in the area. Both officers also staked out areas where they could build drainage ditches, campsites, repair and service facilities, revetments, and a control tower.

Both men agreed, however, that they could probably operate here only until mid-September when the heavy rainy season began. Fraser turned to Sergeant Lumb yet again. "Are there any more potential sites around here for an airfield?"

The Australian non-com once more spoke to the Chimbus. The tribesmen shook their heads. The

Marilinan chief told Lumb that any other sites were much further south, below Wau, while this site was 40 miles northwest of Wau, only 50 miles from Lae, and about 300 miles from Wewak. An airbase on this plain would place American fighter planes within easy round trip distance of the growing Japanese base far up the New Guinea coast.

Sgt. Howard Lumb along with some of the Tsili Tsili natives remained at the site, while Fraser and Robinson returned to Bulolo with the Chimbu tribesmen. But Fraser could not a get a plane back to Moresby for at least a week or two. So Fraser and Robinson trekked for two more days through the jungle, finally reaching Wau almost a week after they found the Tsili Tsili site. The two men boarded the first plane going to Port Moresby and reached the base two hours later. The two officers hurried at once to Lieutenant Colonel Woodbury's headquarters.

"I think we've found a good place," Fraser said. "It's only three hundred miles from Wewak and about fifty miles from Lae. The kunai plain is plenty long enough for a five thousand foot runway, with enough space left over to construct fifty or sixty revetment areas. There's plenty of water from the nearby Watut River."

"You need only improve the old mining camp runway that's already there," Lieutenant Robinson said.

"Fine, fine," Woodbury answered.

"There is one problem, sir," Robinson said. "The drainage is not the best. You can probably deal with the usual rain storms, but I don't know if we can keep an airfield operating during the rainy season in

September and October."

"If the Eckton plan works," Woodbury gestured, "it won't make any difference. We'll have Lae by early September and we can develop an airfield in the Markham Valley. The potential airfield site at this Tsili Tsili is only for one purpose — to support an aerial knockout of Wewak."

"Yes sir."

Woodbury immediately met with Gen. Ennis Whitehead, the ADVON 5th Air Force commander, to report the information brought back by Fraser and Robinson for a potential fighter base at Tsili Tsili, only 300 miles from Wewak. Woodbury warned Whitehead, however, that this base would only do until the heavy rains began in mid-September. Then, all equipment, planes, and men would need to be pulled out. The operations against Lae and Wewak would need to be completed by then.

"It'll be over," Whitehead gestured sharply. "We'll make damn sure it is. Maybe the schedule will be a little tight, but I think we'll have the Markham Valley airfields in operation by mid-September and we can abandon any temporary site at this Tsili Tsili."

Lt. Col. Murray Woodbury loaded a C-47 with a crew of 12 men, a small grader, a small bulldozer, carryalls, grasscutters, and a large number of axes, picks, and shovels. He would press into service as many of the Chimbu natives as were willing to work. By the afternoon of 2 August 1943, a C-47 came into the hastily built strip made by Howard Lumb and the natives. The Gooney Bird bounced over the rough terrain but came to a safe stop. The tough, dependable C-47 transport plane again showed its value in alighting on the worst kind of terrain.

Woodbury immediately ordered his engineers to level the area with their small dozer and grader, while the unique Sgt. Howard Lumb persuaded hundreds of Chimbu tribesmen to work with picks, shovels, and machetes to clear away brush and kunai grass on the square of open plain. Within three days, the small team of airborne engineers and the hordes of natives had leveled a decent 4,000 foot runway, allowing dozens of C-47s to land at Tsili Tsili with more bulldozers, graders, carryalls, grass cutters, and jeeps. The work continued until the men completed a runway, two taxiways, and 40 hardstands to park aircraft.

By the second week in August, the 871st Airborne Engineer Battalion had completed most of its work and the C-47s flew in the 57th Australian Infantry Battalion along with their guns and equipment. The Aussies would guard this new base, especially since Japanese patrols were active in the area. Gooney Birds also flew in a signal company, the 565th Aircraft Warning Battalion, the 119th Quartermaster Company, an airdrome maintenance squadron, and a fighter control unit. These new arrivals quickly established communications networks, a radio station, an ordnance dump, a supply room, and housing for 3,000 men.

The Americans, however, saw one major problem during the construction of the Tsili Tsili airfield. If Japanese recon pilots spotted the frantic activity, their bombers would be over Tsili Tsili at once to destroy the site. Lieutenant Colonel Woodbury thus ordered two ruses.

"First," he told Capt. James Beck, his aide, "everything at Tsili Tsili must be camouflaged, so it looks like a remote patch of nothing from the air. Secondly, I want a dummy airfield at Marilinan: planes, equipment, facilities, the works. I've got a hunch that the Japanese may be suspicious of our activities out here. Among these hundreds of natives helping out, some of them are bound to talk, and rumors will get back to the Japanese at Lae and Salamaua."

"Yes sir."

Lieutenant Colonel Woodbury had certainly guessed right. Chimbu natives did not intentionally run to the Japanese with reports of the airbase construction along the Watut River, but village tribesmen innocently boasted of their work on the airbase. The talk spread to other villages and eventually to Salamaua, where the Japanese heard the news. Almost at once, Japanese recon pilots set off from Lae to reconnoiter the area along the Watut River. They soon enough spotted a target and they sent quick reports to Wewak.

Gen. Yamusi Arisue wasted no time. He called to his headquarters at once Capt. Masihisa Saito of the 751st Kokutai Naval Air Group and Capt. Shinichi Kapaya of the 15th Sentai Army Air Group. "We have received information from our reconnaissance pilots. The enemy is building a secret airfield along the Watut River above Wau. The site is only fifty miles from Lae and three hundred miles from Wewak. The enemy's strategy is obvious. They hope to have an airfield where they can base fighter planes to escort their B-25 strafers to Wewak. A bomber force with escort must destroy this cancer at once. The 18th Sentai will mount a squadron of heavy bombers and the 751st Kokutai will furnish Mitsubishi fighter escorts."

"Yes, Honorable Arisue," Captain Saito said.

Captain Saito quickly alerted his 26th Zero Fighter Squadron from the 751st Kokutai, while Captain Kapaya alerted the 153rd Betty Bomber Squadron from his 18th Sentai. On the morning of August 7th, the attack force took off from Wewak, 26 Zeros under Lt. Comdr. Joyotara Iwami and 24 Betty bombers under Capt. Shinichi Kapaya himself. By 1000 hours, the Japanese planes arrived over their target—the counterfeit site at Marilinan.

"We will attack in one minute, one minute," Captain Kapaya called his bomber crews.

Soon, whistling 500 pound bombs tumbled out of the Betty bombers, shuddering the ground in numbing explosions. Several scattered phony planes on the ground exploded as did dummy buildings, and dummy bulldozer equipment. More bombs chopped holes in the fake runway. The Japanese left a pall of destruction in the area and Captain Kapaya was satisfied. The Americans had cleverly inserted dynamite sticks in the cardboard and plywood targets so they would explode when struck by exploding bombs.

"Fighters will land at Lae to refuel," Kapaya cried into his radio. "Bombers will return to base."

"Yes, Honorable Captain," Lieutenant Commander Iwami said.

The Japanese planes banked away from the Watut River site high in the Owen Stanley Mountains and flew back to Wewak or Lae. Both the bomber crews

59

and fighter pilots grinned with delight after their successful strike on Marilinan.

However, at least one Japanese pilot flew his Zero with a sober face. Lt. Comdr. Joyotara Iwami flew toward Lae with doubt instead of elation. He could not believe that the attack on Marilinan could have come off so easily. Not a single antiaircraft shell nor a single interceptor had challenged them. Surely, if the Americans were building a secret base on the remote highland plain, they would have taken strong defensive measures. The Americans certainly knew that Japanese reconnaissance planes continually patrolled the skies over the Owen Stanleys and the Americans should have guessed that sooner or later snooping Japanese pilots would discover their site. But no antiaircraft guns or fighter planes had interfered with the Japanese attack.

Yet, Iwami had seen the planes, equipment, buildings, and runway below. Had the enemy created a deceptive airfield replica to fool the Japanese, while their real construction site was somewhere else? The 751st Kokutai squadron leader could not dismiss this suspicion from his mind. He would talk to Captain Saito when he returned to Wewak, and he would urge his kokutai commander to conduct a massive recon search in the areas about the Watut River and Wau.

Meanwhile, at Tsili Tsili, the men of the US 871st Airborne Engineers cheered in delight when they got reports of the Japanese attack on Marilinan. "It worked, Colonel, it worked," Captain Beck grinned at Woodbury. "Those Nip idiots took the bait and hit our phony airfield. Maybe we'd better restore the stuff at Marilinan so the Japs can hit them again."

But Lt. Col. Murray Woodbury was not smiling. In fact, a frown had wrinkled his face. "Captain, we're not going to fool those Nips for long. They'll figure out this ruse pretty soon. We need to get those fighter planes up here as soon as possible. And we'd best make sure in the meanwhile that we have anti-aircraft crews on full alert."

"Yes sir."

Lieutenant Colonel Woodbury then called Moresby and spoke to General Whitehead himself, who promised to get 35th Fighter Group planes to Tsili Tsili within a week. "You're not the only one worrying about Tsili Tsili, Colonel," the general said. "We're all anxious to get planes up there. Everybody here in Moresby is worried about the Japanese build-up at Wewak. We want to knock out that base as soon as possible."

"Yes sir," Woodbury said.

Later, when he left his tent, Woodbury squinted to the north, beyond an Owen Stanley ridge. Wewak was somewhere to the northwest and perhaps the Japanese would soon return with more air formations. And next time, they might hit Tsili Tsili instead of the counterfeit Marilinan.

CHAPTER FOUR

The Japanese base at Wewak had been in operation for more than a year, but only recently had the 8th Area Forces begun heavy construction. During most of 1942 and into 1943, the principal Japanese staging area of New Guinea had been Hollandia, far up the coast in Dutch New Guinea, and at Lae in Papua, New Guinea. However, after the Bismarck Sea debacle in March of 1943, the 8th Area Forces staff faced two problems: the serious Allied threat to Lae and the remoteness of Hollandia to the battle areas in Papua. The Japanese therefore needed a base much closer than Hollandia and still far enough away to remain out of range from US 5th Air Force fighter planes.

Wewak, at the westerly end of Papua, had been little more than a native village when the Japanese first occupied the site in early 1942. The area had been an important trading port in the Bismarck Archipelago because of its two fine harbors, Wewak itself, and Hansa Bay, ten miles to the south. When the Japanese sought a likely site for their current needs, 8th Area Forces engineers studied several areas along the northern coast of New Guinea and concluded that Wewak would make an ideal site for an air and sea base.

The Wewak peninsula, jutting into the Bismarck Sea and measuring 15 miles in length and three to five miles in width, offered plenty of dry, flat areas for the construction of airfields. On the left side of the peninsula was Wewak Harbor and to the south was Hansa Bay, a sheltered cove ideal for shipping.

From mid-March until well into July of 1943, the Japanese had worked vigorously at both Wewak and Hansa Bay. They had built excellent jetties, shoreline warehouses, and service buildings at both harbors. Shipping could enter both harbors from Rabaul without fear of getting hit by the dreaded American B-25 strafers because Buna, the Allied base, lay out of range for fighter planes.

8th Area Forces engineers had also begun construction on airfields. Construction battalions, besides using their own equipment, had enlisted the aid of hundreds of Papuan natives, most of them in forced toil. Desertions among the villagers had been rampant, but the Japanese had always rounded up enough new people to replace such deserters.

By July of 1943 the Japanese had completed three sprawling airdromes on the Wewak Peninsula and a fourth airdrome at Hansa Bay. Along the coast at the tip of the peninsula was But Drome, a 4,500 foot runway with hidden revetment areas on the south side. But could house up to a hundred fighters and at least fifty bombers and became the home of the 751st Naval Kokutai. About three miles inland was the main airfield, Wewak Drome, with its long 5,500 foot runway that could accommodate up to 200 aircraft. This drome housed the 253rd Naval Kokutai with its horde of Zero and Oscar fighters along with heavy Betty bombers.

Southeast of Wewak Drome was Dagua Drome, another large airfield with a 5,500 foot runway. Here were the medium Sally bombers and Oscar fighters of the 17th Army Sentai. And finally, ten miles to the south the 18th Army Sentai based its Dinah light bombers and Oscar fighters along with Betty heavy bombers at Boram Drome just beyond Hansa Bay. Boram could house over a hundred planes.

The Americans certainly had reason to worry when US reconnaissance pilots reported the increasing air strength at Wewak. Photographs on 7 August showed more than 125 planes at the Wewak complex, about 30 more than previous photos only a few days earlier, and 50 more than photos taken a week earlier. Based on recon information, American intelligence men believed that the Japanese 7th Air Division planned to house at least 400 planes at the Wewak airdromes.

True enough! Gen. Yamusi Arisue, the CinC of the 7th Air Division, was amassing aircraft on the Wewak airfields as fast as his service troops could accommodate such aircraft, combat crews, and fighter pilots. By the second week in August, he counted nearly 200 planes among his two navy Kokutais and two army sentais. On 5 August, he called into conference his quartet of air commanders: Capt. Masahisa Saito of the 751st Kokutai, Comdr. Shuichi Watakazi of the 253rd Kokutai, Col. Koji Tanaka of the 17th Sentai, and Maj. Shinichi Kapaya of the 18th Sentai.

"Gentlemen," Arisue began, "I need not tell you that the enemy is making a frantic effort to get fighter planes within range of Wewak. Such aircraft could then escort their B-25 low level strafers to attack our airdromes. We fortunately discovered their new construction near a village called Marilinan where the Americans are building their fighter airdrome. Photos of our air attacks yesterday showed that we did considerable damage. Do you concur?" he asked Capt. Shinichi Kapaya of the 18th Sentai.

"Honorable General," Kapaya answered, "we left a swath of fire and smoke in our wake. The Mitsubishi bomber crews did exceptionally well. We caught the enemy off guard since they did not mount a single fighter plane to challenge us; nor did they send up a single antiaircraft shell."

"It must have been a complete surprise," Arisue nodded, "for I have always known the enemy to have excellent early warning systems."

"Honorable Arisue," Captain Saito of the 721st Kokutai now spoke, "I must tell you that Lieutenant Commander Iwami was uneasy. He led our 26th Squadron of fighters to escort the Mitsubishi bombers. He suspects that the so-called construction of the enemy airbase at Marilinan is a ruse. Iwami refuses to believe that such a site would not be protected with large numbers of antiaircraft guns and hordes of enemy fighters."

"But the evidence is obvious," the 7th Air Division commander insisted. "When our intelligence men at Salamaua were informed by reliable natives of this site, our scout pilots verified the enemy construction. Also, reconnaissance photos revealed the presence of these facilities. Our bomber crews saw the equipment, planes, runway, and build-up. All of us must surely know that the enemy is apprehensive because of our build-up here in Wewak. They are desperate to do something about it."

"But Commander Iwami is a wise combat officer," Saito persisted.

"Please, Honorable Saito," Captain Kapaya of the 18th Sentai grinned at the 721st Kokutai commander. "The bomber crews were quite certain of their targets. None had any doubts that a new enemy airfield was under construction at Marilinan. If we should bombard this area again and again, we can surely forestall any American attempt to attack Wewak before we mount our own heavy assaults on the enemy's airbases."

"Perhaps Commander Iwami is wrong," Saito conceded.

Arisue shook his head. "Let us get on with the business at hand." He shuffled through some papers in front of him. "I have taken count of our strength at Wewak at this moment. We currently have thirty-nine fighters and twenty bombers from the 721st Kokutai at But Drome. There are thirty fighters, thirty-four light bombers, and fifteen heavy bombers of the 18th Sentai at Boram; sixteen medium bombers and thirty-three fighters at Dagua Drome, and thirty fighters and thirty heavy bombers of the 253rd Kokutai at Wewak Airdrome. We thus have nearly two hundred and fifty aircraft scattered among the four airfields. It is my hope to have at least three hundred aircraft in Wewak before we launch our massive assaults on the enemy's bases in Buna and Port Moresby. Meanwhile, we should send out aircraft regularly, whenever weather permits, to destroy the enemy construction site at Marilinan."

"How soon will we have the remainder of our aircraft to bring the Kokutais and Sentais of the 7th Air Division to full strength?" Captain Kapaya asked.

"Within a week," General Arisue answered.

"And what of the enemy's air strength?" Captain Saito asked.

"Our latest estimates indicate that the enemy has close to five hundred aircraft based at their several airdromes in Port Moresby and their two airfields at Buna," Arisue answered. "Among the enemy's bombers, however, only sixty of these are heavy B-24s and B-17s that might attack Wewak, and even those would only attack at night. As long as they do not have fighter planes to escort bombers to Wewak, the enemy's light and medium low level bombers will not attack our bases here."

"When do you plan to launch our multiple strikes, Honorable Arisue," Colonel Tanaka asked.

"As soon as possible," the 7th Air Division commander answered. "General Adachi is quite anxious to begin his counteroffensive for recapturing Buna. He has amassed nearly thirty thousand men in the Wewak area, of which thirteen thousand are honed combat troops. He estimates that the enemy has no more than a few thousand combat soldiers in Buna and Port Moresby, where most of the personnel are airmen or service troops. It is the Honorable Adachi's intent to begin a drive overland from Salamaua along the jungle trails, while the bulk of his combat force make amphibious landings on the shoreline at Gona, just above Buna."

"But can he truly succeed in such an operation?" Captain Saito asked.

"He can if we neutralize the enemy's air power," Arisue answered. "That is why we must strike hard at the enemy's airbases in Buna and Port Moresby. We will make our initial attacks on the enemy's fighter dromes to keep interceptors to a minimum. On subsequent missions our aircraft will attack their bomber fields."

"I see," Captain Saito said.

"The 7th Air Division staff has drawn up a tentative plan to begin our air attacks in mid-August," Arisue gestured. "Our meteorologists believe that good weather will prevail over the Bismarck Archipelago at that period, and we should be able to continue daily, sustained assaults over a period of several days. Such frequent, multiple strikes will enable us to stop the enemy from getting his airfields back into operation before our ground troops make their landings in the Buna area."

Arisue looked at the papers in front of him once more before he spoke again. "A new convoy from Rabaul is expected to reach Wewak within the next couple of days. These marus will bring more arms, ammunition, food, medicine, clothing, and other needs to carry out Operation MO II. Meanwhile, all types of aircraft will continue to arrive in Wewak from Rabaul to bolster our four air groups." He scanned the men around him. "I urge you to meet with your own squadron and flight leaders and apprise them of the discussions at this conference. Your fighter pilots and bomber crews must be on alert. Your ordnance men must be certain they have ample fuel and ammunition to load aircraft on a day's notice. They must also make certain that all guns are in good order. Finally, the ground mechanics must be sure the aircraft are in combat readiness for these long flights to the enemy's airbases."

"What about Lae?" Captain Saito asked. "Can our fighter pilots rely on the commander there to land and refuel our fighter planes before returning to Wewak?"

"Yes," Arisue nodded. "Colonel Miyazaki of the Lae Base Force has assured me that he will have at least one thousand men on alert and at least several dozen trucks fully loaded with earth. Miyazaki's work crews will quickly fill any bomb craters in runways should the enemy attack the Lae airfield during our series of bombing raids on Buna and Port Moresby. He will keep these laden vehicles well camouflaged and away from the airfields to avoid destruction by American or Australian aircraft. Colonel Miyazaki has also kept on reserve several hundred drums of gasoline to refuel aircraft that stage out of Lae. The gasoline trucks will also be camouflaged and away from the airfields."

"Good," Captain Saito nodded. "It is imperative that the facilities at Lae are available to our fighter pilots, otherwise these flyers could never return to Wewak."

Arisue looked at his watch. "It is time for the noon meal. We will retire to the dining room. Then you should return to your units and meet with your own officers."

Meanwhile, for the 18th Army ground troops, the build-up at Wewak heightened their morale. The combat troops stationed here, after the disasters at Buna and in the Battle of the Bismarck Sea, now saw a chance to reverse these defeats. They had seen the wilderness of the Wewak Peninsula transformed into a major military base. These infantrymen and artillerymen of Adachi's army had themselves enthusiastically helped construction battalions to build runways, taxiways, storage warehouses, repair and service facilities, revetment areas, and port facilities. Now, after many weeks, these Nippon troops admired the results of their hard labors.

The airmen of the 7th Air Division had also reached new heights in morale. They had seen more bombs, ammunition, aircraft repair tools, and service equipment pour into Wewak. They had seen the steady new arrival of more aircraft: Mitsubishi A6s (Zero) and Nakajima K-43s (Oscar) fighters, Mitsubishi GM-4 (Betty) heavy bombers, Mitsubishi K-21 (Sally) medium bombers, and Mitsubishi K-146 (Dinah) light bombers. Revetment areas were now crammed with planes, and construction crews continually toiled to build new housing for the dozens of fresh fighter pilots and bomber crews who came to Wewak.

Japanese airmen, especially the veterans from the old Tianan Wing in Lae, saw a resurgence of the Japanese Air Force in New Guinea. They envisioned the day not far off when Japan would again control the skies over the Bismarck Archipelago. All of them waited breathlessly for the big week when Japanese bombers and fighters out of Wewak darkened the skies over the Southwest Pacific and flew southward to smash the Allied airfields in Buna and Port Moresby. These men had already heard from crews of the 18th Sentai how Bettys were smashing the American attempt to build an airfield at Marilinan, a raid in which the Japanese had not suffered any losses in planes or airmen.

"We are going back to make certain that not even a barrel of fuel is left intact," one 18th Sentai airman boasted to ground crews.

The 7th Air Division service troops believed the combat airman and on the morning of 8 August, only two days after the first raid, the ground crews at Wewak watched the line of 22 Betty bombers from the 18th Sentai once more lumber toward the main runway on Boram Field to set off on another strike against Marilinan. At the same moment, Lt. Comdr. Joyotara Iwami again led his 24 Zero fighters from the 751st Kokutai toward the main runway at But. The Zeros would again escort the Bettys.

By 0800 hours, the 46 planes from the 7th Air Division had left their airdromes in Wewak. The men left behind watched until the combat planes had disappeared to the south. As they returned to their chores, the ground crews did not keep their minds totally on their work, for they were thinking of Marilinan, and wondering if the combat crews would succeed today as they had two days ago.

Meanwhile, Murray Woodbury of the US 871st Airborne Engineers knew that the enemy might get suspicious; that the Japanese might learn that Marilinan was a deception and that the real airbase was at

Tsili Tsili. As soon as the Japanese raid of the 6th had ended on the sham airfield, Woodbury sent a company of construction men along with several hundred willing natives to "repair" the bombed base of Marilinan. The lieutenant colonel fully expected the Japanese to hit the site again and he wanted to give them another good target.

But Woodbury also considered the lack of defenses at Marilinan. The Japanese might have logically assumed that they had caught the Americans off guard, thus accounting for the lack of AA or fighter opposition. However, if the Japanese faced no opposition on another raid, they would surely suspect that Marilinan was not a real airbase. The lieutenant colonel called on Maj. Jim Coburn of the 470th Automatic Weapons Battalion that furnished the anti-aircraft defenses for the new Tsili Tsili airdrome.

"Major," Woodbury said, "I need some volunteers with a few guns over at Marilinan. I expect the Japanese to bomb that decoy airbase again and it's quite imperative that they meet some flak opposition."

"I agree, sir," Coburn answered. "I'm sure I can find at least a half dozen volunteer crews. I'll fly them in there this afternoon."

"Good," Woodbury said.

"What about fighter plane protection?" Coburn grinned.

"I've thought of that too, Major," Woodbury answered, "and I've done something about it."

Lt. Col. Murray Woodbury had alerted the 35th Fighter Group in Port Moresby. Lt. Col. Malcolm Moore, the 35th Group commander, must keep a squadron of fighter planes over Tsili Tsili-Marilinan areas on two hour CAPs throughout the daylight hours. The P-38s or P-39s would operate in relays since Tsili Tsili was less than an hour's flying time from Moresby. Moore's squadrons could easily maintain two hour patrols. The fighters were to attack any Japanese planes that came into the area, even if the enemy aircraft went after the dummy field of Marilinan instead of after Tsili Tsili itself.

Lieutenant Colonel Woodbury had also met with his own men at Tsili Tsili to make certain they kept all equipment under wraps, all buildings fully camouflaged, all vehicles hidden, and the completed runway and taxiways heavily covered with brush to hide them from the air.

By 1020 hours, 8 August, the Japanese air formations approached the Watut River. Before any bombers came within striking distance of Marilinan, Maj. Curran Jones of the 35th Group's 39th Fighter Squadron cried into his radio. "Enemy aircraft at one o'clock. First and 2nd Flights will take the bombers; 3rd and 4th Flights will attack the escorts."

"I read you, Major," Capt. Tom Lynch answered.

Off to the northward, Lt. Comdr. Joyotara Iwami spotted the American planes to the southwest and he heard the sporadic booms of AA fire in the distance. The Japanese 26th Squadron commander frowned, somewhat confused. The Americans were now waiting with both interceptors and antiaircraft guns. Perhaps Captain Kapaya was correct. Perhaps they had simply caught the Americans asleep on the first bombing attack.

Iwami mulled over these conjectures for only a moment and then cried into his radio. "Interceptors to the southwest. We must protect the bombers. My first flight will attack the interceptors and 2nd Flight will remain with the bombers."

"Yes, Honorable Iwami," Lt. Masami Nakami answered.

The Japanese would not compete with the more powerful P-38 aircraft and the experienced pilots of the 35th Fighter Group. Among the American airmen, Major Jones had been in combat for more than a year and had downed six Japanese planes, half of them during the early months of 1942 when the Japanese had controlled the skies over New Guinea. Jones was now on his 37th combat mission.

Capt. Tom Lynch had been in combat for about six months and during that time he had already downed five Zeros and damaged a score more. Lynch too had gained most of his victories during those hard months of 1942 and early 1943. But Lynch seemed destined to be a fighter pilot for he seemingly did everything right. The young captain would become one of the greatest American aces of the Pacific war.

Jones's flight, 12 planes, immediately waded into the 13 Japanese Zeros under Lieutenant Commander Iwami. In the vicious dogfight north of Marilinan the Americans shot down three Japanese fighters for a loss of one P-38. Major Jones got two kills himself when he blew one enemy plane apart with solid 20mm hits. He got his second kill with short bursts of .50 caliber wing fire that ripped off the tail of the Mitsubishi fighter before the Zero tumbled into the mountainous jungle below.

Scoring the lone kill for the Japanese was Lieutenant Commander Iwami, a veteran of more than two years in combat. He had served first in China, then in the Philippines, and then aboard a carrier in the Central Pacific. He had then served at Rabaul, and he had finally joined the 751st Kokutai in New Guinea to command a naval fighter squadron. Iwami got his score when he maneuvered into position to blast away the cockpit of a P-38 with 7.7 machine gun fire, killing the pilot. The Lightning then tumbled into the jungle and exploded. The kill was Iwami's 14th during his long combat career.

The Nippon pilots protecting the Betty bombers did somewhat better against the flight of P-38s under Capt. Tom Lynch. But here too the Japanese lost two Zeros of their own for a loss of one P-38. As the Lightnings and Zeros battled furiously with each other, the Betty bombers held their positions with little interference and droned over Marilinan. Intense American AA fire downed one of the Bettys, but the bombers never faltered.

From 8,000 feet, the Japanese crews released over 30 tons of 500 pound bombs that sailed into the dummy base and erupted a staccato of explosions. Once more the Betty airmen left behind a huge patch of fire and smoke that almost obscured the target area.

As the Japanese planes made their way back from their target, both Captain Kapaya of the 18th Sentai's 153rd Betty Bomber Squadron and Lieutenant Commander Iwami of the 751st Kokutai's 27th Fighter Squadron were now convinced that the Americans were indeed building an advanced fighter base at Marilinan. Kapaya himself promised to see

General Arisue as soon as he returned to Wewak and to request that Japanese air units return to Marilinan the next day with even more bombers to hit the base again.

Lt. Col. Murray Woodbury, of course, could not have been more delighted with the action over Marilinan on the other side of the mountain ridge from Tsili Tsili. After the two air strikes, he was now certain that the Japanese were convinced that Marilinan was the true site of the new American airbase construction. As soon as the raid ended on the bogus target, Woodbury ordered his airborne engineers to remove all camouflage on Tsili Tsili and to resume construction work.

"I want that strip and those taxiways finished as quickly as possible," Woodbury told Captain Beck. "We can't just keep CAPs up here. We've got to base planes here at Tsili Tsili. If those Nips find out we've been conning them, they'll send their whole damn air force after us."

"What about the 35th Fighter Group?" Captain Beck asked. "Are they ready to come up here?"

"They'd better be," the lieutenant colonel said. He looked at the sky to the west. "I won't feel safe until I see their parked planes up here."

"Yes sir."

CHAPTER FIVE

Lt. Col. Murray Woodbury of the 871st Airborne Engineer Battalion exhorted his men to work harder, toiling on three shifts, 24 hours a day, to get the airfield completed as soon as possible. Meanwhile, Woodbury called Port Moresby almost daily to make certain that the US 35th Fighter Group was ready to move at once into Tsili Tsili when they got the word.

The Japanese conducted two more raids on Marilinan, one on August 10th and another on August 13th. Again, American fighter planes from the 35th Group and American AA gunners from the 470th AW Battery challenged the Japanese air formation, downing seven planes, while losing two P-38s and one AA site. Weather prevented the Japanese from making attacks on the 9th, 11th, and 12th of August. Gen. Yamusi Arisue believed that the multiple strikes had effectively knocked out Marilinan.

"Aircraft continue to come into Wewak," Arisue told his air commanders. "By the time the enemy rebuilds his destroyed base at Marilinan, we ourselves will have smashed their airbases at Buna and Port

Moresby. However," he continued, "we will continue to maintain routine reconnaissance aircraft over the Marilinan area."

Meanwhile, Gen. Ennis Whitehead of the US AD-VON 5th Air Force continued his own reconnaissance flights over Wewak, and each new effort brought more unpleasant reports to the 5th Air Force staff. By 14 August the recon pilots and their passenger observers estimated that the Japanese now had close to 300 aircraft at their four airdromes.

On the afternoon of the 14th, General Whitehead's aide, Col. David Hutchinson, brought the ADVON commander the latest recon report. "Sir, I know you've been waiting for those Nips to build up Wewak to maximum capacity before we strike, but we can't keep Tsili Tsili under wraps much longer. The enemy will find that airbase soon."

Whitehead nodded. "Is Tsili Tsili ready?"

"Pretty much," Hutchinson answered. "The 35th Fighter Control Squadron has been up there for a couple of weeks and they've got the groundwork completed."

"Okay, send up the advance echelon of the 35th Fighter Group to Tsili Tsili tomorrow and their fighter planes can go out the day after."

"Yes sir."

Meanwhile, Japanese reconnaissance planes continued patrols in the Owen Stanley Mountains in the areas west of Lae and Salamaua. The Nippon pilots had always kept an eye on the Australian base at Wau, checking any potential build-up of men and equipment. Any increases in combat strength here might indicate that the Allies were planning an assault on Salamaua or Lae over jungle trails, so the Japanese kept themselves fully informed on such allied activities. The Japanese also worried about the allies developing new bases on the Watut River area that could be a threat to them.

On the afternoon of 14 August a flight of three Japanese recon planes was cruising along the Watut River to observe the wreckage at Marilinan: smashed buildings, wrecked planes, and burned out vehicles. Moderate AA fire challenged the three planes, but the Japanese in their highly maneuverable Zeros easily evaded this flak.

In taking evasive action, one of the recon pilots, F/O Masajiro Kawato of the 721st Kokutai's 27th Squadron thought he detected something wrong. He had been staring at a couple of "wrecked" planes at Marilinan but he noticed that the smashed fuselage did not reflect any sparkle in the afternoon sun. He called fellow pilot F/O Isuma Sasaki.

"Something is wrong down there," Kawato said. "I am flying low for a closer look."

"It is dangerous to do that in view of the enemy's antiaircraft fire," Flight Officer Sasaki said.

"I shall go down anyway."

F/O Masajiro Kawato arced his Zero and came zooming over the Marilinan plain, despite the AA fire. He flew over a 4,000 foot length of terrain at nearly deck level and looked hard at the area around him. As he rose sharply out of the area, his face reflected utter shock and he quickly called Sasaki.

"Isuma, we have been deceived! Deceived! There is no enemy air base below us."

"What?" Sasaki gasped.

"It is a false airfield. The wrecked planes and smashed buildings are made of nothing more than painted plywood and cardboard. The burned out vehicles are wood and not charred metal, and there is no runway or taxiway, but only a brush covered strip of elongated earth. I fear that our attacks on Marilinan have been nothing but useless exercises."

"This cannot be," Sasaki cried.

"I would ask that you and Motomu come down with me at low level and make observations for yourselves."

"We will do so," Sasaki answered.

All three Japanese pilots arced sharply and dove into the area, crossing the Watut River and then skimming over the wide expanse of open plain. Both Sasaki and Motomu stared hard as they swept across the open area before they too gaped in astonishment. There were no airfield, no real buildings, planes, or vehicles; just plywood and cardboard forgeries.

The ack ack fire caught Motomu's plane and the Zero exploded from the solid hits before cartwheeling into the ground in a ball of fire. However, Kasato and Sasaki got away and they rose high in the afternoon sky.

"Isamu," Kawato called his companion over the radio, "Marilinan is an obvious fraud as you have seen."

"Yes," Sasaki answered.

"They have fooled us while they probably built a highland base somewhere else," Kawato said.

"That is a most logical conclusion," Sasaki answered.

"We have fuel for three more hours of flying

time," Kawato said. "We will not fly back to Lae immediately. Instead, we will search along the Watut River, and we will look for another open area that could be an airbase site."

"Very well, Masa," Sasaki said.

The two Japanese pilots flew low along the Watut River for about 15 minutes, skirting mountain ridges until they saw another open plain to the left. The Americans had again camouflaged all construction here, and Lieutenant Colonel Woodbury had ordered his AA gunners to stay under wraps to avoid exposure of his airbase. But Kawato and Sasaki would make a close observation of the open plain.

"We will fly at low level."

"Yes, Masu," Sasaki answered.

The two Japanese pilots then dropped under 100 feet and cruised over the Tsili Tsili flats. From this ground level, the American camouflage tactics could not thwart complete observation. Kawato and Sasaki gasped in awe at what they saw: several service and repair buildings concealed under brush; a half dozen C-47 transport planes, whose metal sparkled even under the heavy grass over them. They also saw at least a dozen vehicles: trucks, bulldozers, and graders—all camouflaged. The two Nippon flyers also detected a brush covered ribbon, long and flat, and they rightly guessed that this lengthy oblong was a runway.

Kawato and Sasaki also noticed the dots of cleared areas under the trees, obvious revetments for planes that would be based here in Tsili Tsili.

Lt. Col. Murray Woodbury, from an obscure shelter, watched the two Japanese planes make two low level passes over Tsili Tsili and he now cursed. He had acted foolishly by withholding AA fire, giving the Japanese pilots a free rein to make careful observations. By the time the two Zeros made their second pass, Woodbury was sure the Japanese pilots had discovered the new airfield.

Capt. James Beck looked soberly at Woodbury. "Well, sir, they know we're here."

"Call Moresby. We've got to have those fighters up here at once. Now that we've been exposed, the Nips will easily guess that we plan to come to Wewak pretty soon. General Whitehead will need to carry out his attacks sooner than he planned."

"Do you think the Nips will hit us soon?" Beck asked.

"It's too late for them to do anything today," the lieutenant colonel answered, "but you can bet your life they'll be here at daylight with a horde of bombers. We've got to work fast."

"Yes sir."

True enough. Within an hour, the recon pilots landed at Lae, and F/O Masajiro Kawato wasted no time in finding a radio. He quickly called his 751st Kokutai commander, Capt. Masahisa Saito and detailed what they had learned: the ruse at Marilinan and the real enemy airbase at Tsili Tsili. Captain Saito listened in shock and asked how far along the Americans had come on the Tsili Tsili airfield construction.

"From our observations," Kawato said, "their project is all but completed and they appear ready to bring in fighter aircraft."

"*Bakarya!*" Saito cursed. "I will consult with General Arisue at once. Meanwhile, you are to remain in Lae. Fly out again with more aircraft this afternoon if you can. You will then fly out at first light to divert the enemy at Tsili Tsili while our bombers arrive over this enemy site."

"Yes, Honorable Saito," Kawato answered.

As soon as the 751st Kokutai commander finished talking with Kawato, the naval air captain called on General Arisue of the 7th Air Division to explain what the recon pilots had learned. Arisue expressed outrage, and he cursed his airmen. After all, they had made several attacks on the alleged enemy airfield during the past week or more. Were all of the Japanese airmen blind? Did not any of the combat fighter pilots or bomber crews notice the deception? The 7th Air Division had expended important time, effort, and ammunition to knock out this supposed enemy field, only to learn that they had simply wasted their labors and resources.

When Saito offered to send out his bombers and fighters at first light, Arisue scowled derisively. "Your airmen are fools. I am disinclined to send out your blind flyers again."

Saito did not answer.

"No," Arisue gestured angrily, "I will send out Colonel Tanaka's 17th Sentai, with his medium bombers and Nakajima (Oscar) fighters. Capt. Kusuma Sakai is an excellent fighter leader and he will give the medium bombers good protection."

"Protection?"

The 7th Air Division commander glared at Saito. "Are you so foolish as to believe that the enemy will not have fighters waiting for us in the morning?

85

Surely, if Kawato and the other reconnaissance pilot made accurate sweeps over Tsili Tsili, the Americans can easily guess that our scouts detected the true nature of their labors. No," the general gestured again, "your airmen will not make the attack. Instead you and the other Sentai and Kokutai commanders are to make ready all bombers, fighters, and airmen. As soon as we have destroyed the American base at Tsili Tsili, we will carry out our massive MO II air operation against the enemy's airfields at Port Moresby and Buna."

"Yes, Honorable Arisue."

Dawn of 15 August broke clear over New Guinea and with daylight a burst of activity erupted at both Wewak and Port Moresby.

At Dagua Drome, Col. Koji Tanaka of the 17th Sentai personally mustered 22 medium Sally bombers from his 146th Squadron and the men boarded their planes for the attack on Tsili Tsili. Tanaka's ground crews had loaded the planes with quartets of 250 pound bombs, including both HE and incendiaries. The colonel intended to bring in his Sallys at a relatively low altitude, no higher than 3,000 feet, for maximum accuracy against the installations at Tsili Tsili. The Sally gunners had made certain that all machine guns were fully loaded with strafing belts.

In the 17th Sentai's 147th Squadron, Capt. Kusuma Sakai mustered 18 Oscar fighter pilots to escort the Sally bombers. Sakai had been a veteran of the Japanese Army Air Force for nearly six years, beginning his career in China where he had downed 17 Russian and Chinese planes during the late 1930s and into 1940 and 1941. At the outbreak of war with the United States, Sakai had fought in Southeast Asia and then in Java and finally in New Guinea. After a year of instruction duty in Japan, the veteran combat pilot had returned to the Southwest Pacific to command an army fighter squadron.

For three months, Sakai had been training new army fighter pilots at Rabaul, but in early July he had left his squadron and flown to Wewak to assume command of the 147th Squadron. At an early morning briefing, he warned his pilots to expect heavy interceptions today over Tsili Tsili, perhaps even from the dreaded P-38 fighter planes. The Japanese pilots must be alert and aggressive if the Sally bomber crews were to do a thorough job on the target.

At 0830 hours, the formation of 22 Sallys and 18 Oscars left Dagua Drome and headed for Tsili Tsili, two hours away. As usual, the bombers would make their runs and return to Wewak, but the fighters would land at Lae to refuel before flying back to Wewak. The Lae Base Force commander had been told to prepare the base to service Oscars today.

At 0600 hours, meanwhile, the first formation of US 54th Carrier Wing C-47 transport planes roared off Ward Drome in Port Moresby. Sixteen Gooney Birds were taking off, carrying the headquarters squadron personnel of the 35th Fighter Group. The transports, escorted by 18 P-39 Aerocobra fighters from the 35th Fighter Group's 41st Squadron, soon cleared the Kokoda Range over the Owen Stanleys and then headed northwest toward Tsili Tsili.

At the new airdrome in Tsili Tsili, the ground crews prepared to meet the first echelon of men from the 35th Fighter Group. Control men readied themselves to bring in the planes, while transportation men waited with trucks and command cars to take the new arrivals to new quarters at the campsites themselves. Mess crews planned on serving a noon meal to the 200 men coming in.

Capt. Francis Dublisher, leading the squadron of Aerocobra fighters, sent three pilots ahead to make sure the area was clear for landings by the 16 Gooney Bird transport planes. Lt. Ed Latine led the trio of van aircraft but he saw nothing. The flight from Moresby had taken more than two hours because the P-39 fighter pilots needed to reduce speed and remain with the slow moving, heavily laden transport planes. The C-47s not only carried 200 men, but these planes also carried several tons of supplies that the headquarters squadron personnel would need: medicine, food, clothing, radio equipment, mess hall gear, filing cabinets, photo paraphernalia, small arms and small arms ammunition, sleeping cots, mosquito netting, and even several pet dogs.

The men aboard the transports occasionally staring out of the windows of the C-47s, did not realize the danger that lay ahead. In fact, the ground personnel of the 35th Group watched with relative confidence as the planes from the first flight of C-47s touched down one after another without incident and taxied toward dispersal areas.

However, as the first plane from 2nd Flight turned to land on the new Tsili Tsili airstrip, a sudden staccato of ack ack fire erupted in the sky. The bombers and fighters from the Japanese 17th Sentai had suddenly come into Tsili Tsili. The cagey commander,

Co. Koji Tanaka, had brought the Sallys and Oscars down to treetop level when they came within 20 miles of target. Thus the Japanese had deftly avoided American early warning systems by coming in under the radar before the planes swept over the mountain ridges and into the Tsili Tsili airdrome.

Colonel Tanaka was astonished when he studied the area ahead. He saw several transport planes taxiing toward revetment areas and he noted two more C-47s turning in the sky to come down for a landing. Tanaka quickly called Capt. Kusuma Sakai.

"Enemy transport aircraft are trying to land. You will shoot them down, while the bombers make their attacks."

"Yes, Honorable Tanaka," Sakai said. He then scanned the sky and saw the eight C-47s over Tsili Tsili. They were huge, defenseless albatrosses waiting for annihilation. Sakai grinned and called his fighter pilots. "Pick your target and shoot it down."

"Yes, Captain," P/O Ito Kayo answered.

The Oscar pilots, in pairs, roared toward the helpless American transport planes that were carrying the second half of the 35th Group's headquarters squadron along with an array of supplies. The 35th airmen stared from the Gooney Bird windows in utter horror. Certain death appeared moments away.

Captain Sakai came down with his wingman, Lt. Shunzo Kodoma, and the two Japanese pilots opened with chattering 7.7 machine gun fire on one of the slow moving transports. The withering fusillade shot off the Gooney Bird's right engine, ripped away part of the fuselage, and ignited the interior of the plane. Cpl. Virgil Dockery, a dental assistant, caught a hit in the shoulder and fellow passengers took him forward as the rear area of the plane burst into flames. Dental officer Capt. Robert Heller worked furiously on the assistant whose shoulder now bled profusely.

The C-47 pilot frantically radioed for help against the Japanese Oscars. He told the field control officer he would try to crash land the crippled transport between two lines of trees. However, as he came down for the precarious landing, Captain Sakai and Lieutenant Kodoma made a second pass and this time the chattering 7.7 fire smashed the cabin of the C-47 and killed the pilot and co-pilot. The out-of-control Gooney Bird then skidded onto the kunai plain and exploded, killing all aboard except Captain Heller who was blown clear of the flaming wreckage. Miraculously, the dentist suffered only minor injuries.

Meanwhile, the Sally bombers hovered over Tsili Tsili in V formation, unleashing their bombs that punched several holes in the airstrip, destroyed two motor vehicles and smashed one of the parked C-47s. 5th Group headquarters personnel who had alighted from these first Gooney Birds had luckily dived into shelters with Tsili Tsili base personnel to avoid the exploding bombs.

A second C-47 that carried more men from the 35th Fighter Group also came under Japanese attack. The Oscar pilots pounced on the American transport plane like wolves after a sluggish water buffalo. The Nippon flyers riddled the plane and set one engine afire. The C-47 carrying more than a dozen men and a ton of supplies wobbled precariously and disappeared into a mountainous area north of Tsili Tsili. Neither the plane nor any of its occupants were ever seen again and all aboard were presumed lost.

With the downing of two loaded Gooney Birds, the elated Japanese fighter pilots arced in the sky to pounce on the remaining C-47s that were still airborne. As the transport pilots made quick 180 degree turns to flee back to Moresby, the Oscar airmen quickly pursued.

But now the Japanese pilots paid dearly for downing two Gooney Birds and blasting the Tsili Tsili airdrome.

Capt. Francis E. Dublisher mustered his P-39 fighter pilots from the 35th Group's 41st Squadron and then cried into his radio. "Get those fighters and bombers before they knock every last transport out of the sky and level the airbase completely. First and 2nd Flights will go after the bombers; 3rd and 4th Flights will attack the enemy fighters."

"Yes sir," Lt. Ed Latine answered.

Now came the Americans' turn. Perhaps the P-39 Aerocobra was not a total match for the Japanese Oscar fighter, but the US pilots were better trained and they now had a score to settle. Lt. Ed Latine, with a mere 11 fighters, waded into the Oscars to ignite a heavy dogfight over the mountainous jungles about Tsili Tsili. Rattling machine gun fire, thumping 20mm shells, and screaming engines echoed across the sky.

The hundreds of men at Tsili Tsili below stared up at the harsh dogfight, watching the planes dart, arc, and zoom about the sky. During the ten minute aerial battle, four American P-39s tumbled out of the sky, while only two Oscars fell from above. The Americans expressed disappointment. However, the 41st Squadron pilots were badly outnumbered by the Japanese fighter squadron.

Lieutenant Latine and his pilots had done their job — keeping the Oscars away while the other 12 planes from the 41st Squadron waded into the formation of Sally bombers. The Japanese mediums, now exposed without escorts, never had a chance.

"Hit them in pairs, in pairs," Captain Dublisher cried into his radio.

The 41st Squadron pilots waded into the Japanese bomber formations with thumping 20mm shells and withering .50 caliber machine gun fire. The American pilots came back in pass after pass to decimate the Sally formations. Within ten minutes, they had downed seven of the Japanese medium bombers and damaged at least four more. Only dense clouds and rugged mountains enabled Colonel Tanaka to escape with the remaining Sallys of his 17th Sentai.

After the initial disappointment, the Americans on the ground had plenty to cheer about. They saw Sally after Sally plop out of the sky. One Japanese medium lost a tail before tumbling downward to crash into a mountain peak. Another Sally exploded in mid-air and fiery fragments fell to earth. A third Mitsubishi KI-21 lost its engines and wobbled badly before hitting a mountainside, exploding, and then skidding downward over the sloping rain forest in a cascade of fire. Another bomber had its wings shot away and the plane cartwheeled into the Watut River, splashing and exploding before sending sizzling fire and smoke upward.

Similarly, another Mitsubishi medium fell out of the sky in flames, and still another Japanese bomber exploded in mid-air. The last downed Sally also plopped into the river after losing a wing from solid 20mm hits.

By 0900 hours, a silence returned to the mountain base of Tsili Tsili, save for crackling fires that ground crews extinguished. Fortunately, the timely arrival of P-39 interceptors against the Sallys and Oscars had prevented the Japanese from doing extensive damage on the airbase or in claiming more transport planes. Before noon, the US troops at Tsili Tsili had completed all repairs to the runway, taxiways, and revetment areas.

Of the four downed American fighter pilots, rescuers found Lt. Fred Topolcany and returned him to Port Moresby. The others were lost.

Lieutenant Colonel Woodbury was nonetheless perplexed and he insisted that the 35th Fighter Group send its planes to Tsili Tsili at once. "The bastards might be back this afternoon," he told the OD at the ADVON 5th Air Force headquarters in Moresby. "We need fighters up here; lots of them."

"Okay," the OD answered. "We'll send the planes right out."

But Lt. Col. Malcolm Moore, CO of the 35th Fighter Group in Moresby, refused to send his planes to Tsili Tsili until ground crews were up there to service the planes. However, he promised to have more fighter escorts to accompany the C-47s that flew up to Tsili Tsili the next day, 16 August. And in fact, not only did Capt. Francis Dublisher muster 22 P-39 fighters for escort duty, but Maj. Curran Jones of the 35th Group's Squadron mustered 23 P-38 pilots to join on escort duty.

On the morning of 16 August, at 0640, 24 C-47 transport planes left Ward Drome for the flight to Tsili Tsili. Not only did these Gooney Birds carry the remainder of the 35th Group's headquarters squadron personnel, but they also carried mechanics, ordnance men, and electricians who could service the Aerocobras and Lightnings that would be based at Tsili Tsili.

The Japanese returned to Tsili Tsili on the morning of 16 August. This time, General Arisue only sent out 25 Oscars from the 751st Kokutai to attack the American highland base as fighter bombers. The Japanese planes, however, never came close to either the US transport planes nor the airbase itself.

Maj. Curran Jones and his pilots from the 39th Squadron were more than a match for the Japanese Oscar pilots. While the 41st Squadron Aerocobra pilots kept a tight ring around the transport planes, Jones and his Lightning pilots roared north of Tsili Tsili to engage the Oscars. Within ten minutes, the Headhunters of the 35th Group downed an astounding 12 Oscars out of the 25 plane Japanese formation. The few Japanese fighters who escaped the P-38 gauntlet then ran into a swarm of P-39s from Capt. Francis Dublisher's 39th Squadron that downed three more Japanese planes. The remainder of the Japanese scattered and flew off.

The Americans had successfully thwarted the second Japanese attack on Tsili Tsili. The 24 Gooney Birds landed safely with all personnel and supplied. And now with their ground crews safely in the highland base, Col. Malcolm Moore, the 35th Group commander, sent his 39th Squadron into Tsili Tsili on the afternoon of 16 August. Service troops at Tsili Tsili, meanwhile, prepared the base to stage fighters out of there.

The US 5th Air Force was now ready for the assault of Wewak.

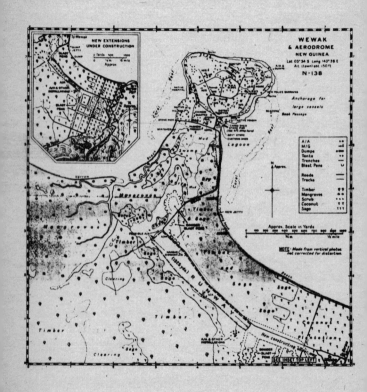

The strong Japanese airbase at Wewak New Guinea.

CHAPTER SIX

The two relatively unsuccessful raids on Tsili Tsili did not discourage the Japanese. In fact, Gen. Yamusi Arisue became more determined than ever to carry out his multiple strikes on the Allied airbases in New Guinea. When Comdr. Hideo Shoji returned to But Airdrome with only half of his Oscar fighter-bombers and explained what happened, the 7th Air Division commander called an immediate conference of his Kokutai and Sentai commanders: Capt. Masahisa Saito of the 751st Kokutai, Comdr. Shuichi Watakazi of the 253rd Kokutai, Col. Koji Tanaka of the 17th Sentai, and Maj. Shinichi Kapaya of the 18th Sentai. Commander Shoji who had led the Oscar fighter-bomber attack on Tsili Tsili had also been invited to the conference.

The 7th Air Division commander first looked at Shoji. "What of these heavy interceptors against your fighter-bombers during the attack on Tsili Tsili?"

"Honorable Arisue," Shoji said, "both their Aerocobra and Lightning fighters made vicious attacks. It is apparent that the enemy is ready to use this new airbase. It would not surprise me if the enemy has fighters at Tsili Tsili by the end of this very day."

Arisue nodded and then scanned his commanders. "We can expect the enemy to be settled at Tsili Tsili within the next day or two, so we ourselves cannot waste an hour in preparing our own air phase of Operation MO II. We will make our first massive assault tomorrow morning."

"In the morning?" Colonel Tanaka asked.

"If, as Commander Shoji believes, the enemy will have fighters at this advanced airbase by even the end of this day," Arisue said, "then we must strike quickly." Tanaka did not answer and Arisue looked at some papers in front of him before he continued. "We have taken stock of our aircraft and I will ask that you confirm my figures. At But Drome there are now thirty-six Mitsubishi fighters (Zeros), twenty Nakajima fighters (Oscars), and twenty-four Mitsubishi heavy bombers (Bettys). Is that correct, Captain Saito?"

The 751st Kokutai commander nodded.

Arisue now looked at a second sheet. "At Wewak Airdrome, we have forty Mitsubishi heavy bombers (Bettys), thirty Nakajima fighters (Oscars), and thirty Mitsubishi fighters (Zeros). Is that also correct, Commander?"

Shuichi Watakazi of the 253rd Kokutai also nodded. "Yes, Honorable Arisue."

"At Dagua Drome," the 7th Air Division commander gestured, "the 17th Sentai has based twenty-four Mitsubishi medium bombers (Sallys) and the same number of Nakajima fighters (Oscars). Would you agree with these figures, Colonel?"

Koji Tanaka nodded. "Yes."

"At Boram Field," Arisue continued, "the 18th Sentai has twenty-four light Mitsubishi bombers (Dinahs), twenty-four heavy bombers, and thirty-six Mitsubishi fighters (Zeros). Correct?"

"Yes," Maj. Shinichi Kapaya said.

"That means we have over three hundred aircraft to carry out these multiple strikes," Arisue said. "The 7th Air Division staff has fortunately drawn up its plan for the air attacks on Port Moresby, Buna, and Tsili Tsili. We have decided that the 721st Kokutai and the 17th Sentai will attack the Port Moresby airfields. We must especially attack Durand Drome, Ward Drome, and Jackson Drome from which they can send their heavy bombers and the dreaded B-25 strafers. The heavy bombers of the 721st Kokutai will attack Durand Drome at Port Moresby under escort of Mitsubishi fighters. The Nakajima fighter bombers (Oscars) will then follow the heavy bomber attacks to make low level fighter-bomber attacks on Durand Drome. This is the drome that houses the B-25s and it must be destroyed. Can you do that?" he asked the 721st Kokutai commander.

"Yes, Honorable Arisue," Captain Saito said.

"The 17th Sentai aircraft will follow the 721st Kokutai to attack the Ward and Jackson Dromes that house the enemy's heavy bombers," Arisue said. "The medium bombers under escort of their Nakajima fighters must make low level sweeps over these airdromes to destroy as many B-24s and B-17s as possible, without concerning yourselves with the runways themselves. We must leave at these airdromes as few heavy bombers as possible for such enemy bombers could be used to attack Wewak at night." He looked again at Colonel Tanaka. "Can your medium bombers attack below two-thousand feet?"

"Yes," Tanaka said. "I will be leading the bombers myself and I will take them down to one-thousand-five-hundred feet, if necessary. If we do not meet interceptors, I will ask the pilots of my Nakajima fighter squadron to also make attacks against these enemy heavy bombers at Port Moresby."

"Good," Arisue said. He then looked at Maj. Shinichi Kapaya of the 17th Sentai. "Besides the enemy's strafer bombers at Port Moresby, the enemy maintains another sentai of these low level B-25 bombers at the Dobodura airfield in Buna. The enemy is also moving P-38 fighter planes to the Horanda Drome at Buna, no doubt to escort the B-25s to Wewak when or if an opportunity comes. These Buna airfields, along with their B-25s and P-38s must also be destroyed. I would ask, Major, that you begin your strikes with high level attacks with your heavy bombers and then follow with low level attacks by your light bombers. You will use your fighter planes as escort."

"I understand," Major Kapaya said.

"Now," Arisue gestured again, "we must also deal with this new enemy air base at Tsili Tsili." He looked at Comdr. Shuichi Watakazi of the 253rd Kokutai. "You have one hundred aircraft at your disposal, Commander, and you must use all of them to destroy this forward enemy base. It is important that your squadrons succeed, for only with the destruction of this airfield can we be certain that no enemy

B-25s will attack our own bases in the Wewak area."

"We will make every effort, Honorable Arisue," Major Kapaya said.

"May I suggest that you begin your attacks with heavy bombers to destroy the Tsili Tsili runway so they cannot mount fighter planes, no matter how many they have at this Watut River field. Your Mitsubishi fighter planes can furnish escort for the heavy bombers. After the initial attacks, your Nakajima fighter-bombers may swoop over the target areas in straffing attacks to destroy as many parked aircraft and installations as possible."

"We will follow your instructions," Major Kapaya said.

"I cannot emphasize too strongly the need to carry out these strikes successfully," Arisue said. "We must return to these targets day after day and as often as weather permits to make sure that the enemy's airdromes are no longer in operation, and that the bulk of their fighters and strafer bombers have been destroyed. Once we have completed our task, General Adachi can begin his invasion of Buna in the ground segment of the MO II operation."

Arisue looked at the sheet in front of him still again and then continued. "We will be using about one hundred thirty aircraft in the attacks on Port Moresby, one hundred aircraft at Tsili Tsili, and some eighty aircraft at Buna. Surely, this overwhelming number of planes should be sufficient to successfully destroy the enemy's bases, especially if we conduct such strikes over a three or four day period."

"Please, Honorable Arisue," Colonel Tanaka now

spoke, "what of their fighters at Port Moresby? Does not the enemy possess a large number of them at this massive base? Could they not cause serious losses to our bombers?"

"We can only do so much," General Arisue said. "Our objective is to destroy their bomber capacity. We must be certain that the enemy does not have the means to attack Wewak. We must also make sure that the enemy is denied the means to attack a counterinvasion convoy to Buna or an overland march from Salamaua to Buna. The enemy aircraft most likely to cause us problems are these B-25s and their B-17 and B-24 bombers. If we eliminate them, we need only worry about American fighter planes. Since we have targeted their fighters at Buna and Tsili Tsili, such fighters at Port Moresby would be ineffective in hurting our ships at sea or at our bases in Wewak, even if they could fly this far."

"But perhaps the fighters from Moresby could cause serious damage to our bomber formations," Major Kapaya said.

"Perhaps," Arisue said. "That is why the bombers will be under strong fighter escort, is that not true?"

Kapaya did not answer.

"Of course," Arisue went on, "if we eliminate the enemy fighter planes at Port Moresby in aerial combat with our own fighter pilots that would be a bonus. We will attack these fighter aircraft fields at Port Moresby and their parked fighter aircraft in subsequent raids. And, as I said, perhaps our own fighter escort airmen can eliminate many of them." He scanned his officers and then sighed. "Please return to your airdromes and work swiftly. All aircraft must be ready to take off at the first light of morning. There can be no delay. Every squadron airman must understand his mission. If we coordinate our attacks efficiently, we will succeed."

"Yes, Honorable Arisue," Captain Saito said.

The Japanese spent the rest of the day, 16 August 1943, to prepare 320 bombers and fighters for multiple strikes the next day against Allied airbases. These swarms of Bettys, Sallys, Dinahs, Oscars, and Zeros constituted a formidable air force and if Arisue acted swiftly he could no doubt badly deplete the Allied 5th Air Force.

But the Americans were not idle.

If the Japanese felt confident because they counted over 300 aircraft at Wewak alone, the Allied 5th Air Force possessed a horde of its own bombers and fighters in New Guinea. By mid-August, Gen. George Kenney, CinC of the 5th Air Force had nearly 600 aircraft.

A big shipment of new P-38s had arrived in the SWPA by late April of 1943. The US 475th Fighter Group had been activated only a few months ago in May of 1943 and the unit had been ready by mid-June, using a cadre of experienced pilots from other fighter groups in the Pacific. By mid-April, the Satans Angels, under the command of Lt. Col. Meryl Smith, had 87 Lightnings among the group's three squadrons. By 15 August, the group began moving its Lightnings from Port Moresby to Horanda Drome in Buna in anticipation of furnishing escort for the B-25 attacks on Wewak. By the end of the day, 16 August, the 475th Group had completed this move to Buna.

The veteran 35th Fighter Group, under the command of Lt. Col. Malcolm Moore, had received 28 P-38s for its 39th Squadron under Maj. Curran Jones, while the 35th's 40th and 41st Squadrons retained 70 P-39 fighters.

Among the other US fighter groups in the SWPA, the 49th Fighter Group's 9th Squadron at Buna also got new P-38s as did the 8th Fighter Group's 80th Squadron at Port Moresby. The other squadrons of the 49th and 8th Groups had an array of P-40 and P-39 fighters, about 130 of them between them. Over half of these fighters had more than 300 hours of flying time and by mid-August most of the P-39s and P-40s were in service or repair depots in Australia and not available for combat.

The newly arrived 348th Fighter Group was still in Brisbane undergoing orientation before moving up to New Guinea with their 90 P-47 fighter planes. They would station themselves in Buna, but the group would only play a minor role in the mid-August air battles.

Among the bombers, the Grim Reaper 3rd Attack Group based at Dobodura Airdrome in Buna possessed 37 B-25s among three squadrons and 21 A-20 light bombers in its fourth squadron. The Sunsetter 38th Bomb Group, based in Moresby, had 26 B-25s between two of its squadrons, the 71st and 405th. The other squadrons from the 38th Group were without planes at the moment. Also at Buna was the 22nd Bomb Group with 43 B-26 medium bombers that were used mostly in attacks on Japanese bases in New Britain. The 22nd would also play only a minor role in the mid-August New Guinea air battles.

Among the heavy bomber units, the 43rd Group had all four squadrons in operation. The 65th and 403rd Squadrons counted 21 B-17s between them, while the 63rd and 64th Squadrons had 26 B-24s. The 90th Bomb Group counted 47 B-24s among its four squadrons. Both of these heavy American bomber groups were based at Port Moresby.

The job of eliminating the Wewak airdromes fell obviously to ADVON 5th Air Force under the command of Gen. Ennis Whitehead. For this effort, Whitehead planned to use his heavy bombers, his P-38 fighters, and most important his B-25 strafers, the commerce destroyers. The 21 B-17s and 26 B-24s of the 43rd Bomb Group, the 47 B-24s of the 90th Bomb Group, the 63 B-25s of the 3rd and 38th Groups, and the 115 P-38s of the 475th Group, 39th Squadron of the 35th Group, 80th Squadron of the 8th Group, and 9th Squadron of the 49th Group would need to be ready. Whitehead thus counted 273 fighters and bombers, considerably less than the more than 300 planes the Japanese intended to use for their assaults on the American airdromes.

But the P-38 fighter plane far surpassed the Japanese Oscar and Zero fighter both in firepower and dogfighting ability. The B-25 medium bomber strafers could cause tremendously more damage in low level strafing-parafrag attacks than could the Japanese Dinah light bomber or Sally medium bomber. The US B-17 and B-24 heavy bombers carried considerably heavier bomb loads than did the Japanese Betty heavy bomber.

Further, all of the American planes were armor plated. Both Japanese fighter pilots and AA gunners had a much more difficult time in knocking down American planes compared to American counterparts knocking down Japanese planes that had little or no armor in favor of better maneuverability.

The question was not who had the stronger air weapon, the Japanese 7th Air Division or the US 5th Air Force, but who could strike the first successful blow. The side which scored the initial numbing attack would so weaken the other that subsequent air assaults would merely be efforts to complete the job — like one boxer who stuns his opponent with a hard blow and then methodically punches him to the canvas for a knockout.

On the late afternoon of 16 August 1944, Gen. Ennis Whitehead called his own air commanders into conference at his ADVON headquarters in Port Moresby. Among those present were Lt. Col. Malcom Moore of the 35th Fighter Group, Lt. Col. Meryl Smith of the 475th Fighter Group, Lt. Col. Larry Tanberg, acting CO of the 38th Bomb Group, Col. Donald Hall of the 3rd Attack Group, Col. Harry Hawthorne of the 43rd Bomb Group, and Col. Arthur Rogers of the 90th Bomb Group. Whitehead silently read a radio communication in his hand before he spoke.

"Gentlemen, this is a recon report that just came into Port Moresby. It's timed at 1300 hours today. The observers flying over Wewak sent this on the spot coded message. They say the Japanese now have over three hundred planes on their four airbases up there and they've begun frantic activity. Japanese ordnance personnel are apparently gassing up and loading planes. The best guess is that they intend to launch multiple air strikes against our bases, possibly as early as tomorrow morning."

"Which bases, sir?" Lieutenant Colonel Moore asked.

"I'd say all them — Tsili Tsili, Buna, and Moresby. They've made two strikes on Tsili Tsili and now they're in a state of panic. They know that we'll strike Wewak as soon as our fighters can stage out of Tsili Tsili and that moment is right now." He gestured to Moore. "Have your fighter planes left yet?"

"Yes, sir," the 35th Fighter Group commander answered. "Maj. Curran Jones has taken the P-38s of the 39th Squadron up there and Capt. Francis Dublisher has taken his 41st Squadron P-39s to Tsili Tsili. They should be landing just about now. I'm keeping my 40th Squadron here in Moresby in case they're needed for interceptor duty."

"Good," Whitehead nodded. The ADVON commander now looked at Lieutenant Colonel Smith of the 475th Fighter Group. "How about your Lightnings?"

"We plan to use all three P-38 squadrons as escort to Wewak. They've been flying into Horanda Drome at Buna since yesterday and all of our P-38s should be settled there by this afternoon."

Again, Whitehead nodded. "The P-38s from the 8th and 49th Groups are here in Moresby. That should give us enough fighters to escort B-25s to Wewak. We'll have nearly 80 P-40s from the Australian 9 Operational Group to protect Moresby along with the P-39s and P-40s of the 35th and 49th Groups. I'll be sending two squadrons of P-47s from the 348th Fighter Group to Buna in the morning to protect the airbases there in the event of enemy attacks." Whitehead looked at another sheet in his hand before he spoke again. "Meanwhile, the P-39s of the 41st Squadron can protect the Tsili Tsili base."

Whitehead gestured. "In view of the recon reports, it's obvious that we've got to strike at once. We'll begin the assault on Wewak with heavy bomber strikes tonight by the 43rd and 90th Groups. How many B-17s and B-24s can you mount, Colonel?" he asked Harry Hawthorne.

"About a dozen Flying Forts and twenty Liberators are ready to go."

"What about you, Colonel?" the ADVON CO now looked at Art Rogers.

"I would say about thirty Liberators," the 90th Group commander answered.

General Whitehead gestured to an aide who pulled down a wall map of Wewak. "You can see the three airdromes on the peninsula itself and Boram Field down the coast," he ran a finger over the map. "I want the heavies to hit all four airdromes. Colonel," he looked at Hawthorne, "your 63rd and 64th squadrons are to hit Dagua with their B-24s. The 64th and 403rd Squadrons will hit But with their B-17s."

"Yes sir," Hawthorne said.

Whitehead then looked at Art Rogers. "Colonel, your 319th and 321st Squadrons should hit Boram while the B-24s of the 400th and 320th Squadrons hit Wewak Drome."

"I understand, sir."

"All eight heavy bomb squadrons have only one mission," Whitehead scowled emphatically, "and that is to punch plenty of big holes in the runways. I want you to carry two thousand pounders as well as incendiaries to light up targets. The one tonners can leave huge pits in the runways, so big that the Japanese will need at least a day to fill them. The heavies should start taking off at 2200 hours so that your bomb runs can begin shortly after midnight. We don't want a single Wewak runway in operation by the time the B-25s come in for attacks at daylight. If the Japanese can't mount interceptors, the Mitchell strafers can do one hell of a job."

"Yes sir," Colonel Rogers said.

"As soon as this meeting is over," Whitehead said, "Colonel Rogers and Colonel Hawthrone should return to their units at once, assign crews for the evening mission, give the men early chow, and then give them a little sleep. They could be airborne for as much as six hours during this night flight to Wewak. I would guess that it might take an hour and a half or even longer for all aircraft to cross the target and make bomb drops. I don't think you'll run into any interceptors, but you'll probably meet plenty of AA fire. So keep your formations loose once you reach the target and begin your runs."

General Whitehead glanced at Lt. Col. Larry Tanberg and Col. Donald Hall. "Obviously the attacks tonight are a prelude for the main show at daylight by the B-25 strafers. If you're lucky, if the heavies knock out the runways, your B-25 crews should have a field day against parked aircraft with your strafing guns and parafrag bombs. Remember, the principal reason for your mission to Wewak is to neutralize that base so they cannot mount planes to interfere with Operation Eckton."

Whitehead glanced at the map again and then turned to Don Hall. "Colonel, the targets for your group will be Wewak and But Dromes. How many planes can you get off?"

"Among our three squadrons of B-25s, well over thirty Mitchells," the Grim Reaper 3rd Attack Group commander answered.

Whitehead then looked at Larry Tanberg. "I'm sorry that Colonel O'Neil is ill at the moment, but we can't stop the war, can we?"

"No sir."

"You have about thirty B-25s in the 38th Group's 71st and 405th Squadrons, is that correct?"

"Yes sir."

"Send one of these squadrons over Dagua Drome and the other squadron over Boram Field. Again, if the heavies do their jobs, you should not meet interceptors and your Mitchell strafers should score well against parked aircraft." Whitehead then looked at Lt. Col. Meryl Smith of the 475th Fighter Group. "You're to mount your P-38s from Horando Drome at dawn, land at Tsili Tsili to refuel, and then fly on a 320 degree course to rendezvous with the Mitchells above Finchhaven."

"Yes sir," Smith said.

"Meanwhile," Whitehead pointed to Colonel Moore, "you should have your P-38s off the Tsili Tsili field before the 475th Group Lightnings arrive. The airbase will be jammed enough and we want as little confusion as possible."

"Will do, sir."

"Your P-38 squadron will also join the B-25s over Finchhaven, here," the general pointed to the map of

New Guinea on the wall behind him. "Rendezvous point is 5.3° south by 147.7° west. Once the P-38s have joined the B-25s, the formation will continue on a 310 degree course toward Wewak. The P-38s from the 35th Fighter Group will furnish escort for the 38th Bomb Group squadrons and the Lightnings from the 475th Fighter Group will furnish escort for the 3rd Attack Group squadrons. If possible, we'll also send out the P-38s from the 80th and 9th Squadrons to escort the 38th Group Mitchells. Are there any questions?"

None.

"I suggest you get back to your units to brief your own squadron and flight leaders. If we're lucky, we'll hit the Nips hard tonight and tomorrow to start a successful air campaign against Wewak."

At Wewak, the Kokutai and Sentai commanders of the 7th Air Division had put all airmen to work. At But Drome, ground crews loaded bombs on 24 Bettys, while also loading six 7.7 machine gun belts on both the bombers and 36 Zeros. They also loaded Oscars with both bombs and strafing belts, two 250 pound bombs under each fighter-bomber wing. Other ground crews checked electrical equipment or gassed up aircraft.

At Wewak Drome, personnel loaded fuel into 30 Oscars, 30 Zeros, and 30 Bettys that would assail Tsili Tsili in the morning. The Bettys carried 2,000 pound bombs that would also punch huge holes in the main runway to make the airfield inoperable. At Dagua Drome, hordes of ground forces gassed up and loaded the 24 Sallys and 30 Oscars that would also strike Port Moresby.

Ten miles to the south, at Boram Field, more Japanese service troops loaded 24 Betty bombers, 24 Dinah light bombers and 37 Zero fighters. These planes from the 18th Sentai would attempt to smash the American airfields at Buna.

Three hundred miles to the south, at Lae, Col. Takashi Miyazaki made certain that more than 200 barrels of fuel sat well hidden under trees. He would need this gasoline to refuel the fighters that landed here before returning to Wewak. Miyazaki also prepared the 37 dump trucks piled with dirt to fill holes in the taxiways and runway in the event of air attacks on the airfield.

At Tsili Tsili, Lt. Col. Malcolm Moore of the 35th Fighter Group arrived at the advanced base at about dusk. He immediately checked with Maj. Curran Jones of the 39th Squadron, reminding him to make certain his P-38s were fully armed and loaded for take off the next day. Jones assured the 35th Group commander that the planes and pilots were ready. Moore then made certain that Tsili Tsili ground crews had prepared gas trucks to fuel P-38s from Buna and perhaps more Lightnings from Moresby before these P-38s also went off to escort the B-25s to Wewak.

Moore also made sure that P-39 pilots from his 41st Squadron were on full alert to intercept any Japanese planes that attempted to attack Tsili Tsili. The lieutenant colonel also made certain that gunners of the 470th Automatic Weapons Battery had their AA guns on the ready and that radar operators were on full alert.

At Dobodura, Col. Don Hall, who had returned

to the base from Moresby by late afternoon, made sure that bomber crews were ready to take off in the morning: strafing guns loaded and bomb bays loaded with clusters of parafrags.

Also at Buna, Lt. Col. Meryl Smith had checked with his ground crews and pilots. Planes must be ready by daybreak and the Satans Angels pilots must be fully awake to take off at dawn. At Durand Field in Moresby, Lt. Col. Larry Tanberg spoke with his B-25 commerce destroyer squadron and flight leaders, while at Ward Drome, Col. Arthur Rogers readied 26 B-24s from the 90th Bomb Group for a 2200 hour take off. At Jackson Drome, Col. Harry Hawthorne had prepared 12 B-17s and 14 B-24s. These planes would also take off at 2200 hours. Both Rogers and Hawthorne had made certain that all crews had sacked out for several hours sleep before they left Moresby. Then the two heavy bomber group commanders retired themselves for a few hours slumber.

By 2000 hours, a quiet had finally descended over New Guinea in both the American and Japanese bases. The only question: which side would get in the initial and perhaps fatal blow?

The powerful Allied airbase at Port Moresby, New Guinea.

CHAPTER SEVEN

The 43rd Bomb Group, Ken's Men, had been activated as a heavy bomb group in 1941, several months before the onset of World War II in the Pacific. The group had trained progressively with A-29s, B-30s, B-18s and finally the B-17 Flying Fortress. The group had been operating on anti-submarine patrol out of Langley Field, Virginia, and they conducted Atlantic coastal patrols out of Bangor, Maine. The 43rd moved to the SWPA in May of 1942 to relieve the decimated 19th Heavy Bomb Group that had been riddled in the Philippines and Java early in the war. About a hundred veteran flyers from the 19th Bomb Group had joined the 43rd at Sidney, Australia, as an experienced cadre for the unit.

When the Japanese invaded Java in July of 1942, General MacArthur had sent elements of the Ken's Men to Port Moresby with their B-17s. The entire group personnel and its aircraft had completed the move to New Guinea by September of 1942. Under the command of Col. Roger Ramsey, the 43rd had conducted some of the most dangerous missions of the war during a period when the Japanese controlled the skies over the Bismarck Archipelago. The group had made attacks against Japanese shipping, Netherlands East Indies bases, New Guinea targets, and even against the stronghold of Rabaul. Ken's Men crews rarely flew missions without getting jumped by Zeros so that 43rd Group gunners had invariably found themselves in life or death aerial battles. Ken's Men gunners probably shot down more Japanese fighter planes than the average American fighter group.

The 43rd had played a major role in the Battle of the Bismarck Sea, sinking three of the enemy ships and damaging several more, to earn themselves a DUC. Only two months later, during a photographic mapping mission over the Solomons in June of 1943, both pilot Jay Zeamer and navigator Joseph Sarnoski won Congressional Medals of Honor for their valiant efforts against 20 enemy interceptors. Sarnoski had remained on the nose guns until he died from enemy strafing fire, and Captain Zeamer, badly wounded, completed his mission and brought the crippled B-17 home with its vital photos during a flight of more than 500 miles.

In May of 1943, Col. Harry Hawthorne took command of the 43rd Group. Hawthorne had been in the USAAF since 1939, training in the States and joining the 19th Bomb Group when that unit had moved to the Philippines in the fall of 1941. He had been among the few combat airmen who had survived the Japanese onslaught in the Philippines and Java. The California native had joined the 43rd as a captain in

October of 1942, won promotion to major by December, and CO of the 65th Squadron in January of 1943. In May, after Colonel Ramsey won promotion to a staff position with 5th Air Force headquarters, Hawthorne took command of the 43rd Group.

At 2045 hours, 16 August, Hawthorne held a final briefing with his squadron commanders before the group took off on its night mission to Wewak. Those present included Maj. Ken McCullar of the 63rd Squadron, Maj. William Benn of the 64th Squadron, Capt. Ray Gowdy of the 65th Squadron, and Maj. Robert Fuller of the 403rd Squadron.

"I hope that all of you understand your assignments," Hawthorne said, referring to a map on the wall behind him. "Our group has the Dagua and But Dromes as targets. The 63rd and 64th will attack Dagua with their B-24s, and I'll personally lead this element. Major McCullar's squadron will come in first, and then Major Benn's 64th Squadron will follow. The B-17s of the 65th and 403rd Squadrons will attack But Drome in tandem with Major Fuller leading this second element. The major's own 403rd Squadron will come in first and the 65th Squadron under Captain Gowdy will follow."

"Will we run into opposition, sir?" Capt. Ray Gowdy asked.

"I don't know how many night fighters the Nips have, if any, but we should be ready for anything. I can tell you, however, that ack ack fire is likely to cause us more damage than fighters."

"We'll go over target at eight thousand feet. Lead navigators will drop incendiaries to light up the objectives for elements that follow."

"How about the route in, sir?" Maj. Ken McCullar asked. "Will we follow the usual flight patterns?"

"Yes," Hawthorne answered. "We fly over the Owen Stanley hump, northwest by west, cross the Watut River above Wau, and then out to sea into the Vitiaz Strait. Then we move up the coast. As soon as we cross the shoreline, all gunners should be on full alert. We could get some enemy night fighters out of Lae or even out of their small base at Finchhaven. We'll be flying at fifteen thousand feet and we'll drop to attack level at IP, about twenty miles from target." He scanned the crews again. "Any more questions?"

"I guess not, sir," Major Fuller said.

"Okay, let's mount up. Transportation to aircraft is outside of this briefing tent."

The command cars and jeeps of the 43rd Bomb Group would carry the Ken's Men crews to the airstrip. Two hundred sixty combat airmen scrambled into the long line of waiting vehicles for the ride to Ward Drome revetment areas where crew chiefs had revved up the heavy bomber engines, and where ordnance men and mechanics were making last minute checks on aircraft before they took off. Hawthorne would lead a total of 14 B-24s from the 63rd and 64th Squadrons to hit Dagua, and Major Fuller would lead 12 B-17s from the 65th and 403rd Squadrons to hit But Drome.

Night bombing raids had become routine for the 43rd because their planes often made long range attacks where they could not enjoy fighter escorts. In mid-1943, the Japanese could still mount hordes of aggressive fighter interceptors so 5th Air Force did not like to send out Flying Fortresses and Liberators in the daytime without escorts.

About a mile away from the Ken's Men campsite, Col. Arthur Rogers of the 90th Jolly Rogers Bomb Group conducted a last minute briefing of his own. The 90th Group had been activated in April of 1942 at Key Field, Mississippi, where some 50 returning veterans from the old 19th and 7th Bomb Groups had formed the nucleus of the new heavy bomber unit. The 90th had trained with B-24s from the onset, moving to several airbases within the United States while the Jolly Rogers prepared for combat, especially in night bombing tactics. The group had finally moved to Hawaii in September of 1942, where the USAAF assigned them to patrol and reconnaissance duties around the island. Finally, in November of 1942, the 90th moved to the SWPA, settling in a new airbase at Iron Range on the northeast tip of Australia.

The Jolly Rogers had entered combat almost immediately, staging out of Port Moresby. The group had carried out its first combat mission on 24 November 1942 when seven B-24s from the 319th Squadron made a night bombing raid on the then important Japanese airbase at Lae. Reconnaissance photos taken the next day showed that the Jolly Rogers airmen had caused considerable damage to the runway and to four service buildings.

The group had then carried out a series of missions during the latter months of the vicious Papuan campaign that had ended in the Japanese defeat at Buna. The 90th had twice attacked shipping convoys that sailed from Rabaul to Lae, sinking two destroyers. In December, the group assailed a large enemy convoy out of Gasmata, New Britain, but the Jolly Rogers had run into a swarm of Japanese interceptors. However, none of the bombers had been lost, while the 90th Group gunners had downed four of the attacking Zeros.

In January of 1943, with a dozen B-24s, the 90th Bomb Group carried out its first bombing attack on the Japanese stronghold of Rabaul, led by Lt. Col. Arthur Rogers who was then the deputy group commander. The mission had been one of the most dangerous in the SWPA up to that time. Several of the Liberators had taken damaging hits because the B-24s had run into extremely heavy AA fire and hordes of Zeros. The Jolly Rogers airmen had destroyed several parked aircraft, three buildings, one runway, and the troop transport *Kuraruku Maru*.

Despite the damage to aircraft, most of the B-24s survived and this daylight mission had set the pattern for subsequent air attacks on Rabaul.

Although the Jolly Rogers did not play a large role in the famed Battle of the Bismarck Sea in March of 1943, it was a 90th Group aircraft that spotted the huge Lae resupply convoy when Lt. Walter Higgins and his crew from the 321st Squadron spotted the convoy off the coast of New Britain in the Bismarck Sea at 1500 hours on 1 March 1943. The 90th had then drawn the job of stalking the convoy over the next three days, while other 5th Air Force Units attacked and virtually destroyed the large Japanese flotilla.

The 90th had also made the first attack on Wewak on 10 April 1943 with seven planes from the 400th Squadron. But weather and interceptors proved fatal, forcing back six planes. General Kenney thus decided that the heavies would only make night attacks on the base until the B-24s and B-17s had fighter escorts.

Col. Arthur Rogers, the Jolly Rogers commander, had come from West Virginia. After graduating from North Carolina College, he had joined the USAAF and earned his wings at Kelly Field in 1934. For the next several years, the young officer had been stationed at Langley Field, flying old B-6s, then the B-40, and finally a B-17. By 1940, Rogers was a squadron commander in the 25th Bomb Group stationed in Puerto Rico, and flying B-18 heavy bombers. In early 1942 he returned to the States to join first the 92nd Group and then the 90th Bomb Group, moving overseas with the Jolly Rogers in the fall of 1942.

Rogers had been a squadron commander and then deputy commander with more than 30 missions between the fall of 1942 and the summer of 1943, earning a DFC and two Bronze Stars for his aerial exploits. He had assumed command of the 90th Group only a month ago, 16 July, and now, on the evening of 16 August, he held a final briefing before going off to Wewak with 26 Liberators.

"By now," the colonel told the 260 seated airmen, "you know we're going to Wewak and Boram Dromes. The 319th and 321st Squadrons will attack Boram Field, while the 400th and 320th Squadrons will hit Wewak Drome. I'll personally lead the elements hitting Boram Field and Maj. Paul Gotke of the 320th Squadron will lead the elements hitting Wewak Drome."

"Do we go in first, sir?" Capt. Everett Wood of the 321st Squadron asked.

"No," Rogers answered. "We follow the 43rd who will hit Dagua and But. My element will come in next to strike Boram and Major Gotke's element comes in last to hit Wewak Drome. As usual, lead aircraft will carry incendiaries to light up the targets."

"Sir," Lt. Tom Fetter of the 400th Squadron asked, "can we expect interceptors on this mission?"

"No more than usual on a right raid," Rogers said. "The Nips never did have much of a night fighter force, so they aren't likely to have many fighters out tonight. Of course, all gunners should be alert." He looked at a sheet in his hand before he spoke again. "We'll fly the usual route at fifteen-thousand feet. We cross the mountains, fly north of Wau and Lae, and then go off the coast near Finchhaven to the Vitiaz Strait. Then we fly northwest by west to our target."

"What about flak, sir?" Captain Wood asked.

"Yes," the colonel nodded, "you can expect plenty of AA fire. We'll be making our runs over target at eight-thousand feet, so you could get hit with flak. Pilots will need to jinx aircraft pretty good to avoid AA fire."

"Yes sir."

"As you know," the Jolly Rogers commander gestured, "our principal mission is to destroy the runways, to put enough holes in them so the Nips can't mount interceptors when our medium strafers go after parked aircraft tomorrow morning. If we put the runways out of commission, the Japanese can't jump the Mitchells with Zeros and Oscars. The B-25s will have a much easier time. All navigators have maps of their targets. Please study them well. We want this mission to be as successful as possible."

"What time do we take off, sir?" Major Gotke asked.

"Take off will begin at 2200 hours," the colonel answered. "We should be over target shortly after midnight. If we follow our usual bombing pattern, the attacks could continue until after 0200 hours."

"Could the Nips mount any night fighters out of Lae or Gasmata, sir?" Capt. Everett Wood asked.

"They might," Colonel Rogers conceded, "but it's not likely. Nonetheless, I would ask all gunners to stay on their guns." He then scanned the crowd of airmen in the jammed briefing tent. "If they're are no more questions, we'll mount up. Vehicles are waiting outside to take us to revetment areas."

As with the 43rd Group, 260 airmen from the 90th Group spilled out of a briefing tent and scrambled aboard jeeps and trucks for the ride to the airstrip at Ward Drome. At the hardstands of the 90th Group, ground crews were completing final checks on electrical systems and mechanical equipment. Ordnance men made final checks on guns and bomb bays, while crew chiefs warmed up the big Liberator engines.

At the control tower, a blinking light winked through the dark night, waiting for the word to send off the 26 Jolly Rogers bombers. At Jackson Drome, control tower personnel waited for word to send off the 26 Ken's Men bombers.

At 2200 hours, the first B-24, Col. Harry Hawthorne's lead Liberator, wheeled to the head of

Jackson Drome's main runway. On signal from the control tower, Hawthorne released the brakes and zoomed down the 6500 foot runway, hoisting the heavily laden bomber off the airstrip only a few hundred feet from the end of the runway. At 30 second intervals, one after another, other B-24s from the Ken's Men 63rd and 64th Squadrons roared down the runway.

Then came the B-17s from the 43rd Group's 403rd and 65th Squadrons. Maj. Bob Fuller wheeled his lead Flying Fort from the 403rd Squadron onto the head of the runway and waited for the green flare to shoot out of the control tower. Fuller then released the brake and the Flying Fortress roared down the runway before hoisting itself into the air. Eleven B-17s followed. Soon the 14 Liberators and 12 Flying Fortresses from the Ken's Men group were cruising over the Owen Stanley Mountain range.

Two miles to the east, Col. Arthur Rogers of the 90th Group turned his lead B-24 to the head of Ward Drome's main runway. The Liberator rocked like a huge dinosaur and when the flare skyrocketed from the control tower, Rogers released the brake. The B-24 shot forward, struggling under its heavy weight of bombs and finally rising into the sky. Thirteen more B-24s from the Jolly Rogers' 319th and 321st Squadrons followed.

The incessant roar of engines on Ward and Jackson Dromes kept awake the hundreds of men stationed at Port Moresby. The men understood the significance of the mission by these US heavy bombers. Few men complained.

When Rogers element of B-24s left the field, Maj.

Paul Gotke came into position at the head of the apron at Ward Drome before he too roared down the strip. Thirteen more Liberators from the 320th and 400th Squadrons followed Gotke until all 26 Jolly Rogers aircraft had left the field.

By 2230 hours, all of the heavy bombers were gone, the deep growl of their engines fading into silence as the planes crossed the Owen Stanley Mountains. Ground crews from the 43rd and 90th Groups reboarded vehicles and rode back to campsites. They would return just before daylight to meet their B-17s and B-24s, hoping that all 52 planes and more than 500 crewmen came back safely. In the dozens of other campsites around Port Moresby, many of the American and Australian ground troops remained awake inside their tents and discussed the Allied plan to knock out Wewak. Could the plan really work?

Even as the heavy bombers disappeared to the north, activity had begun at the Durand Airdrome campsite in Port Moresby. Many of the ground crews from the 38th Bomb Group were already awake for the big show in the morning, when the B-25 strafers from the Sunsetter group took off for Wewak.

By midnight, a peaceful quiet prevailed at the sprawling bases at Wewak. The frantic activity of preparing 320 bombers and fighters for the morning missions against Allied airfields had finally ended. Dozens of Bettys, Sallys, Dinahs, Oscars, and Zeros were now lined up wing tip to wing tip along the four airdromes. The planes had been checked out: mechanical and electrical equipment in good order. Strafing guns on both fighters and bombers had been fully loaded as were 20mm cannon shells, 250 and

2,000 pound bombs set inside the bomb bays of Dinahs, Sallys, and Bettys, or under the wings of Oscar fighter-bombers. Most of the aircraft had been fueled although gas trucks would be back at daylight to finish this job.

In the dark night, the planes resembled huge penguins in quiet dormancy.

Save for routine sentinels and night ODs, the airmen of the 7th Air Division, both combat and ground crews, had retired for the night. The OD personnel would awaken them at daylight to resume their frantic activities in servicing crews and planes before take off on the missions against Tsili Tsili, Buna, and Port Moresby. Wewak was quite remote from any Allied base, and the sentinels knew that only the night Kiwi birds in surrounding gloomy rain forests would challenge them in the darkness with their high pitched squeals. In the AA pits, flak gunners also sat in boredom. They expected nothing to happen during this quiet night. And finally, inside the various kokutai and sentai headquarter huts, night OD officers and non-coms sat at their stations, reading or talking, or occasionally looking up at the clock in the hope that time would pass swiftly so they would be relieved. But, as usual in the case of clock watchers, time dragged.

By 0030 hours, 17 August 1944, the dark silence at Wewak had reached an apex. Even the echoing squeals of Kiwi birds in surrounding forests had abated. And gratefully, New Guinea insects that plagued men unmercifully in this tropical hellhole, had vanished for the night into the desolate jungle darkness.

At 0035 hours, Japanese technicians on the early warning systems apparatus at Boram Field got a call from a coastwatcher to the south: enemy bombers coming northwest, no doubt on the way to Wewak. The technicians quickly radioed the information to 7th Air Division headquarters near Wewak Drome and within moments wailing sirens shattered the night time silence. And a moment later, searchlights exploded in blinking lights and speared arrows of beams into the dark sky before vacillating back and forth in a full 180 degrees. Finally, a dozen dark shadows darted toward But Drome to man Irving night fighter planes. These pilots would take off to challenge the interlopers.

The sirens and searchlights jerked men out of their sleep and they bounded from their beds of matted straw before darting toward air raid shelters. They knew that enemy bombardiers would aim for the runways, taxiways, and parked planes, but errant bombs often fell into surrounding campsites.

At 0045 hours, 17 August, the first B-24 roared over Dagua Drome. Col. Harry Hawthorne blinked from a sweeping searchlight beam that struck the windshield of the plane's cabin and nearly blinded Hawthorne and his co-pilot. Then the colonel winced from a close exploding AA shell that shuddered the big Liberator. However, the 43rd Bomb Group commander never altered his course and soon, he heard the bombardier cry into the intercom.

"Bombs away!"

A confetti of incendiary bombs fell out of the Liberator's belly and tumbled to earth before bursting in a series of blinking lights 8,000 feet below. The explosions ignited dozens of fires and brightened the Dagua runway like a brilliantly lighted stretch of highway. Following B-24 crews could see the airstrip perfectly and they could see the dozens of planes that lined both sides of the runway.

Maj. Ken McCullar in the second 63rd Squadron plane grinned at the target below. He was tempted to lay his bombs on the inviting line of Sally bombers or the line of Oscar fighters on the other side of the strip. But his job was to disable the runway. The major knew that his drop from 8,000 feet would luckily knock out only a few of these planes, if any, compared to what the B-25 strafers could do from tree-top level. If these Japanese fighters got off the ground, they could decimate the low flying B-25s that were due to arrive over Dagua at daylight.

"Sergeant," McCullar called his bombardier, "are you on target?"

"Yes sir. Bombs away in ten seconds," Sgt. Karl Snyder answered.

"Good," the major answered. McCullar had been with the 43rd Bomb Group since the unit first came overseas in 1942. The handsome, square-faced officer from Courtland, Mississippi, had scored many firsts with the Ken's Men. He had been among the first 43rd Group pilots to hit a Japanese warship, a cruiser off Milne Bay. He had been the first 90th airman to hit the Waropi Bridge at Buna, knocking out the middle span. He had been on the first mission to Rabaul where his plane had been hit badly but which he had brought home with dead and wounded aboard.

McCullar's co-pilot, Lt Hank Derr, watched anx-

Gen. George E. Kenney, CinC of US 5th Air Force, planned the air phase of Allied operation Eckton II.

Gen. Ennis Whitehead, CO of ADVON 5th Air Force directed attacks on Wewak.

(L to R) Lt. Everette Fraser, Sgt. Howard Lumb, and Lt. Ed Robinson found site in Owen Stanleys for an advanced American fighter base.

Maj. Curran Jones commanded 39th Squadron, 35th Fighter Group, for Wewak attacks.

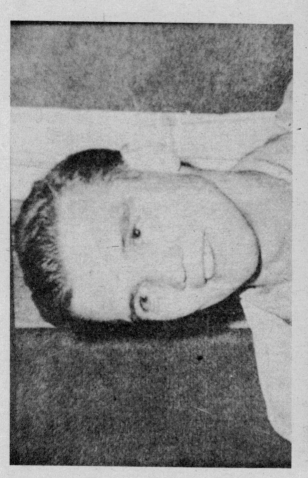

Capt. Tom Lynch of 39th Squadron downed two Japanese planes over Tsili Tsili.

Lt. Col. Meryl Smith (L) and Maj. Furio Wagner (R), the CO and deputy CO of the 475th Fighter Group that downed more than 30 Japanese planes in Wewak raids.

Col. Harry Hawthorne led 43rd Bomb Group heavy bombers in night attacks on Wewak

Col. Donald Hall, CO of the 3rd Attack Group that caused devastating losses to the Japanese at Wewak. 3rd Group won a DUC for Wewak efforts

Lt. Col. Larry Tanberg of the 38th Bomb Group led attack in Hansa Bay on 21 August

Maj. Ken McCullar of 43rd Bomb Group scored heavily
in night attack on Wewak.

The crew of 90th Bomb Group's "Crosby's Curse," that hit Wewak in night raid. (L to R) St: Lt. Eugene Bell, copilot; Capt. Everett Wood, pilot: Lt. Hamilton Chisolm, navigator; Lt. Joe Guidry, bombardier. Kn: Sgt. Sey Hutto, radioman, Sgt. Norm Janke, engineer, Sgt. Vic Green, tail gunner, Sgt. Sab Tenski, turret gunner, Sgt. Art Hamilton, waist gunner, and Sgt. Phil Yrigoyen, nose gunner.

Capt. George Welch led the 8th Fighter Group's 80th Squadron over Wewak.

Maj. Jerry Johnson led the 49th Fighter Group's 9th Squadron on Wewak raids.

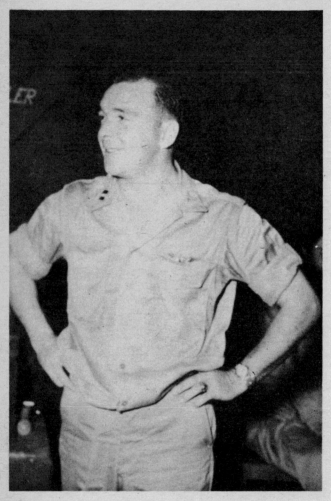

Maj. Howard Paquin led the 38th Bomb Group's 71st Squadron on Wewak raids.

Crew of 38th Bomb Group's "Pacific Prowler." L to R, St: Lt. William Traver, pilot; Lt. Ed Gervais, bombardier, Lt. Jim Craig, copilot, Lt. Rich Robertson, navigator: Kn: gunners Jim Piper, Edward Koch, and George Lane.

Crew of 38th Group's "½ Pound Mary." L to R, St: Lt. Ken Deltz, Lt. Ed Murphy, Lt. Frank Nelson, Lt. Robert Crooks, pilot. Kn: gunners Hal Mendelson, Larry Ward, and Jim Carrauthers.

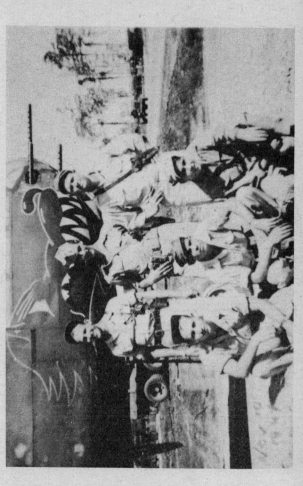

Crew of 38th Group's 71st Squadron: L to R, St: Lt. Rich Kaydso, navigator; Lt. Paul Morse, copilot; Capt. Robert Blair, pilot. Kn: gunners George Suter, Fred Rawlins, and William Hawes.

Maj. James Down led the 3rd Attack Group's 13th Squadron on Wewak raids.

3rd Attack Group B-25 crew: L to R: Lt. Phil Patton, pilot; Lt. Robert Wilkes, copilot; Sgt. Harry Kiser, gunner.
This crew destroyed 12 Japanese planes on the ground.

Grim Reaper crew from the 13th Squadron: L to R: F/O Jack Harrington, copilot; Capt. Don McClellan, pilot; Sgt. Woodrow Butler, gunner. This crew ravaged Boram Drome.

Sgt. Frank Timberlane, gunner aboard Colonel Hall's lead 3rd Attack Group B-25. He had formerly been the gunner for Maj. Ed Larner in Bismarck Sea battle.

Maj. Ralph Celli led 38th Group attack over Wewak on 18 August when he won the Congressional Medal of Honor.

Capt. Tom McGuire had a field day in shooting down Japanese planes over Wewak. The 475th Group Fighter pilot became one of America's top Pacific air aces.

Lt. Francis Lent, another Satans Angel pilot who shot down several planes at Wewak.

Gen. Hitoshi Imamura, CinC of Japanese 8th Area Forces, had hoped to recapture Buna.

Gen. Hatazo Adachi, CinC of 8th Army, would lead counteroffensive in New Guinea.

Gen. Yamusi Arisue, CinC of 7th Air Division, planned a series of air strikes out of Wewak to destroy Allied air bases in New Guinea.

Capt. Masahisa Saito commanded the 751st Kokutai Wing in Wewak. His units were supposed to knock out B-25 air-fields in Port Moresby, but his bombers never got air-borne.

Lt. Comdr. Joyotara Iwami of the 751st Kokutai scored heavily against American P-38s, but all in vain.

Maj. Shinichi Kapaya (r) of the 18th Sentai attempted to knock out the new American Tsili Tsili airbase, but he and his airmen failed. Lt. Tadashi Shizizui at right.

Col. Koji Tanaka of the 17th Sentai. His job was to knock out the American heavy bomber airfields in Port Moresby. But Tanaka never got off his planes, either.

L to R, P/O Shunzo Kodoma, P/O Kusuma Sakai, and F/O Ito Kayo of Japanese 147th Fighter Squadron. They discovered the secret American base at Tsili Tsili while on a reconnaissance mission.

Pilots of the 751st Kokutai's 26th Fighter Squadron. Lower, Lt. Yosihiko Kuroe (L) and Comdr. Hideo Shoji (R). They failed to stop B-25 raids on Wewak airdromes.

Lt. Suzuki Yonai of the 253rd Kokutai's 70th Fighter Squadron. He and his pilots also failed to stop B-25 raids on Wewak airdromes.

B-25 revetment areas of the 3rd Attack Group at Dobodura Drome, Buna.

Hordes of Chimbu tribe natives in New Guinea help to build airfield at Tsili Tsili.

Natives pull C-47 transport plane out of ditch at Tsili Tsili.

Japanese Zeros of the 152nd Squadron drone over skies of New Guinea.

Nose of a B-25 strafer while mechanics work on the plane. These commerce destroyers were the most devastating air weapon of the Southwest Pacific war.

B-25 strafers of the 38th Bomb Group drone at low level over Dagua Drome, Wewak.

Heavy US B-25 attack on Wewak drome leaves holocaust against parked Japanese planes.

Boram Field engulfed in fire and smoke after 3rd Attack Group attack on 17 Aug. 1943.

Grim Reaper Mitchells unleashed parafrag bombs on parked Japanese planes at Wewak Drome. 3rd Group airmen destroyed most of them.

3rd Attack Group B-25s attack more parked Japanese planes with parafrags at Wewak.

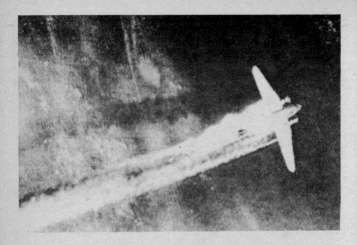

Japanese Sally going down in Solomon Sea, victim of American fighter pilots.

Japanese vegetable garden at Wewak. They grew own food for lack of supplies.

Japanese campsite at Wewak just before low level American B-25 strafing attack.

But Drome, Wewak: 71st Squadron of the 38th Bomb Group devastated this airfield and its parked planes on 18 August.

Parked Japanese planes burn furiously after 3rd Attack Group attack on Wewak Drome.

Scattered wrecked Japanese planes after US B-25 strafing attacks.

38th Bomb Group Mitchell attacks a Japanese Sugar Charlie freighter in Hansa Bay.

Sunsetter Mitchells rip apart Japanese ship in Hansa Bay with strafing fire and parafrag bombs.

A B-25 crashes into Hansa Bay after getting hit by Japanese ack ack fire.

Gen. Thomas Blamey (L) and Gen. George Lasey (R) review their Australian ground troops before the invasion of Lae.

American paratroopers of the 503rd Parachute Regiment jump into Nadzab Valley.

iously as the pair of two thousand pounders fell out of the bomb bay and exploded in numbing concussions squarely atop the Dagua runway, gouging two huge holes in the apron. The major and his co-pilot exchanged grins.

"Goddamn, Snyder was perfect," McCullar said.

More B-24s came over Dagua Drome, dropping more 2,000 pounders and gouging more abysses in the runway. By the time the last of the 14 Liberators from the 43rd Group's 63rd and 64th Squadrons left the area, the Dagua apron looked like a huge punchboard, while two Sallys had been destroyed in the assault.

Next came the Ken's Men B-17s over But Airdrome. Maj. Robert Fuller of the lead 403rd Squadron watched the skyful of incendiaries fall downward and explode in a chain of blinks along the But airstrip, brightening the runway like a glistening downtown area. Then came the other B-17s of the 403rd and 65th Squadrons, dropping 2,000 pounders out of their bellies. Two bombs struck a pair of parked Oscar fighters and two Betty bombers from the 721st Kokutai. However, most of the heavy bombs landed squarely on the runway. Thus the second element of planes from the 43rd Group had also done its job. The Japanese would need considerable man-hours to fill the holes, and the work would not likely be done before the B-25s arrived at daybreak.

However, ack ack fire took a toll against the 43rd Bomb Group. One B-17 exploded from a solid flak hit and tumbled into a fiery mass into the jungle, killing all aboard. A second B-17 caught serious hits, but the pilot brought the plane home.

By the time the 90th Bomb Group Liberators began their run over target, eight Irving night fighters were airborne. However, the Japanese pilots only made half-hearted passes at the Jolly Rogers B-24s in the face of heavy fire from Liberator gunners. The Japanese had scored a few minor hits but caused no serious damage. In turn, Jolly Rogers gunners downed two of the Irvings. Intense AA fire proved deadly. The 90th Group lost two of their planes and crews. Ack Ack caught the B-24 "Yank from Hell" from the 400th Squadron and the plane fell in flames, killing all ten crewmen. A second B-24, shot up badly, flew awry, collided with a 403rd Squadron B-17 and then tumbled into the jungle. Luckily, the Flying Fortress had not been damaged badly and the pilot brought the ship home.

Despite the losses, the Jolly Rogers bombardiers proved as able as those from the 43rd Group. Incendiary bomb clusters accurately hit the Wewak and Boram airdromes. Again, American airmen saw the rows of bombers and fighters on both sides of the runways: Bettys, Dinahs, Oscars, Sallys, Zeros. These parked planes tempted the Jolly Roger airmen, but they too knew that the job of destroying aircraft belonged to the commerce destroyers of the 38th Bomb and 3rd Attack Groups. So the 90th Group airmen also carried out their assignments of punching holes in the Wewak and Boram runways. The Holly Rogers airmen left the two airstrips as badly potholed as the 43rd Bomb Group had punctured the Dagua and But Dromes.

A few bombs did strike parked aircraft. As Jolly Rogers crews knocked out six fighters and four heavy bombers, the 43rd Group destroyed six fighters in their bombing attacks. The two American units had also rendered unserviceable all four Wewak fields.

When the raid ended, Col. Harry Hawthorne, the OTC for the mission, cried into his radio. "Okay, let's go home. Keep formations tight and all gunners stay alert. They could send night fighters after us all the way to Port Moresby."

"Yes sir," Maj. Ken McCullar answered.

And true enough: by now, Japanese everywhere in the Bismarck Archipelago knew that American heavy bombers had made devastating night bombing assaults on the Wewak runways. Further, the Japanese suspected that the US heavy bombers had come from Port Moresby, so the Nippon air commanders plotted the probable flight route of the B-24s and B-17s as the Americans flew back to their bases, Ward and Jackson Dromes.

Japanese Irvings came out of Gasmata, some came out of Madang, and a few came from Finchhaven. But most of the Japanese pilots failed to find the American air formations. The few Nippon airmen who did locate the tight diamonds of Liberators and Flying Fortresses kept their distance. With up to twelve .50 caliber machine guns aboard each of the 49 planes, the total American fire power was awesome. The handful of night fighters that came near the American 5th Air Force heavy bombers made only squeamish passes and did not materially harass the crews heading for Moresby.

By 0400 hours, 17 August, the US heavy bombers began landing at the Port Moresby runways. Ground crews directed the planes to dispersal areas, before transportation men carried the returning crew members to their campsites. Here, the flyers ate a hearty breakfast and then went to their tents to sleep. These heavy US bomber crews did not know how much damage they had caused. And, ironically, the Ken's Men and Jolly Rogers airmen would be sacking out when the main show took place over Wewak on the morning of 17 August 1943.

CHAPTER EIGHT

By the time the American heavy bombers had left the Wewak area, every man at the big Japanese base was wide awake. Gen. Yamusi Arisue rode in a command car with Comdr. Shuichi Watakazi of the 253rd Kokutai, and together they drove from the camp area to the Wewak Drome airstrip. The two men studied the wisps of smoke and globs of fires as they approached the runway. By 0300 hours, they alighted from the car and took a close look. Arisue stared at the damage in a mixture of anger and frustration, while Watakazi pursed his lips in distress.

The 7th Air Division officers strolled along the potted runway for some 30 or 40 yards, looking at the huge bomb craters on the main runway or peering at several wrecked planes.

"The enemy bombers were uncannily accurate this time," Arisue said.

"They must be using the new bombsight that we have heard so much about," Watakazi said. "Our intelligence said the sight is controlled by radar that enables the bombardier to almost see in the dark."

"Fortunately," Arisue said, staring at the line of planes on both sides of the runway, "the enemy did not damage too many aircraft. While they did extensive damage to the runway, we can still mount considerable fighters and bombers if we can quickly fill these bomb craters."

"They obviously used one ton bombs," the 253rd Kokutai commander said, "so they have left unusually large craters. It would take many hours, perhaps one or two days before we can put this runway into operating condition. I fear we will need to call off the planned morning strikes."

"No," Arisue gestured sharply. "We will begin repairs at once. The entire garrison at Wewak was awakened by this air raid and they will not go back to sleep. We will use every man, every vehicle, and every shovel to fill in holes. I will ask General Adachi to use every airman in the 7th Air Division and every soldier in the 18th Army, and every sailor in the naval detachment to help out. We will even enlist any natives we can find. The only men who will be exempt from such labors will be the combat fighter pilots, bomber crews, and such ground crews that are needed to get off our aircraft."

"Even with such effort, it could still be noon before the runways can be used by our fighters and bombers."

"Then we will make our strikes this afternoon instead of this morning."

"Yes, Honorable Arisue."

When Comdr. Shuichi Watakazi took stock of his aircraft he learned that he had only lost four Betty bombers, three Oscar fighters, and one Zero fighter.

He could still use 36 heavy bombers, 27 Oscar fighter-bombers, and 29 fighter escorts to attack Tsili Tsili. Watakazi learned later, in fact, that the other 7th Air Division units had lost even fewer aircraft in the night time attacks.

As soon as Watakazi returned to his 253rd Kokutai headquarters, he called at once into conference his three squadron commanders: Lt. Suzuki Yonai of the 70th Oscar Fighter Squadron, Lt. Hiramma Toyoda of the 71st Zero Fighter Squadron, and Lt. Comdr. Togo Ikeda of the 72nd Betty Bomber Squadron.

"No one need tell you of the damage that the enemy's heavy bombers caused us this evening. Their B-17s and B-24s left many huge bomb craters on our Wewak runway. Fortunately, they did not damage or destroy too many of our aircraft so that we can still use most of our fighters and bombers for the attacks on Tsili Tsili."

"But it could take as much as two days before the runway can be repaired," Lieutenant Yonai said.

"General Arisue has decided to put to work every available man in Wewak," the commander said. "Every vehicle that can move will haul earth to runways to fill the craters. It is our hope that the main runway at Wewak Airdrome will be ready for use by mid-morning, and surely no later than noon. We will then carry out our attacks on the enemy's new airdrome at Tsili Tsili as planned."

"Will it not be too late in the day, Honorable Commander?" Lieutenant Toyoda asked.

"No," Watakazi said. "We are less than one and a half hours from our target point. That means we can make the flight, carry out our attacks, and return to base within four hours. Since Tsili Tsili is only three hundred miles distance from Wewak, both our bombers and fighters can return directly to Wewak after our mission. We need not stage our fighters as must other units of the 7th Air Division."

"I see," Toyoda said.

Commander Watakazi now looked at a sheet in his hand, squinting in the relatively dim, lamp-lit hut. "You all know your assignments. The Mitsubishi heavy bombers will make the first attack on Tsili Tsili from eight thousand feet and their duty is to destroy the runway so that no fighters can take off." He looked at Comdr. Toga Ikeda. "Are the bomber crews ready?"

"They have been awake since the bombing raid began a few hours ago," Ikeda answered. "Yes, they are ready and the crews understand their mission."

"Good," Watakazi said. He then looked at Lt. Suzuki Yonai. "And what of your Nakajima aircraft that will conduct fighter-bomber attacks? Are pilots and aircraft ready?"

"Yes, Commander," the 70th Squadron leader answered. "Every aircraft carries a pair of two-hundred-fifty pound bombs, fully loaded machine guns, and fully loaded 20mm cannons. As soon as the Mitsubishi bombers have completed their high level bomb drops, our fighter-bombers will come down at low level to bomb and strafe any aircraft we can find parked at the airdrome. My pilots will not fail."

The 253rd Kokutai commander nodded and looked at Lt. Hiramma Toyoda. "And what of the Mitsubishi fighter pilots?"

"They too are ready, Honorable Watakazi," the

71st Fighter Squadron commander said.

"You and your pilots will have an important function," Watakazi said. "We do not know how many fighters the Americans have brought into Tsili Tsili. It will be necessary for your airmen to be extremely alert. You should send at least half of them ahead of the bombers and fighter-bombers to engage any enemy fighters in the event the Americans attempt to send up interceptors. It is vital that these enemy fighters do not interfere with the bombing runs."

"I understand," Toyoda said. "Since we have nearly thirty Mitsubishi fighters ready for combat, I will keep half of them ahead of the bomber formations and the others in a protective ring around the bombers."

Watakazi pursed his lips and then looked again at Lieutenant Yonai. "If it becomes necessary, you will use some of your Nakajima fighter-bombers to also engage enemy fighters."

"Yes, Honorable Watakazi."

The 253rd Kokutai commander looked at his watch. "It is now 0330 hours. Please return to your encampments. You should see that your fighter pilots and bomber crews go back to sleep. They should get as much rest as possible while we are repairing the runways, which could take anywhere from four to ten hours, depending on how swiftly we work. Breakfast of rice, tea, and fish cakes will be ready for the combat airmen as soon as they are awake. We do not want to lose any more than a half hour between the time they awake and the time they mount their aircraft." Watakazi then sighed. "Are there any more questions?"

None.

"Fine," Watakazi said.

Two miles away, at the 751st Kokutai headquarters near But Drome, Capt. Masahisa Saito also held a conference in his headquarters hut after the American heavy bomber raid. In attendance were Comdr. Hideo Shoji of the 26th Oscar Fighter Squadron, Lt. Comdr. Joyotara Iwami of the 27th Zero Fighter Squadron, and Lt. Comdr. Yoshi Kido of the 28th Betty Bomber Squadron.

"I have examined the damage to our airfield," Saito began, "and I can report that the enemy caused few casualties among our aircraft that are parked at the field. We have lost but two Mitsubishi bombers and two Nakajima fighters. This means that the bulk of our aircraft are still available for combat. To my dismay, however, I found the runway quite badly damaged with bomb craters and I do not know how long it will take before the runway is repaired."

"I cannot believe the astounding accuracy of this night time attack," Commander Shoji said.

"In a sense, we were quite fortunate," Captain Saito said. "While damage to the runway is bad, we lost very few planes."

"It almost seems that the enemy airmen were only interested in damaging the runway and not the aircraft," Lieutenant Commander Ikeda said.

"It was simply a remarkable coincidence," Saito gestured. However, he frowned when he saw the deep scowl on Commander Iwami's face. "What is the matter, Toyotara?"

"You must excuse me if I disagree with you, Honorable Saito," the 27th Squadron commander said.

"I am more inclined to believe that the enemy's intent was deliberate and not coincidental."

"Deliberate?"

"Captain," Iwami pointed, "It is almost impossible for a fleet of heavy bombers, dropping explosives on an airfield from as high as ten thousand feet, to cause extensive damage to a runway, but only minimal damage to aircraft that are lined up along this runway."

"What are you suggesting, Joyotara?" Lieutenant Commander Kido asked.

"We know the enemy has a new bombsight that is very accurate in night bombing," Iwami said. "Such accuracy was seen during this raid. I think the enemy's heavy bombers had the sole mission of destroying our runways so that our aircraft could not take off. I think the American heavy bombers had a mission of preparing the ground work for a dreaded B-25 strafer attack. What could be a more desirable target than a long line of exposed aircraft that is immobile and nakedly available for low level strafing and parachute bomb attacks?"

"Are you saying, Commander, that the enemy will soon be here with B-25s?" Commander Shoji asked.

"Yes," Iwami nodded, "perhaps at daylight."

"Impossible," Shoji gestured. "They would need to send their B-25s to Wewak without escorts. And while the enemy may have completed the airstrip at Tsili Tsili, he is not ready to send out fighter escorts from this highland base. It would be a few days at least."

"But if they destroyed our runways so that they are inoperable, they may have no fear of intercep-

139

tors. Thus, their B-25s may come to Wewak without any escorts."

"No," Captain Saito now spoke sharply. "I agree with Commander Shoji. The enemy has no way of knowing how much damage they caused to our runway during this night time attack. They will first need to send over reconnaissance planes to determine such damage, and that would not happen until sometime during the daylight hours. The enemy is not that foolish as to send B-25s to Wewak in an unpredictable gamble. Our intelligence reports that the Americans only have about fifty to sixty of these B-25 strafers and they would not brazenly endanger this small complement of aircraft. I am sure it will be a few days before they attempt any such low level strike on Wewak, by which time we will have completed our own mission."

"I would say that Captain Saito speaks logically," Commander Shoji said.

"Perhaps," Iwami conceded.

Saito sighed. "Let us get on with the business at hand. As I said, our aircraft losses at But Drome were minimal. We can still mount at least twenty heavy bombers and eighteen Nakajima fighter-bombers, and all of our thirty-six Mitsuibishi fighters." He looked at Kido. "Are your bomber crews ready?"

"Yes," the twenty-eighth Squadron commander said. "I took the liberty of telling my crews to go back to sleep after the air attack. They will need as much rest as possible before the mission."

"That was wise," Saito said. "You should tell your pilots to do the same," he gestured to Iwami and Shoji.

"I suspect that most of my pilots have already gone back to sleep," Commander Shoji grinned.

Capt. Masahisa Saito nodded and then looked at a sheet in his hand. "I wish to go over our assignments once more. We have the most important mission of destroying the enemy's B-25 strafer base at Port Moresby. If we knock out the Durand Field and its aircraft, the Americans cannot mount their B-25s to attack Wewak, no matter how many fighters they have at the new base in Tsili Tsili. I do not know when we will take off this morning, whether in four hours or ten hours. It depends on how soon they can repair But Airdome."

"We will be ready whatever the time," Lt. Comdr. Yoshi Kido said.

"Our bombing pattern has been established," Saito said. "The Mitsubishi bombers (Bettys) will make the first assault from eight thousand feet, and these heavy bomber crews will be responsible for destroying the Durand Airdrome runway. The Nakajima fighter-bombers (Oscars) will come in next to destroy as many of the B-25 strafers as you find parked about the airdome."

"I understand, Captain," Shoji said.

Saito looked at Iwami. "Joyotara, we know quite well that American and Australian fighter planes abound at Port Moresby. There is every reason to expect heavy interception. It is important that you contain such enemy fighters until our bombers and fighter-bombers have made their attacks. You should follow the usual tactic, keeping half of your planes far ahead of the formation, while the other fighters remain with the bombers."

"Of course," Iwami nodded.

"We will fly toward our target at fifteen-thousand feet as far as the Kokoda area in the Owen Stanley Mountain range. Then we will drop our formations as low as possible to sweep over Imita Ridge and come into Port Moresby. With this strategy, we can avoid enemy radar and reach our targets before the Americans or Australians can mount fighters to intercept us. In fact," Saito pointed to Iwami, "if the vanguard fighters reach Port Moresby undetected and without meeting interceptors, they should strafe the enemy's main fighter strip at Kola Airdrome to thwart any interception."

"I will so instruct my flight leaders," Iwami said.

"Are there any questions?"

"If we leave for our mission late in the day, Honorable Saito, will it not be dark before we return to Wewak?" Commander Shoji asked.

"The fighters and fighter-bombers, of course, will need to land at Lae to refuel," the 751st Kokutai commander said. "If it is too late to leave that base, then these aircraft will remain overnight and leave at first light, before a possible enemy air attack on Lae. General Arisue has made arrangements with Col. Takashi Miyazaki, who commands the 4th Lae Base Force. The Mitsubishi bombers, of course, will fly directly back to Wewak and they should return before dark."

Commander Shoji nodded.

"I would suggest that you now return to your units and relay to your flight leaders the plans we discussed here. Make sure that all bomber crews and fighter pilots get more sleep, while others here in Wewak are repairing the But runway. As soon as we have been told that the runway is operable, we will awaken the combat crews, feed them a good breakfast, and take them to the runway. We want to be off within a half hour after the runway is repaired."

"Yes, Honorable Saito," Lieutenant Commander Iwami said.

In the headquarters tent of the 17th Army Sentai near Dagua Drome, Col. Koji Tanaka called his two squadron leaders to a meeting: Maj. Hayashi Arao of the 146th Medium Bomber Squadron, and Capt. Kusuma Sakai of the 147th Oscar Fighter Squadron. The colonel told his two squadron leaders that the enemy air attack on Dagua Drome had caused the same kind of damage as the assault on the other Wewak dromes. Aviation engineering officers had counted 16 large bomb craters in the main runway, but men, trucks, and equipment were already at work to fill these holes and the runway could be repaired within the next four to six hours.

"Fortunately," Tanaka told his commanders, "the enemy caused few losses to our aircraft, only two of the medium bombers. It will be our duty, of course, to attack the heavy bomber Ward and Jackson Dromes at Port Moresby. I would ask that you divide your squadrons into two groups of a dozen bombers and fighters each. One unit will attack Ward Drome and the other Jackson Drome. You must destroy the runway and as many parked B-17s and B-24s as possible."

The two 17th Sentai commanders listened as Tanaka continued. He reminded the squadron leaders that they would be flying to Moresby at 15,000 feet, but would drop near treetop level over the Owen Stanleys, once they came within 20 or 30 miles of Port Moresby. The 17th Sentai units would follow the 721st Kokutai units that went into Moresby first to attack the B-25 strafer airfield.

"I do not know when we will take off," Tanaka said, "but I want our bomber crews and fighter pilots at their aircraft within a half hour after the runway is repaired. The bombers will return directly to Wewak after the air attacks and the fighters will fly to Finchhaven where we have made arrangements to refuel the fighters and even keep them overnight if necessary."

"Yes, Honorable Colonel," Captain Sakai said.

"Return to your quarters," Tanaka gestured. "See that your combat crews get some sleep and you get some sleep yourselves."

Ten miles to the south, at Boram Drome, Maj. Shinichi Kapaya spoke to his own squadron commanders of the 18th Army Sentai: Capt. Inaba Tsukomoto of the 151st Dinah Light Bomber Squadron, Lt. Tadashi Shizizui of the 152nd Zero Fighter Squadron, and Capt. Ando Akada of the 153rd Betty Heavy Bomber Squadron.

"We are already repairing our main runway," Kapaya began, "and I suspect that we will be ready to take off by mid-morning or even earlier. I issued immediate instructions after the all clear sirens that bomber crews and fighter pilots should go back to sleep. They must have as much rest as possible before they make the long flight to Buna. I would urge you three to do the same thing as soon as this meeting is over, since you will also be on this mission."

"How bad was our damage, Honorable Kapaya?" Lieutenant Shizizui asked.

"Minimal to our aircraft, but eleven bomb craters on the runway," the 18th Sentai commander answered "However, work crews are expected to have the runway repaired by mid-morning. I have called you here only for a final review of instructions. Of all the scheduled missions against enemy airfields, ours is perhaps the most important. A full sentai of enemy B-25 strafers are based at the Dobodura Drome in Buna and for the past two days a full sentai of American long range P-38 fighters have been coming into the Horanda Airdrome at Buna. We can easily guess the reason for such movements. The B-25s and P-38s at Buna are obviously preparing for an attack on Wewak. I would even say that the enemy heavy bomber attack during this very night was designed to put our airdromes out of commission, so the enemy's B-25 strafers can attack our airfields without fear of interception."

"But even from Buna these P-38s cannot fly the four-hundred-fifty mile round trip to Wewak," Captain Tsukomoto said.

"We have now confirmed the fact that the Americans have completed their base at Tsili Tsili and the P-38s from Buna will simply stage there before escorting the B-25s to Wewak. I believe the enemy will attempt to attack Wewak within the next day or two. So it is imperative that we destroy the enemy airdromes at Buna before they can do so."

The squadron leaders did not answer.

"All of you know what to do," Kapaya said. "Our sentai has been divided into two groups, each to attack the Dobodura and Horando Dromes respectively. I will personally lead the A element of twenty-four bombers, and twelve heavy Mitsubishis GM 4s and twelve light Mitsubishi K-164s to attack Dobodura Drome. We will endeavor to chop up the runway and to destroy as many of the B-25 strafers as possible. Since we have only lost two Mitsubishi fighters in this recent air attack, we can still use sixteen fighters to escort the A element. Lieutenant Shizizui will lead these fighters."

"Yes, Honorable Kapaya," Shizizui said.

Kapaya looked at Captain Akada. "You will lead the B Element. You will first bomb Horanda Drome with the other Mitsubishi heavy bombers of the 153rd Squadron. You will then use the Mitsubishi light bombers of the 151st Squadron to attack any parked P-38s that you find along the Horanda runway. Meanwhile the other sixteen fighters will act as escort for this B Element."

"That is clear, Major," Captain Okada said.

"If all goes well, we should do considerable damage," Kapaya gestured. "As usual, we will fly to our target at fifteen-thousand feet and drop to near tree-top level once we are south of Salamaua. We can then make these sweeps over Buna under their radar network to attack before they can mount interceptors." He scanned his officers and sighed. "Please return to your units and be ready to mount aircraft on a half hour's notice."

"Yes, Major," Tsukomoto said.

Thus the commanders of the four 7th Air Division units at Wewak prepared their leaders and airmen for the first multiple air blows in the Japanese MO II op-

146

eration.

Meanwhile, General Arisue moved quickly after he inspected the Wewak Airdrome. He immediately called on his 7th Air Division aide and an 18th Army headquarters officer to release as many men, graders, trucks, shovels, and tractors as possible to fill bomb craters on the four airdromes. Every man at the Wewak complex save for certain air crews and a few select ground crew personnel soon went to work.

Less than a half hour after the American heavy bomber raid, dump trucks and vehicles towing trailers growled throughout the area with scores of men who quickly loaded them with dirt. Within an hour after the work began, trucks unloaded the first squares of dirt into the bomb craters. Other men also dumped trailer loads of dirt into the holes.

As soon as trucks and trailers and even wheelbarrows unloaded earth into bomb craters, graders quickly leveled off the dirt, with the help of thousands of men who packed down earth with tampers, stones, or even shovels. No man in the 18th Army did not jump into the job without enthusiasm and purpose. Every Nippon soldier, airman, and sailor knew that the sooner they got their 300 or more planes off the runways, the sooner the 7th Air Division could extract vengeance against the enemy. In fact, groups of men even broke into song as they labored, while others smiled and joked. Few of them could recall when a mutual camaraderie had prevailed among various unit personnel at the huge Wewak base.

Both General Adachi and General Arisue were more than satisfied with the swift progress in repairing the four main runways at Wewak. The work moved much faster than expected and Arisue, who had hoped to get off his planes by noon, now felt that he could mount his bombers and fighters by 0700 hours or by 0800 hours at the latest.

"We can thank our troops, Honorable Adachi," Arisue told the 18th Army CinC as they watched the progress at Wewak Airdrome.

"The men have responded well," Adachi agreed.

"There is little doubt that we will be over our targets by noon in these first raids on the Allied airbases."

"Good, good," Adachi said. "Will there be follow up raids?"

"As often as weather permits," the 7th Air Division commander said.

By daylight, the job of filling the bomb craters was almost finished, to the surprise of Adachi, Arisue, and every man at Wewak. By the time the sun rose over the mountains at 0800 hours, the graders and hordes of men would be finishing the job of leveling the runways. Arisue called the headquarters huts of the two kokutai and sentai units and ordered air crews to prepare themselves for take off. The Nippon combat airmen responded and within a half hour many of them would be on the way from the campsites to the airdromes at But, Wewak, Dagua, and Boram.

Soon aircraft were lined up wing tip to wing tip on all four fields. By 0830 hours bomber crews and fighter pilots began boarding planes, while ordnance men began gassing up planes that had not yet been fully fueled. The men who had worked hard during the early morning hours to repair the runways could now relax and some even headed for the beaches.

There were 40,000 18th Army troops, 5,000 7th Air Division airmen, and 1,000 naval personnel at Wewak. At 0830 hours, 17 August 1943, not a single one of them could guess that the most devastating air raid ever seen in New Guinea was only moments away.

CHAPTER NINE

By the time the first streaks of dawn had emerged over the Owen Stanley peaks on the morning of 17 August, frantic activity prevailed at the three Allied air bases in Papuan New Guinea. Ground crews readied P-38 fighters and B-25 medium bombers for the mission to Wewak this morning. The Japanese, except for a few men like Lieutenant Commander Iwami, were sure the Americans would wait for reconnaissance reports before attempting to attack the base. However, Gen. Ennis Whitehead, CinC of ADVON 5th Air Force, now had 115 Lightnings that could stage at Tsili Tsili and this number of fighters could hopefully contain any Zeros or Oscars that tried to intercept the Mitchell strafers.

At Tsili Tsili, Maj. Curran Jones briefed 13 pilots for the morning attack on Wewak, since only 14 of the 35th Group's planes had thus far arrived at the new highland base. The Lightning pilots of the 39th Squadron had eaten an early breakfast, before daylight, and they now listened to these final instructions from their squadron leader.

"If all goes well," Jones began, "we should have a fine day over Wewak. Let's hope that the heavies did a good job last night and we won't run into many Zekes or Oscars. However, that's why we're going along—to protect the B-25s. Those low flying Mitchells are very vulnerable at tree top level." He referred to a map behind him. "We'll be picking up the Mitchells here, just north of Finchhaven in the Vitiaz Strait. Our squadron will need to take off as soon as possible because we have other P-38 squadrons coming in to refuel at Tsili Tsili before they join us in escort duties."

"How many P-38s are going, Major?" Capt. Tom Lynch asked.

"All six squadrons," Jones said. "Our own, a squadron from the 8th Group, one from the 49th Group, and the three squadrons from the 475th Group. There'll be well over a 100 Lightnings on this mission."

"How many B-25s?"

"Around sixty from what I was told," Jones answered. "They'll be hitting all four dromes with about fifteen planes at each airfield. If the enemy does not send out too many interceptors, we may do some strafing of our own."

"On which airdromes?" Lynch asked.

"That'll be up to the OTC," Jones said. He looked at the sheet in his hand again. "That would be Col. Donald Hall of the 3rd Attack Group. Our own squadron will furnish top cover for this same group." He looked at his watch and sighed. "Okay, let's get some breakfast and then mount up. We've got to be out of Tsili Tsili in a half hour because P-

38s from Moresby will be coming into Tsili Tsili in about forty-five minutes."

"Yes sir," someone answered.

Daylight had not emerged in the skies over New Guinea before Maj. Curran Jones wheeled his first P-38 from the 39th Squadron to the head of the Tsili Tsili runway. He waited until the green flare shot upward from the control tower. Then he and his wingman zoomed down the runway and took off. Twelve more Lightnings followed and moments later the 14 P-38s were out of sight and flying northwest to join the B-25s over the Vitiaz Strait.

Two-hundred miles to the southeast, at Port Moresby, even before daylight, other American air units were ready. At the 80th Squadron campsite of the 8th Fighter Group, Capt. George Welch gave last minute instructions to 15 fellow P-38 pilots. The 8th Group had been one of the first air units to reach the SWPA when they arrived in Australia in March of 1942. Within weeks, units of the Headhunter Group were operating out of Moresby and by September of 1942 the entire group had moved to Moresby to support operations in the vicious six month Papuan campaign.

The 8th had been among the early US fighter units that continually fought against superior numbers of Japanese planes in the skies over the Owen Stanley Mountains, where they endeavored to escort bombers against the Japanese at Kokoda, Buna, and Lae. The Headhunter personnel had been so racked with malaria that in February of 1943, after the Papuan campaign ended, the group personnel returned to Australia to recuperate and rebuild its disease-riddled squadrons. The 8th had returned to New Guinea in June of 1943 with the 80th Squadron equipped with P-38s.

The Headhunter Group had produced several air aces, such as Jay Robbins, Ken Ladd, Dick West, and Buzz Wagner. Capt. George Welch had already downed four Zeros during his short combat career and he would become one of America's air aces. In fact, he had been at Pearl Harbor during the 7 December 1941 attack, where he had downed a Japanese Kate torpedo bomber.

"We'll be taking off before daylight," Welch told his fellow pilots, "because we'll need to land at Tsili Tsili to refuel before flying on to Wewak. I don't know what we're likely to find over the target, but we'll need to be ready for anything."

"Who's going with us as escort, sir?" Lt. Ed De-Graffenreid asked.

"All six P-38 squadrons, with one squadron from the 49th Group, one from the 35th Group, all three 475th Group squadrons, and our own 80th Squadron." He looked at a sheet in his hand. "We've been assigned top cover for the 38th Bomb Group Mitchells right here out of Port Moresby. The 39th Squadron will be top cover for the 3rd Attack Group Mitchells out of Dobodura."

"How much opposition can we expect?" another pilot asked.

"We have no idea," Welch shook his head. "We do know there are over three hundred planes in Wewak and at least half of them must be fighters. If the heavies did their job, maybe these Nip fighters can't get off to intercept. If so, we'll be going down to do some strafing ourselves."

"Yes sir."

The mess hall is open for us," the 80th Squadron commander said. "Let's get some breakfast and then we ride out to the field. We land at Tsili Tsili by sun up, refuel quickly, and then fly on to pick up the B-25s over Vitiaz Strait."

"Yes sir," Lieutenant DeGraffenreid said.

About a mile away, at the campsite of the 49th Fighter Group, Maj. Jerry Johnson of the group's 9th Squadron also held a briefing. Johnson would take 17 P-38s from the Forty-Niner Group on this mission to Wewak. The 49th was perhaps the earliest American unit to begin combat operations in the SWPA. The group had been activated at Selfridge Field, Michigan, in January of 1941, to begin training with P-35 fighter planes. By January of 1942, the group moved overseas and landed at Melbourne, Australia, where the USAAF assigned the group P-40s to enter combat.

Only a month later, the group's 9th Squadron had moved to Darwin to fight the hard, losing Java campaign, while they effectively protected Darwin in northwest Australia. To the northeast, the group's 7th and 8th Squadrons had moved to Cape York on the tip of the Cape Horn Peninsula. From here the two Forty-niner squadrons had staged at Port Moresby to engage in the exhausting battle against superior numbers of Japanese planes. They had regularly fought air battles against the famed Nippon Tianan Wing out of Lae, but they had fared badly in their P-40s against the superior Zero that usually outnumbered them in dogfights over the Owen Stanleys by two to one.

Eventually, however, 49th Group pilots had learned to deal with Zero pilots and the Americans had finally contained these Nippon airmen. For their valiant efforts in New Guinea during the early months of the war, the 49th had won a DUC. They would earn three more DUCs before the war ended in the SWPA.

Maj. Jerry Johnson, the 9th Squadron commander, had been in combat for more than six months, and he had already downed six Japanese Zeros and Oscars. The baby-faced Forty-niner from Eugene, Oregon, had been in the air corps since 1940. In May of 1942 he had joined a US air unit in Alaska and here, over the Aleutians he had shot down his first Japanese plane. A few months later he was transferred to the SWPA to join the 49th Fighter Group. During the early months of 1943 he had run up a score of six more kills. He would down a total of 22 planes before he ended two tours of duty in the SWPA. He would win two DFCs, a Silver Star, a Legion of Merit, and several other awards.

"Since only the 9th Squadron from our group has P-38s, we'll be on this mission to Wewak," Johnson began. "We've drawn the assignment of vanguard in the air formation. That means we'll be the first unit to meet enemy interceptors. We'll not only need to take on such enemy fighters, but we must keep other 5th Air Force units informed on the strength and dangers from such interceptors. So, we've got quite a responsibility."

"How many interceptors can we expect, Major?" Lt. Theron Price asked.

"God only knows," Johnson shook his head. "We know from recon reports that the Nips have well over three hundred planes in Wewak, so we can guess that at least one hundred fifty of them are probably fighters."

"Goddamn, Major, that's a lot of fighters."

"General Whitehead is using all of the P-38 squadrons this morning," the 9th Squadron CO said. "So we should have well over a one hundred fighters of our own."

"We'll probably need every one of them," Price said.

"Maybe not," Johnson answered. "If the heavies did a good job, those Wewak runways should be well potted. Zeros and Oscars may not be able to get off. In that event, we'll probably make some strafing runs of our own against parked enemy aircraft." The major looked at a sheet in front of him and then continued. "We'll be taking off within the next half hour along with the 80th Squadron and we'll be landing at Tsili Tsili to refuel. Then we head out to sea to meet the bombers over the Vitiaz Strait."

The first streak of daylight had barely emerged over the Owen Stanley range when the two P-38 squadrons at Port Moresby began taking off from the Kola Drome fighter strip. Maj. Jerry Johnson and his wingman whirled to the head of the runway and the two Lightnings from the 49th Group's 9th Squadron roared down the runway on signal from the tower. Fifteen more Lightnings from the squadron followed. Then came the 80th Squadron. Capt. George Welch and his wingman turned to the head of the same Kola runway and within minutes the 16

157

Lightnings from the 80th Squadron also took off. Then the 33 P-38s from the Forty-niner and Headhunter squadrons disappeared into the darkness over the Owen Stanleys. The US fighters would land at Tsili Tsili, refuel, and then continue on for its rendezvous with the bombers.

Three miles away from the Kola Drome, at Durand Drome, Lt. Col. Larry Tanberg conducted a briefing in the operations tent of the 38th Bomb Group with the bomber crews of the 405th and 71st Squadrons. Tanberg held the briefing because the group CO, Col. Brian "Shanty" O'Neil had come down with stomach poisoning and now lay in the Port Moresby base hospital. The B-25 strafers of the 38th Sunsetter Group would hit But and Dagua dromes in low level attacks with their 27 Mitchell strafers.

The Sunsetters, activated in 1941 at Langley Field, Virginia, had trained with B-18s, B-26s, and B-25s. Ground echelons from two squadrons had arrived in Australia in early 1942, but they remained inactive for months because they had no planes. Two other squadrons from the 38th had been at Hawaii where they had participated in the Battle of Midway. Not until August of 1942 did the Sunsetters finally get their B-25s in the SWPA, finally moving to Port Moresby in September of 1942 to begin operations with their medium bombers.

Although the Sunsetters had been in combat for nearly 11 months, the 38th Group had always operated in the shadow of the glamorized 3rd Attack Group that also used B-25s in the SWPA. However, the 3rd had won all the accolades during the hard fought early New Guinea battles. Still, although the 38th Group had also participated in the Battle of the Bismarck Sea in March of 1943, the 3rd Group with its skip bombers had won the honors and a DUC in the destruction of the Lae resupply convoy. In fact, with each new innovation for the B-25, the 3rd Group had always used such improvisations first: nose strafing guns, the parafrag bomb, the skip bomb, and the 75mm nose cannon.

However, by August of 1943, the Sunsetter B-25s were equipped as fully as the 3rd Group. The 38th Group, on this morning of 17 August 1943, would finally operate with the 3rd Group on an equal basis for this vital air operation against Wewak's airdromes.

Larry Tanberg had come overseas with the 38th bomb Group in mid-1942 as a flight leader, rising progressively to squadron commander and then deputy group commander. He had been in the USAAF for more than three years and from the start, he had always displayed excellent leadership qualities and a unique aggressiveness in combat. Now, in perhaps the Sunsetters' most important mission since coming to the SWPA, Tanberg would direct the 38th Group operations. The deputy group commander scanned some papers before he spoke.

"This is the big one. More than three hundred planes are sitting on the deck at Wewak. Preliminary reports say our heavies did a good job in knocking out runways, leaving the parked Japanese planes stranded along the airstrips. We'll never find a better target than the one we're likely to see this morning."

"Are we getting enough fighter cover?" Maj.

Howard Paquin of the 405th Squadron asked.

"Over one hundred P-38s," Tanberg answered. "However, I would certainly suggest that gunners remain on full alert." He paused and looked at the sheet in his hand before he continued. "As you know, for the first time, we'll be using turret auxiliary tanks before we reach target. We've been practicing, so I hope we'll have no problems with such release."

"Sir," Capt. Ray Middleton said, "that plywood cover doesn't always hold too well and when it loosens, we get an awful lot of cold air inside the plane."

"Then keep your fur lined jackets tight," Tanberg grinned. "What else can I tell you?"

Middleton did not answer.

"All of you know our target," Tanberg continued. "The 71st Squadron, which I'll lead, hits Dagua Drome; the 405th under Major Paquin will hit But Drome. We'll be flying at eight-thousand feet to target, but we'll break off at IP, southeast of Wewak. Then we'll drop to treetop level for bomb runs; 71st to Dagua and 405th to But. Any questions?"

"Sir," Lt. Bill Travers of the 71st Squadron asked, "any chance we'll catch Jap fighters out of Lae or Gasmata?"

"I don't know," Tanberg, answered. "As I said, gunners must be alert."

"Yes sir," Travers answered.

The 38th Group acting CO then looked at his watch. "Okay, let's get breakfast and then head for the field. Our rendezvous with the fighter escort will be at Bena Bena, then we join the 3rd Group over the Vitiaz Strait. Expected time of attack is 0900 hours. Any questions?"

"No sir," Capt. Bob Blair of the 71st Squadron said.

At 0600 hours, the 27 Mitchell strafers from the 38th Bomb Group's 71st and 405th Squadrons lumbered toward the head of the runway at Durand Drome. On signal from the control tower, Lieutenant Colonel Tanberg and his wingman, Lt. Bill Travers in the plane "Pacific Prowler", released the brakes of their B-25s and zoomed down the runway to take off. Then came Lt. Bob Crooks and his wingman. Soon, these two B-25 strafers also took off.

At 30 second intervals, the other B-25s from the 71st and 405th Squadrons also took off. Finally, all 27 Mitchells had risen into the gloomy, cloud covered skies over the Owen Stanley range. Ground crews at Durand Drome now shuffled to waiting vehicles for a ride back to their campsite. They would return to the airstrip in four hours to meet returning Sunsetter crews, hoping that all of them came back.

Over the Owen Stanleys, Lieutenant Colonel Tanberg frowned as he stared at the dense gray clouds. He feared that heavy thunderstorms were imminent and he might have to abort this mission. In the same formation, Lt. Herman Crooks in his plane "½ Pound Mary" also squinted uneasily at the dense clouds that had closed in the entire Owen Stanley range. Crooks's aircraft had been named after a prostitute in Townsville, Australia, who charged ½ pound to take on airmen who came down to that town on leave from New Guinea.

Crooks again looked at the threatening clouds and

he then checked with his crew: co-pilot Lt. Ken Deitz, navigator Lt. Tim Murphy, gunners Sgt. Bob Anderson and Sgt. Hal Carpenter, and two passengers, photographer Lt. Joe Nelson and observer Lt. Tom Morris. The crew responded positively: all instruments in good order, aircraft operating smoothly, equipment fine, radio okay, guns in good operating condition.

As the 27 Mitchells from the Sunsetter Group continued over the Owen Stanley Mountains toward Bena Bena, the rendezvous point with their fighter escorts, the clouds grew denser and more ominous. Pilots soon found themselves shrouded in heavy mists, unable to see fellow aircraft. Finally, Maj. Howard Paquin called Larry Tanberg.

"Colonel, we'll never make it through this soup. It keeps getting worse and we may soon crash into each other. We can't hold formation much longer. I suggest we abort."

Tanberg looked at the gloomy, several miles thick clouds and he then answered Paquin. "You're right, Howie, we'll have to turn back." Tanberg then gave the order to abort. The lieutenant colonel felt bitter because his Sunsetters had finally gotten a chance to perform on a par with their friendly competitors, the 3rd Attack Group. But Tanberg could not jeopardize the planes and crews aboard these 27 medium bombers.

Not everyone heard the order to return to Port Moresby. Capt. Ray Middleton, leading a V of B-25s with Capt. Rowen Gay and Lt. Bob Lacenis, had apparently failed to get the instructions. While 24 Mitchells turned and headed back to Moresby,

Middleton's trio of planes continued on toward the rendezvous point at Bena Bena.

Earlier, at 0600 hours, at the 3rd Attack Group campsite near the Dobodura Airdrome in Buna, Col. Don Hall, the group commander, held a last minute briefing with 37 three man crews who would make the flight to Wewak this morning.

Perhaps no other US air unit in the Pacific enjoyed the prestige of the 3rd Attack Group Grim Reapers. The 3rd had developed from the old 104th Aero Squadron of World War I that had fought in the Marne. The 104th returned to the States to become the nucleus of the 3rd Attack Group in 1921. Over the next two decades, the USAAF had used the 3rd for experimenting with new combat innovations: low level bombing, bomber strafing tactics, antisubmarine techniques, and low flying patrol missions. The group had come to the Pacific in February of 1942, landing at Townsville, Australia. They began combat operations immediately, staging out of Port Moresby.

The 3rd Group had used A-20s, A-24s, and B-25s during their missions in the six month Papuan campaign, where the Grim Reapers had suffered terrible losses above the Owen Stanleys against swarms of enemy fighters. Yet the group had scored telling blows against Japanese shipping, airfields, supply depots, and troop concentrations. The 3rd, as the most successful air group in New Guinea, had been singled out by the Japanese Tianan Fighter Wing as the American air group that must be destroyed.

The Grim Reapers had carried on a two decade tradition of innovation, using new techniques in the Papuan campaign to stop the Japanese offensive and to send them into headlong retreat. The 3rd had been the first unit to use the heavy strafing nose guns on their A-20s and B-25s. The Reapers had been the first to use the parafrag bomb to make low level bombing attacks with medium bombers, and they had been the first unit to use the skip bomb against Japanese shipping. These tactics by the Grim Reapers had broken the back of the Japanese during the Papuan campaign and had been the principal factor in destroying the Lae resupply convoy during the Battle of the Bismarck Sea victory.

By July of 1943, after 17 months of combat, the Grim Reapers had destroyed over 200 enemy planes in the air and on the ground, nearly 50,000 tons of shipping, several airfields, and they had slain more than 10,000 enemy troops. Small wonder that the Japanese considered the Reapers their most deadly enemy in the Southwest Pacific.

The 3rd Attack Group had already won three DUCs and they would win more before the war ended in the Pacific. The 3rd had been the only combat air unit in World War II designated an attack group instead of a fighter or bomber group.

The 3rd had produced some of the greatest air heroes in the SWPA: Col. John "Big Jim" Davies who had escaped the Philippines in early 1942 and taken command of the 3rd during the successful Papuan campaign; Lt. Col. Bob Strickland who led the group after the Buna campaign; Maj. Ed Larner who led the group in the Bismarck Sea victory; and now Col. Donald Hall who had carried out the first parafrag attack against Japanese troop concentrations.

Hall had been with the 3rd Group since the unit came overseas in early 1942 and he had distinguished himself on several missions, winning two DFCs, a Silver Star, and a Purple Heart. He had risen quite rapidly in rank and by April of 1943 he had won promotion to colonel and command of this famed aerial attack group. Thus far, he had shown the same high combat and leadership qualities as had commanders before him, and he was confident now that his Grim Reapers would do a good job today.

Unlike the 38th Bomb Group that used five man crews on their Mitchells, the 3rd Attack Group used three man crews on their B-25 strafers. They had operated with reduced crews for several months, ever since January of 1943 when the Grim Reapers had converted all of their Mitchells to strafers. From then on, the 3rd had conducted only low level parafrag and machine gun attacks on any combat mission. Thus 5th Air Force had seen no need for waist gunners. The pilot served as bombardier and the co-pilot as navigator, with the single top turret gunner also the radio man. The system had worked quite well for the Grim Reapers. Now, on this early 17 August morning, Colonel Hall scanned his crews before he spoke.

"You know your targets, the Wewak and Boram Dromes. The 8th Squadron, which I'll lead myself and the A Element of the 13th Squadron under Lieutenant Beck will hit Boram. The 90th Squadron under Capt. Phil Hawkins and the B Element of the 13th Squadron under Maj. Jim Downs will hit Wewak Drome. We'll fly straight up the Solomon Sea in company with the P-38s from the 475th Fighter Group. So we'll have escorts all the way. We join the 38th Group Mitchells in the Vitiaz Strait at the rendezvous point of 5.3 south by 147.7 north. The remainder of the P-38 escorts will meet us there."

"How many escorts will we have, sir?" Capt. Don McClellan asked.

"Well over a hundred," Hall answered. "I was told that all six Lightning squadrons would join us on this mission."

"How well did the heavies do, sir?" Lt. Phil Patton of the 90th Squadron asked.

"We don't know yet," the Grip Reaper CO said, "but reports from crews say they did quite well. However, all gunners better stay alert. The Nips might be waiting for us after the night attack by our B-17s and B-24s. We could run into a swarm of interceptors."

"Yes sir."

"We fly at eight thousand feet for most of the way," Hall continued, "and then drop at IP to treetop level, with my element going to Boram and Captain Hawkins's element veering off to Wewak. At least one squadron of P-38s from the 475th Group will accompany each attack unit."

"Will that be enough?" Maj. Jim Downs of the 13th Squadron asked.

"There'll be plenty of P-38s with us if we need them," Hall answered. He looked at his watch. "Okay, let's get some breakfast and then mount up."

"Yes sir," Captain Hawkins answered.

About a mile away, at Buna's Horando Drome, Lt. Col. Meryl Smith of the 475th Fighter Group called 52 pilots of his three squadrons into a briefing. They would take off as soon as the 3rd Attack Group Mitchells got off, and they would accompany the Grim Reapers all the way to Wewak. The 475th Satan's Angels Group had had as little combat experience as the

3rd Attack Group had extensive combat experience.

The Satans Angels had not been activated until the spring of 1943, and not even in the United States, but in Australia under a special edict granted by the 5th Air Force. The new fighter group under the command of then Maj. Meryl Smith began its training at Ambery Field, Australia, and its personnel included a mixture of veterans and green pilots just over from the States as replacements.

Smith had been a veteran pilot in the New Guinea war, serving in both the 8th Fighter Group and the 35th Fighter Group for several months before returning to Australia for a rest. He had been a fighter pilot for seven years, since he joined the USAAF. The major had surrounded himself with excellent, experienced combat pilots when he was asked to form this new group: men like Maj. Daniel Roberts, Capt. Tom Henry, Capt. Bill Weldon, Capt. Tom McGuire. These veterans had done a good job in training replacement pilots who had recently arrived from the States. The Satans Angels, the only US air unit initiated outside of the continental United States, received a full complement of P-38s.

In August of 1943, just before the planned Wewak air operation, the entire group had moved to Port Moresby with all of its planes, personnel, and equipment. However, they had not even unpacked because General Kenney, CinC of 5th Air Force, ordered them to the newly completed Horanda Airdrome in Buna. By the afternoon of the 16th, the entire group had settled there. The group's first mission had been a routine escort mission with the 22nd Bomb Group on a B-26 bombing mission to Gasmata, New Britain, yesterday.

Even as the 475th was completing its move to Buna, the group's 431st Squadron under Capt. Tom McGuire had done a creditable job at Gasmata, downing two Zeros to no losses for the Americans, and Smith hoped his pilots would do as well at Wewak on this second escort mission.

"All three squadrons are going off this morning," Smith told his fighter pilots. "We take off as soon as the 3rd Group is gone. I needn't tell you what you might expect at Wewak. Our latest intelligence reports say there are well over three hundred Japanese planes up there. We could also run into Zekes and Oscars out of Lae, Finchhaven, Madang, or Gasmata on the way to Wewak. So stay alert."

"Do we just cover the 3rd Group, sir?" Capt. Bill Weldon of the group's 432nd Squadron asked.

"No," Smith answered. "The 38th Group's B-25s will rendezvous with us off Finchhaven in the Vitiaz Strait. There, Major Roberts's 432nd Squadron will maintain close cover around the 38th Group, while our 431st and 432nd Squadrons maintain close and near cover for the 3rd Attack Group. Among the other three squadrons of P-38s on this mission, one will give the 38th Group top cover, one will furnish top cover for the 3rd, and the other Lightning squadron will maintain the vanguard position." He looked again at a sheet in his hand. "The 3rd Group will break into two units, one going to Boram and the other to Wewak Drome. Our 432nd Squadron will accompany the Mitchells to Boram and Captain McGuire's 431st will accompany the 3rd Group unit that goes to Wewak. Major Roberts's squadron will accompany the 38th Group Mitchells to But and Dagua Dromes."

"I understand," Major Roberts said.

"Any questions?" Smith asked. When no one answered the 475th Group CO nodded. "Let's get some breakfast and then mount up."

By 0645 hours, both the 3rd Attack Group and the 475th Fighter Group had left Dobodura and were now well to the northwest over the Solomon Sea. Because of the heavy traffic at Tsili Tsili this morning, 5th Air Force had ordered the 475th Group to stage at the mountain base to refuel on the way back from the mission. By 0700 hours the swarm of American planes from 5th Air Force had rendezvoused at the scheduled point of 5.3°south by 147.7° west, off the New Guinea coast over the Vitiaz Striat. Colonel Hall was shocked when he learned that only three Mitchells from the 38th Group had joined the formation, but he told Capt. Ray Middleton to fall in behind the Grip Reaper planes.

Meanwhile, Maj. Curran Jones of the 39th Squadron, along with Capt. Tom Welch of the 80th Squadron, assumed top cover over the B-25s. Maj. Jerry Johnson of the 9th Squadron zoomed ahead in the van position, while the P-38s from the 475th Group jelled around the 32 B-25s, all that had made it from the 63 planes that had taken off from Durand Drome in Port Moresby and Dobodura Drome in Buna. Among the fighters, 16 had turned back with varying degrees of mechanical difficulties and only 85 P-38s were still with the bombers.

However, Col. Don Hall was sure that 85 Lightnings would be enough cover. And if the Americans met only minor interception, he would send down the P-38s in strafing runs against parked Japanese planes.

For another hour, the 117 American planes sped on. Luckily, they had not met any fighters out of Lae, Madang, or Gasmata, and by 0745 hours, the US air formation approached the coast of Wewak.

Both fighter pilots and bomber crews grew uneasy. All of them knew that the Japanese had based more than 300 planes on their four Wewak airdromes. The skies over Wewak could be black with enemy fighter planes that waited for the Americans. None of the US airmen had ever been to Wewak before and they had no idea what to expect at this formidable base.

As the American planes approached IP, Don Hall looked at is watch: 0850 hours. They were less than 15 minutes from target. Hall stiffened and he felt perspiration dampen his face. The colonel was a veteran pilot who had challenged death on several occasions. Yet he was obviously nervous, unsure of what lay ahead. Similarly, other American airmen felt uneasy, even veterans like Lt. Col. Meryl Smith, Capt. Tom McGuire, Capt. John Welch, or Maj. Jerry Johnson. The newer men to combat no doubt felt even much more apprehensive. They had heard enough about Wewak and just the number, 300 planes, had been sufficient to leave them extremely nervous.

However, these American airmen could not guess that they would catch the Japanese completely off guard.

CHAPTER TEN

The sun had finally risen from the eastern horizon of the Solomon Sea as the 32 B-25s of the 3rd and 38th Groups neared Wewak after their long flight from the south. Copilot Miles Green aboard Lt. Don Hall's lead Mitchell squinted from the starboard window of the cabin and then turned to his pilot.

"Not a cloud in the sky, sir."

Hall nodded.

Then Green rubbed his face. "Sir, do you think we'll get jumped by Zeros?"

"I don't know," Hall answered, "but at least we've got plenty of fighter cover." Then as an afterthought, the Grim Reaper commander called his gunner. "Sergeant, do you see anything?"

"No sir," Frank Timberlane answered, "just our escort upstairs."

"Stay sharp."

"Yes sir," the gunner answered.

Hall looked at his watch and then at the map on his lap. He next checked his compass and then his altimeter: 310 degree bearing and 8,000 feet respectively. He glanced at the fuel gauge that showed slightly more than a half tank. He knew he was close to target and he called his squadron commanders.

"Target fifteen to twenty miles ahead. Stay alert. Check all guns and check release buttons. Remember, we drop to treetop level as soon as we spot the coast. Thirteenth Squadron A Element will follow the 8th Squadron to Boram Drome. Thirteenth Squadron B Element will follow 90th Squadron to attack Wewak Drome. That's where most of their fighters are likely to be, so Captain Hawkins's unit will need to hit the Wewak Drome quickly and thoroughly."

"We'll get them before they know what hit them, sir," Capt. Phil Hawkins of the 90th Squadron said.

"We'll be right behind you at Boram, Colonel," Maj. Jim Downs of the 13th Squadron said.

Hall flew on for a few more minutes and then craned his neck to stare at the formation of P-38s overhead. He then glanced at the Lightnings that hung around the tight diamonds of B-25s. Finally he called Jerry Johnson of the 9th Fighter Squadron.

"Major, we'll be reaching target within a few minutes. Please make certain your vanguard planes report any interceptors."

"Already done, sir," Johnson answered. "I've got six Lightnings as far as twenty miles ahead of us and on a ten mile spread. They'll warn us in plenty of time."

"Good," Hall answered. Then the 3rd Attack Group colonel called Lt. Col. Meryl Smith who led the 475th Fighter Group. "Please stay close to us, Colonel. Target is just ahead."

"We'll stick to you like glue," Smith said. "We'll be with you all the way in and out."

Hall next called Maj. Curran Jones of the 39th Squadron and Capt. George Welch of the 80th Squadron, reminding them to maintain their top cover to meet any interceptors that might try to attack the bombers from upstairs. Finally, Hall called Capt. Ray Middleton of the 38th Bomb Group's 405th Squadron. Middleton, who was leading the only three Sunsetter B-25s that had managed to make it across the Owen Stanleys from Port Moresby, felt uncertain and almost embarrassed. He worried all the way to the target, wondering what he could do with a mere three planes.

"Captain," Hall said, "if those Wewak dromes are as jammed with planes as recon reports say they are, we're going to need every bomber we've got. I want you to hit your target at Dagua. Maybe three planes aren't much, but there's a lot of firepower on these B-25 strafers. I think you can do a lot more damage than you imagine."

"Yes sir," Middleton answered.

Hall's affirmation reassured the Sunsetter flight leader who had been quite discouraged. He called his two other pilots, Capt. Jim Gay and Lt. Frank Lacenis. "Colonel Hall has confirmed our target as Dagua. The colonel thinks we can make a real contribution even with three planes. We break off from formation as soon as we see the coast."

"Okay, Ray," Captain Gay answered.

About the B-25 formations, the P-38s of the 475th Fighter Group hung like dangling spiders. Lt. Col. Meryl Smith, the Satans Angels commander, peered at the diamonds of fighters around him. Then he squinted to the north, but still saw only the wide expanse of water ahead. He called his pilots.

"Just a reminder: 433rd Squadron will accompany the 3rd Attack Group bombers over Boram, 432nd Squadron will accompany the 3rd Group units over Wewak Drome, and 431st Squadron will accompany 38th Bomb Group bombers over Dagua Field. Keep your formations tight, and keep a pair of fighters ahead. We don't know what we might run into at Wewak."

"Yes sir," Capt. Bill Weldon of the 432nd Squadron said.

"I read you, Colonel," Capt. Tom McGuire of the 431st Squadron answered.

"As soon as the mission is over," Smith continued, "we hang about the B-25s all the way home. If you have any trouble, you can make an emergency landing at Wau. The others land at Tsili Tsili to refuel."

"Yes sir," Captain Weldon said again.

Among the 39th Squadron P-38 pilots, Maj. Curran Jones again stared ahead and he also saw nothing but open sea. He too called his pilots. "We stay upstairs when we cross the coast. Our squadron aircraft will hang at eight thousand feet and 80th Squadron aircraft will hang at ten thousand feet."

"Yes sir," Capt. Jim Welch of the 80th Squadron answered.

In the cabin of his lead B-25, Col. Don Hall once more peered from his window at the empty sea ahead. He again glanced at his watch: 0840. Target was only five minutes away. He turned and grinned at Lieutenant Green who had stiffened in his seat and the grin relaxed the copilot.

In the bright morning sun, the huge formation of 5th Air Force planes continued on: 32 B-25s with 85 P-38s around and above the Mitchells. The bomber crews had become more and more apprehensive because 14 of the Lightnings had turned back. They hoped that no more P-38s left them before the Mitchells reached targets, and they hoped that the remaining fighters would be enough to contain any Japanese interceptors that rose from the Wewak dromes to challenge the Americans. General Whitehead had not convinced more than a few of them that they could catch the Japanese napping, and the airmen on this mission expected Zeros to be waiting in the sky to meet them. So Mitchell gunners and Lightning pilots made certain that their guns were in good order.

Astonishingly, the Japanese at Wewak were indeed unprepared for any low level B-25 commerce destroyer strikes. Earlier, at 0730 hours, the combat airmen of the 7th Japanese Air Division had just completed breakfast at an array of mess halls about the sprawling base. The pilots and crews had eaten their usual fare of hot rice, tea, and a little fish. The officers, who generally ate better than enlisted personnel, had enjoyed an added item of juice. As the combat clad flyers ate, the mess hall personnel had served them with admiring looks. Finally, these combat crews would strike hard at the Yankee dogs. Over 300 fighters and bombers would be off within the next hour, the biggest air formation ever to leave a Japanese base for an air strike.

By 0850 hours, rattling, growling trucks carried the combat crews of the 253rd Kokutai to the Wewak

Drome where ground crews had lined up the 27 Oscars, 29 Zeros, and 36 Bettys on both sides of the runway. The Zeros would escort the flights of heavy bombers and Oscar fighter-bombers that attacked Tsili Tsili. Lt. Suzuki Yonai would lead the 70th Oscar Squadron, Lt. Hiramma Toyoda would lead the 71st Zero Squadron and Lt. Toga Ikeda would lead the 72nd Betty Squadron. All along the route from the campsite to the airfield, soldiers waved to the combat fighter pilots and combat bomber crews.

"Destroy the Yankee dogs!"

"A victory for the Emperor!"

"Remember Yamamoto!"

The combat airmen of the 253rd smiled and waved back. Yes, they would extract vengeance today—avenge the defeat at Buna, the losses in the Bismarck Sea, and the murder of Yamamoto. The Japanese naval airmen were eager, stirring restlessly on the hard rear seats of the trucks until they finally alighted and hurried to their waiting Oscars, Zeros, and Bettys. Ground crews who still served the fighter planes and bombers in last minute checks, or who still poured fuel into the aircraft, bowed and cheered before helping pilots and crews into their planes.

To the south, Capt. Shinichi Kapaya of the 18th Army Sentai wore a stern look on his face as he rode in the back of a truck with some of his airmen toward the Boram airstrip. He seemed unaware of the jounces over the rough roadway. About him, Dinah and Betty bomber crews stirred with ardent zeal as did Zero pilots in other trucks. Most of the airmen had been on several missions against Dobodura or Moresby during the past couple of months and they expected this 17 August 1943 day to become a most fruitful one. They would crush their enemies in these multiple strikes.

Some of the young airmen joked and clapped and sang, causing a numbing din in the rear of the trucks. But the sober Captain Kapaya made no effort to subdue the almost childlike behavior. Perhaps, inwardly, Kapaya was as eager as his men to strike a severe blow against the Allies.

Finally, the trucks wheeled up to the waiting Dinahs, Bettys, and Zeros at the airstrip. Only now did Kapaya speak harshly, as did Lt. Tadashi Shizizui of the 152nd Zero Squadron and Captain Tsukomoto of the 151st Dinah Squadron.

"Move quickly! Man your aircraft!" Kapaya barked.

"Hurry, we will be taking off soon," Shizizui cried.

"You must not loiter," Tsukomoto prodded his men.

As the crews scrambled to their planes, they could see the endless rows of aircraft on both sides of the main runways. The horde of Zeros would cover the Bettys and Dinahs on the Horanda and Dobodura targets at Buna. Here at Boram, ground crews also cheered and waved at the combat crews and pilots as the airmen shuffled toward the heavy bombers, light bombers, and fighters that lined both sides of the runway.

To the northeast, more trucks growled toward Dagua Field, where Sally medium bombers and Oscar fighters from the 17th Sentai sat in straight lines on both sides of the runway. Col. Koji Tanaka would take off with both squadrons: the 146th medium Sallys and the 147th Oscar fighters. Tanaka was eager to fly this mission because he surely recognized the threat from heavy bombers at Moresby's Ward and Jackson Dromes. B-24s and B-17s had hit them only last night. As his bomber crews tumbled out of the rear of trucks, the colonel directed them swiftly to waiting planes.

Tanaka then squinted toward the campsite of the 147th Squadron, but he did not see the trucks coming. Capt. Kusuma Sakai and his fighter pilots were not yet on the way. But then, Tanaka shrugged. It didn't matter. Sakai's fighter planes could catch up to the bombers long before the Sallys reached Port Moresby. The colonel merely glanced at the rows of Oscars on the opposite side of Dagua Drome's runway before he turned to his bomber crews.

"Hurry to your stations," he barked. "We do not have all day."

And in fact, Captain Sakai was still eating breakfast with his fighter pilots of the 147th Squadron. The Sally bombers of the 17th Sentai would not take off until 0900 hours to make the long flight to Moresby. Sakai and his pilots would surely be in their planes by then, and even if the fighters landed at Finchhaven to refuel they would easily catch up to the medium bombers over the Owen Stanley Mountains before continuing the journey to Port Moresby.

By 0840 hours, many of the Japanese pilots and bomber crews had boarded their planes, while more 7th Air Division airmen were getting ready to board planes. A few stragglers were still riding toward the airfields to their waiting planes. Not a single Japanese airmen, sailor, or soldier in Wewak had the slightest idea that dreaded US B-25 strafers were only moments away from striking their airfields at low level.

At 0845 hours, the Wewak coast finally loomed to the northwest for the Americans. Lt. Jim Reynolds of the 9th Fighter Squadron was leading the vanguard P-38s and he quickly called Jerry Johnson. "Major, target straight ahead."

"Okay," Johnson answered. The major in turn called Don Hall. "Sir, your target is straight ahead. You can break off for attacks."

"Thank you," Hall answered. The Grim Reaper commander then called his squadron leaders. They would drop to 100 feet, cross the coast and skim over the treetops to attack at low level with strafing fire and parafrag bombs. Hall would lead the 8th Squadron over Boram with the A Element of the 13th Squadron following in tandem. 90th Squadron would veer right to attack Wewak Drome with B Element of the 13th Squadron. The three B-25s of the 38th Group would also veer right to hit Dagua Field. Fighters from the 80th and 39th Group would hang upstairs, the 9th Squadron Lightnings would forge ahead, and the P-38s from the 475th Fighter Group would hang around the B-25s.

Amazingly, not a single Japanese plane rose to meet the bombers because the attack by the US 5th Air Force planes would be a complete surprise.

"It was too much to ask," Hall would later tell a foreign correspondent. "To expect to catch the Japanese off guard after the heavies made their attacks in the dark was absolutely amazing. But that's exactly what happened."

179

Col. Don Hall crossed the coast first in his lead B-25 and he grinned when he looked down. He saw Japanese soldiers swimming in the surf, even at this early morning hour. Other soldiers simply lolled on the beaches, with some of them wearing colorful robes. When these bathers spotted the oncoming Mitchells flying almost directly overhead, they panicked and scattered. But Hall would not waste ammunition on them. He wanted every bullet in his forward strafing guns reserved for parked Japanese planes.

Hall and his fellow B-25 pilots zoomed over the rolling terrain and forests beyond Wewak's shoreline, before the planes crossed and recrossed the winding, roughly hewn roads that led from the beaches to supply areas, campsites, repair shops or airdromes. Hall and copilot Mike Green saw several vehicles on the roads, mostly trucks whose rears were loaded with Japanese soldiers, obvious work parties. The trucks stopped abruptly as the whine of planes echoed overhead and the men in the rear of the vehicles froze in awe as they stared at the low flying B-25s. Gunner Frank Timberlane grinned at the rigid Japanese soldiers who had seemingly been frozen by some kind of paralyzing ray guns. But, again, Hall withheld fire against these tempting targets and he told his pilots not to strafe the loaded Japanese trucks. He wanted aircraft.

Less than a minute after the US 5th Air Force Mitchells crossed the coast, Boram Drome loomed open and clear. Both Colonel Hall and Lieutenant Green peered at the sight in astonishment as they spotted the more than 80 planes nakedly exposed and lined up wing tip to wing tip on both sides of the main runway: Zeros and Dinahs on the right and Zeros and Bettys on the left. The two 3rd Group airmen could see crews still scrambling about the bombers and fighters in last minute checks, while ordnance men were still pouring fuel into some of the Bettys from gasoline trucks.

"Goddamn it, Colonel," Green hissed, "I don't believe this."

"Son of a bitch," Hall grinned. "They're getting ready to take off and hit us." Hall called Timberlane. "Sergeant, do you see any Zekes?"

"Nothing, sir, not a thing," the gunner answered, "and they haven't fired as much as a rifle at us: no ack ack, no machine guns, no nothing. Goddamn, sir, looks like we caught them sound asleep."

"How about our own fighters?"

"They're upstairs with nothing to do," Timberlane said. "They're just flying around like loitering birds."

"Stay alert, anyway," Hall said. He then peered up at the swarms of P-38s that arced lazily and idly about the sky. Why let them stay there? He quickly called Lt. Col. Meryl Smith who led the 432nd Squadron from the 475th Fighter Group. "Colonel, it looks like you won't need to take on any Zekes or Oscars, so you may as well come down and get some licks yourself. If the same thing is true on the Peninsula, I'll tell the other P-38 Squadrons to also do some downstairs strafing themselves against enemy aircraft."

"I'll check," Smith said. Less than a moment later, he called back Hall. "Sir, no enemy fighters airborne up ahead either. "I've told the 39th Squadron to hit

181

Dagua Drome in strafing runs behind the 38th Group Mitchells, while the 9th Squadron will hit troop concentrations. The 80th Squadron will hit But Drome, and my other 475th squadrons will seek out and destroy ammo and fuel dumps."

"Very good," Colonel Hall said.

The 3rd Group commander then called Major Downs of the 13th Squadron. "Jim, you take the parked aircraft on the right; we'll hit the aircraft on the left."

"Okay, colonel," the 13th Squadron commander answered.

Maj. Shinichi Kapaya, CO of the 18th Sentai, had just settled himself into the pilot's seat of his Betty bomber when he heard and then saw the swift flying Mitchells coming straight into Boram runway at almost deck level. He froze in astonishment for there was nothing he could do. Lieutenant Shizizui was more fortunate. He had not yet boarded his Zero fighter in the 152nd Squadron when he saw the Mitchells he quickly signalled to his fighter pilots.

"Run! Run!"

Colonel Hall began the holocaust when he opened with strafing fire from the ten forward machine guns on his commerce destroyer. The withering fire caught a Betty bomber that was trying to take off and the plane blew up on the runway. Hall then swept over the line of Bettys and fighters, unloading his bomb bay of parafrag bombs. A staccato of explosions erupted along the left side of the airstrip, destroying at least two more Bettys and damaging some three other Japanese bombers.

As Hall arced away, Lt. William Beck swept over

the same line of planes with heavy strafing fire and descending parachute bombs. Once more, a string of explosions erupted over Boram Field. Two Bettys blew up, emitting raging fires and palls of smoke.

Immediately behind Beck, came Capt. Charlie Howe. He and his copilot watched in ecstasy and both men grinned as Howe unleashed his streams of strafing fire on the fish-in-the-barrel targets. The two men saw one plane explode and another catch fire. Howe released his parafrags that burst atop two Zeros. The blasts ignited both planes. As Howe arced away, his gunner stared at the debacle below. Nearly half of the planes on the left side of the runway were burning furiously.

Aboard Beck's plane, Sgt. Norman Gates, the gunner, looked upward, but he did not see a single Japanese fighter plane in the sky; only the forked tailed P-38s that were waiting their turn to hit Boram. Gates could not believe they had caught the Japanese so utterly unprepared.

More 8th Squadron Mitchells from the 3rd Attack Group swept over the Boram airstrip, spitting more heavy strafing fire into the line of 7th Air Division bombers and fighters and dropping more deadly parafrags on the helpless targets. More fire ignited, more smoke curled upward, and more planes blew up. By the time the 8th Squadron had left the target area, only a row of destruction lay in the wake of the B-25 commerce destroyers.

Now came Maj. Jim Downs with the nine Mitchells of the 13th Squadron. Downs cried into his radio. "Pick your targets and hit in tandem."

"Lead the way, Jim," Capt. Don McClellan said.

The 13th Squadron commander opened with chattering machine gun fire that caught two Zeros that were trying to break away from the line of Japanese fighters. One zero blew up and the second lost a tail from Downs's accurate machine gun fire. Then the major swept over the field and released his bombs that ignited at least two more Zeros.

Behind the squadron leader came Capt. Don McClellan with strafing fire and falling parachute incendiary bomb clusters that exploded like a string of firecrackers over the mass of parked Zeros and Bettys. The captain could not assess his damage, so he called his gunner as the B-25 arced away.

"Sergeant, how did we do?"

"Just beautiful, Captain," Sgt. Woodrow Butler answered. "We knocked out at least three planes and maybe more."

Lt. Bob Widener came in next to unleash withering strafing fire and then parafrag bombs that damaged three planes and destroyed at least three more. As Widener arced away, Sgt. Jim Leffler, the gunner, stared at the conflagration behind him. He then looked upstairs where P-38s still waited patiently in the sky. The Grim Reaper gunner had expected to meet a skyful of enemy fighters and he was simply astonished. Further, he could not believe that not a single ack ack gun had challenged them.

Six more B-25s from the 13th Squadron roared over the line of Japanese fighters and bombers on the right side of Boram Field. The other Mitchells wrecked, ignited, or damaged still more 7th Air Division planes. By the time the last of the nine Mitchells departed the right side of the airstrip, they also left a mass of smoke and fire in their wake.

Lt. Col. Meryl Smith came down with his P-38s from the Satans Angels 432nd Squadron to cause even more havoc with strafing fire: destroying or damaging more planes, vehicles, and supply or repair buildings.

Meanwhile, Capt. Phil Hawkins led his ten Mitchells of the Grim Reaper's 90th Squadron over Wewak Drome, the airfield to the north. Hawkins too had failed to meet a single interceptor or a single round from ack ack guns. When he spotted the drome, he could not believe what he saw. Here also, Japanese aircraft were lined up wing tip to wing tip on both sides of the runway: 27 Oscars, 29 Zeros, and 40 Bettys. Hawkins could not understand why these fighters had not been airborne to intercept the B-25s. He would also learn that they had caught the Japanese utterly unprepared. Hawkins called Lt. Phil Patton.

"Phil, you take the planes on the right and we'll take those on the left."

"I read you, Captain," Patton answered.

"Gunners, stay alert," Hawkins cried into his radio. "Some of the Zeros may have taken off."

And indeed Lt. Susuki Yonai of the 253rd Kokutai's 70th Squadron had acted with uncanny swiftness. Almost instinctively, as soon as he saw the Mitchells approaching, he swung his lead Oscar onto the Wewak runway with his wingman and zoomed down the strip to take off. Twelve more Oscars had followed him and also got off. However, the next pair of Oscars had not made it. Phil Hawkins was over the airstrip and his strafing fire battered both

Japanese fighters that blew up on the apron. Then Hawkings released his parafrags over the line of Oscars and Bettys to destroy three more planes on the ground.

Four more Mitchells from Hawkins flight also unleashed a fusillade of heavy strafing fire and bomb bays full of parafrags. By the time the quintet of B-25s arced away, they left a mass of burning planes behind them. Lt. Phil Patton now roared over the lines of planes at Wewak Drome with five Mitchells from the 90th Squadron. The five Mitchells swept over the right side of the runway and unleashed strafing fire and a skyful of bomb clusters that looked like descending cotton balls. The ground shook from the sustained pops of 23 pound bombs. Exploding planes rocked the earth. By the time the Mitchells arced away, the 90th Squadron had left a second holocaust at Wewak Drome. Finally, the B Element of the 13th Squadron swept over Wewak to destroy or damage still more Japanese planes.

Luckily, Col. Koji Tanaka had not been among the victims of the B-25 attack on the line of Sallys. The 253rd Kokutai commander sat rigidly in the cockpit of his plane and simply gaped at the fire and smoke around him.

Meanwhile, Lieutenant Yonai, who had gotten off with a dozen Oscars, found himself with an almost impossible task. Capt. Tom McGuire who was leading the 475th Group's 431st Squadron called his pilots. "We've got a few bandits up here. Let's get them."

"Yes sir," Lt. Francis Lent answered.

Within five minutes the Satans Angels pilots

downed five of the Oscars, while damaging several more. Lieutenant Yonai had no choice but to scoot away before he lost the remaining airborne Zeros of his squadron. McGuire then spoke to his pilots again. "Okay, we've cleared the skies. Let's get down there for our own licks on those Wewak Drome targets."

"We're with you," Lieutenant Lent answered.

Meanwhile, Capt. Ray Middleton led his three B-25s from the 38th Bomb Group over Dagua Field. When the captain saw the sight in front of him, he scowled. Both sides of the runway were lined with hordes of Sally bombers and Oscar fighters, and Middleton only had three planes. However, he would do what he could. He called his two fellow pilots.

"Go in low and hit them hard."

"Okay, Captain," Lt. Bob Lacenis said.

The trio of 38th Group Mitchells then swept over the field, but hit only the right side of the runway. Captain Middleton loosed his streaking strafing fire that ignited three planes that became funeral pyres for the Japanese Sally crews inside. Then Middleton dropped his clusters of para-incendiaries that set afire at least three more Sally bombers. As the B-25 arced away, Sgt. Jim Reese, the turret gunner, stared in awe at the raging fires that his single Mitchell had caused.

Behind Middleton, Capt. Rowen Gay roared over the line of Sallys. He first unleashed blistering machine gun fire from his ten forward guns. The heavy fusillade tore apart three Sallys and killed several Japanese crew members who had tried to escape from the planes. Gay then dropped his parachute bomb clusters that drifted downward like huge white dandelions before exploding in bursting pops. Four more Sally medium bombers went up in smoke.

Behind Gay, Lt. Bob Lacenis zoomed over the same line of planes. Lacenis struck several Sallys with rattling machine gun fire before dropping his parafrags. He knocked out four more bombers and damaged two more Japanese planes. Lacenis grinned with delight, glad now that he had decided to continue on toward Wewak with Captain Middleton and Captain Gay. The young B-25 pilot had enjoyed a field day against the parked Japanese planes.

As soon as the three Mitchells from the Sunsetters' 405th Squadron arced away, Maj. Curran Jones came down with his P-38s from the 39th Squadron. The American fighter pilots unleashed blistering wing fire as they swept over the Dagua airdrome in pairs. By the time the Headhunter squadron arced away from target, these US fighter pilots had destroyed or damaged an additional 15 to 20 planes at Dagua Drome.

Meanwhile, other P-38 units were also carrying out ground attack missions. The P-38s from the 80th Squadron swept over But Drome along the Wewak coast. Hastily assembled AA Japanese gunners tried to intervene, but they did not hit a single Lightning as Capt. George Welch and his pilots unleashed heavy strafing fire on both sides of the runway. Fire and smoke erupted as the American fighter pilots knocked out at least a half dozen planes and damaged six to eight other Japanese fighters and bombers.

"Nice job," Welch told his pilots, "but no more

runs. We may need the rest of our ammo for interceptors."

Meanwhile, the other two squadrons from the 475th Fighter Group skimmed over the Wewak Peninsula until they saw both ammo and fuel dumps. Maj. Daniel Roberts of the 433rd Squadron led one unit over the fuel dumps and after chattering incendiary tracer fire, he and his pilots ignited the stacks of ammo, shaking the Wewak landscape like a severe earthquake as the bombs and ammo exploded. By the time Daniels and his Satans Angles pilots arced away, two huge ammo dumps had been utterly destroyed. Two miles away, the other element from Daniels's squadron under Capt. John Henning swept over two fuel dumps. Rattling machine gun fire from the P-38 wing guns soon ignited countless barrels of gasoline that exploded like a string of heavy firecrackers. Huge columns of smoke and roaring fires erupted from both dumps, as the Satans Angels pilots destroyed both targets.

And finally, Maj. Jerry Johnson led his 9th Squadron pilots over Japanese campsites, hitting huts, buildings, and vehicles with withering machine gun fire. The attack erupted explosions and flames, flattened structures, and killed hordes of fleeing Japanese soldiers and airmen. The 49th Group pilots left a swath of smoke and fire in their wake.

As the American planes arced away from their targets, the 38th Group Mitchells got jumped by the half dozen Zeros that had escaped the dogfight with the US 431st Squadron P-38 pilots. Lieutenant Yonai damaged one of the B-25s with blazing machine gun fire but the following Zero caught solid machine gun fire from Sgt. Jim Reese aboard Captain Middleton's plane. The tracers struck the Zero's gas tank and the plane blew up before plunging to earth in a ball of fire.

"Nice going, Sergeant," Captain Middleton called his gunner.

"Lucky, sir," Reese answered.

"No," the captain said, "good; damn good."

In fact, the loss of the Zero prompted the other Japanese fighter pilots to momentarily break off their attacks on the B-25s. However, they never got a second chance because a formation of escorting P-38s from the 80th Squadron hurried to the aid of the 38th Group commerce destroyers. The Zero pilots scooted away.

By 0915 hours, less than a half hour after the B-25 and P-38 attacks began, the assault was over. Within moments, the roar of American planes diminished to the south. Only crackling fires, dense smoke, and the moans of dying and wounded now prevailed at the sprawling Japanese base.

CHAPTER ELEVEN

If the Japanese at Wewak felt dismay after the B-17 and B-24 attacks on the night of 16-17 August, they reeled in shock after the rampant destruction on the morning of 17 August.

When the raid by the B-25 strafers and P-38 fighters ended, Gen. Yamusi Arisue ventured from his shelter, again accompanied by Comdr. Shuichi Watakazi of the 253rd Kokutai. They stared in awe at the crackling fires and palls of smoke that rose from every part of the Wewak Drome. But now, the smell of burning flesh intermingled with the smell of burning oil, gasoline, and scorched metal. Arisue could not even guess how many planes and men along the Wewak runway had escaped the devastating American attacks.

The 7th Air Division commander squinted to the north and southeast where he could see more palls of smoke from the B-25 and P-38 attacks on Dagua and But Dromes. These airfields had not suffered as badly as Wewak Drome, but the Americans had caused serious damage there, even with a mere three

B-25s and the strafing P-38s. And finally, faintly, Arisue and Watakazi could see the smoke ten miles to the south where the enemy had hit Boram Field. Also, the two men could see the uncannily thick smoke from the burning fuel dumps and the raging fires from the two ammo dumps.

General Arisue obviously realized that the US Mitchells and Lightnings had caught the Japanese at the worst possible moment. As he walked along the smoking Wewak runway in a near state of shock, Arisue could not believe that B-25s could strike so soon. The 7th Air Division commander had been certain that the enemy would have needed at least two or three days before B-25s came to Wewak with needed fighter escorts.

Arisue also recognized another distasteful irony in these raids. The American heavy bombers, he now realized, had conducted their night raid to chop up the runways so the Japanese could not mount fighters at daylight to harass the B-25s. Even though the general had put every able bodied man to work in repairing the runways by daylight, he had placed his men and planes in a most vulnerable position when the B-25s and P-38s struck Wewak.

Commander Watakazi tried to count the number of wrecked planes along his runway, but he could only make a rough guess because of the widespread fires and smoke. He suspected that at least half of his 253rd Kokutai aircraft had been destroyed or damaged.

"Honorable Arisue," Watakazi said, "it will be some time before we can assess our losses, perhaps not for a couple of hours."

Arisue nodded.

"I fear we have lost a large number of combat airmen," the 253rd Kokutai commander continued. "Unfortunately, many of our pilots and crews were already in their fighters and bombers when the enemy bombers and fighters struck our parked aircraft."

"Horrible, horrible," Arisue shook his head. "There will be consternation at Rabaul when we report this damage."

Watakazi did not answer.

Two miles away, at But Drome, Capt. Masahiso Saito and Comdr. Hideo Shoji of the 751st Kokutai were also walking along their own runway. They counted about 15 fighters destroyed or damaged and several Betty bombers destroyed from the P-38 strafing attack by Capt. George Welch and his 39th Squadron pilots.

"We were more fortunate than the other units," Commander Shoji said, "Only their fighters attacked our airfield."

"It is obvious that the enemy has a limited number of these B-25 strafers," Captain Saito said. "They could only attack two or three of our fields with these low level bombers."

"We did lose about twenty men killed, Honorable Saito," Shoji said, "for they could not escape the cockpits of their fighters or the interior of their bombers before the enemy strafing attack."

"Unfortunate," Saito said. He scanned the damage about the field and then turned to his 26th Squadron commander. "We must clear the wreckage at once and then fill in quickly any craters on the runways or taxiways. Then you and Lieutenant Commander Iwami must have your fighter pilots on full alert. It is always possible that the enemy may attack again soon, and this time we must be ready for them. In fact, I believe we should keep combat air patrols over Wewak at all times from now on. As soon as we have completed our tour here, I will call on General Arisue and ask that he agree to these continual patrols over Wewak."

"A wise suggestion, Captain," Commander Shoji said.

At Dagua Drome, Col. Koji Tanaka and Capt. Kuzuma Sakai of the 17th Army Sentai made their way along their runway after the attack by the three B-25s and a dozen P-38s. The two Japanese officers stared in horror at the destruction caused by a mere handful of B-25s and P-38s.

"I have been taking count," Captain Sakai said, "and it appears that we lost about a dozen bombers and an equal number of fighters."

"A serious loss," Tanaka nodded, "but not total."

"We have also lost considerable men," Sakai said, "but I do not know how many. It will be some time before we can make an accurate count."

Again Tanaka nodded. Then he studied the ten or fifteen potholes in the runway, where some of the 38th Group parafrag bombs had struck. "We will fill in these bomb craters at once," he gestured. "We will then clear away wrecked and damaged planes. Meanwhile, Captain, you are to keep your fighters on full alert. The enemy struck us this morning with surprising suddenness and we cannot afford to allow this to happen again."

"Yes, Honorable Tanaka."

"As soon as you determine how many fighters are in combat condition," the 17th Sentai commander said, "you will call a meeting of your pilots and brief them for combat air patrols."

"I will do, Colonel."

To the south, Maj. Shinichi Kapaya of the 18th Sentai emerged from his shelter and stared at the destruction along his Boram Field runway. Fire and smoke was so thick here that Kapaya could not even see any planes. No doubt, Boram had suffered the worst damage on this 17 August morning. Fire trucks were racing up and down the airstrip to put out fires as swiftly as possible, so that flames from burning planes did not reach out to destroy undamaged planes that were lined up wing tip to wing tip.

Even as Kapaya and Lt. Tadashi Shizizui of the 16th Sentai's 152nd Squadron came within close proximity of the holocaust, they could not make an accurate count of losses because of dense palls of smoke. Major Kapaya watched the fire crews sending streams of water into the burning planes while other men sprayed the flames with C20 foam to put out fires. Kapaya then turned to Shizizui. "It is unfortunate that the enemy struck first, and at a most inopportune moment."

"I cannot believe that they were ready for an attack on Wewak so soon."

"The American attack was well planned," Kapaya scowled. "They used their heavy bombers to chop up our runways then sent in those dreaded B-25 strafers with swarms of fighter cover."

"I have no idea how many of our Mitsubishi

fighters, if any, are still in operating condition," Lieutenant Shizizui said.

"We will take count as soon as these men put out fires," the 18th Sentai commander said. "Then we will remove the wrecked aircraft and scatter the others. We must not leave them lined up along the runway again. Once we have taken stock," he gestured to Shizizui, "I want you to meet with your fighter pilots and keep them on full alert. There is no doubt the enemy will return."

"But what of our own air operation?" Shizizui asked. "Will we still carry out attacks against enemy airfields?"

Maj. Shinichi Kapaya looked at the lieutenant with a derisive grin before he spoke. "Do you honestly believe that the 7th Air Division is now in a position to carry out such attacks? We do not even know if we have enough planes or any fuel and ammunition after the enemy's P-38s destroyed these dumps. And I suspect that other units in Wewak have suffered the same extensive losses in aircraft as we ourselves. I would say that the best we can hope for at the moment is to protect our airfields against a second devastating attack."

"But if we do not destroy their airfields—"

"Not today, or even tomorrow," Kapaya shook his head. "The Honorable Arisue would surely need to bring in more aircraft, fuel, bombs, and supplies from Rabaul and Hollandia to strengthen the 7th Air Division. Only then can we carry out this planned air offensive against the enemy's airfields."

"Yes, Honorable Kapaya."

By about 1030 hours, on this 17 August morning,

the Japanese had finally taken an accurate count of their losses.

At But Drome, the 751st Kokutai had lost six bombers and 15 fighters destroyed with the death of 30 combat flyers and ground crews who were caught in the sudden P-38 strafing attack. At Boram Field, Col. Don Hall and the B-25 crews from his 13th and 8th Squadrons had destroyed an astonishing 23 bombers and 12 fighters, while killing 142 men who had either been in their planes or who were working about the airstrip. At Dagua Drome, the three B-25s from the 38th Group and the 16 P-38s from the 39th Squadron had destroyed 14 bombers and 11 fighters, while killing 42 Japanese combat flyers and ground crews. And finally, at Wewak Drome, Capt. Phil Hawkins unit of Mitchells had destroyed 21 bombers and 18 fighters, while killing 16 men about the air-field.

Totally, the 7th Air Division had lost a phenomenal 121 planes and 336 men killed at the four Wewak airdromes.

The other squadrons on this mission, fighter units, had caused devastating damage of their own. Since the Lightnings had encountered few interceptors, the P-38 pilots could concentrate on ground targets. In destroying two ammo and two fuel dumps, the Lightning airmen had killed about 100 Japanese, while destroying some 500 barrels of gasoline and over 50 tons of bombs and ammunition.

Capt. Jerry Johnson and his Forty-niners from the 9th Squadron had raked the two campsites, destroying about a dozen huts and killing some 60 Japanese. These addenda attacks had killed an additional 163

Nipponese, while causing more widespread damage at Wewak.

By 1100 hours, General Arisue and Gen. Hatazi Adachi of the 18th Army met in Adachi's headquarters to consider their next step. Adachi knew that the debacle this morning meant he could not carry out the planned air attacks on Tsili Tsili, Buna, and Port Moresby. Adachi needed to postpone his own offensive MO Operation to recapture Buna. Without doubt, the devastating raids had left the Japanese at Wewak hanging on the ropes and they needed to recover swiftly or face a possible knockout blow. Arisue pleaded with Adachi.

"We must contact Rabaul for immediate reinforcements in supplies, men, and arms, as well as aircraft. Two of our fuel dumps have been destroyed as have many bombs and ammunition boxes."

"The Honorable Imamura will be furious," General Adachi said.

"Still," Arisue said, "if you hope to carry out the MO II operation, General Imamura must send reinforcements. I hope you will call him."

The 18th Army CinC nodded.

When Gen. Hitoshi Imamura heard of the losses at Wewak on this August morning, the 8th Area Forces CinC was shocked: 121 planes destroyed? Over 500 men killed? Damage to supplies, buildings, and other installations? Two fuel dumps and two ammunition dumps destroyed? How could this happen? Why weren't the men at Wewak on full alert against such a low level enemy air assault? After all, the Americans had conducted heavy bombing raids during the night, where the B-17s and B-24s had concentrated on destroying runways with the obvious intent of stopping planes from taking off, especially fighters. Why didn't anyone at Wewak see the obvious logic of the enemy's plans?

However, despite his wrath, General Imamura could not dwell on what had already happened. He could only replace these heavy losses in planes, men, and provisions. He immediately called on Adm. Takeo Takagi of the Japanese 9th Transportation Fleet. Takagi must carry at once a supply convoy to Wewak, at least a dozen ships loaded with fuel, ammunition, food, equipment, tools, vehicles, and airmen for the 7th Air Division.

"I will leave as quickly as possible, Honorable Imamura," Admiral Takagi said, "as soon as we can load the marus. We should be able to set sail by this time tomorrow and we should be in Wewak in about three days."

"Very good," Imamura said.

Adm. Junichi Kusaka, CinC of the 25th Air Flotilla, had also expressed shock when he learned of the losses to the 7th Air Division in Wewak. But he could not waste time dwelling on this stunning news any more than could General Imamura. Kusaka called General Arisue immediately. "Clear away any rubble," he told the 7th Air Division commander, "and keep your fighter pilots on alert. You will maintain combat air patrols over Wewak at all times."

"Yes, Honorable Kusaka."

"I will send more fighters, bombers, and airmen to Wewak from Hollandia within the next day or two. Make certain that you have readied revetment areas for such new aircraft."

"I will not fail," Arisue assured Kusaka.

Admiral Kusaka then reported to General Imamura, explaining his plan to replenish the losses at Wewak. Imamura was satisfied. He believed that increased vigil at Wewak would thwart any further surprise attacks. As soon as the replaced men, planes, and supplies reached Wewak, the Japanese could carry out the air phase of the MO II operation. Then Adachi could invade Buna. At worst, Imamura hoped, they would merely need to delay this operation.

The Americans were not so naive as to give the Japanese a respite after the murderous blow against Wewak on the morning of 17 August. Returning pilots and crews from the 5th Air Force were elated with the excellent results on the morning attack; they told and retold their accomplishments to anyone who would listen, and they expressed an eagerness to lash out with a second blow.

The returning Mitchells and Lightnings had landed at Tsili Tsili, Buna, or Port Moresby by late morning, although the P-38s from the 475th Fighter Group had needed to alight at Tsili Tsili to refuel before flying back to Buna. At noon, Gen. Ennis Whitehead, CinC of ADVON 5th Air Force, ordered a briefing of all group commanders. He asked Colonel Hall of the 3rd Attack Group and Lt. Col. Meryl Smith of the 475th Fighter Group to fly at once to Port Moresby from Buna.

Hall and Smith, despite the tiring day on the long mission to Wewak, did not hesitate. They remained in Buna only long enough for a post mission briefing and quick noon meal. Then the two men flew off to Moresby in Smith's P-38, with Hall riding piggy back. By 1400 hours, they landed at Kola Airdrome in Moresby and by 1500 hours, Whitehead opened a meeting at his ADVON headquarters.

In attendance besides Hall and Smith, were Col. Arthur Rogers of the 90th Bomb Group, Col. Harry Hawthorne of the 43rd Bomb Group, Lt. Col. Larry Tanberg of the 38th Bomb Group, Capt. George Welch of the 80th Fighter Squadron, and Maj. Jerry Johnson of the 9th Fighter Squadron. Whitehead waved a sheet in his hand before he addressed the officers.

"Gentlemen, this is the first recon report from PBY pilots over Wewak. The reports are uncanny. Our observers have seen huge fires, palls of smoke, smashed buildings, and wrecked planes all over the huge enemy base. We obviously dealt the Japanese a telling blow on this first raid." He gestured emphatically. "But we can't give them a chance to recover."

"What do you suggest, sir?" Colonel Hall asked.

"The same thing we did today," Whitehead answered. "I want the heavies out again tonight to knock out the Wewak runways, putting as many holes as possible into the aprons. I want the B-25s out again early tomorrow morning." He looked at Lieutenant Colonel Tanberg. "I hope all of your Mitchells make it this time."

"Yes sir," Tanberg answered.

"We'll be sending out five more P-38 squadrons tomorrow," Whitehead continued. "I think we should leave the 39th Squadron at Tsili Tsili to bolster the

P-39s already there. I suspect the Nips may try to knock out that base because they must know we've staged our fighters out of here."

The air commanders listened.

"Rendezvous will be at the same point off the New Guinea coast in the Vitiaz Strait," Whitehead said. "The 9th and 80th Squadrons will escort the 38th Group Mitchells out of Moresby and the 475th Group will escort the 3rd Attack Group. For the morning mission, Colonel Hall will again be the OTC. For tonight's mission, Colonel Hawthorne will be the OTC. I should remind all of you that we cannot expect to catch the Japanese off guard twice. Heavy bomber gunners must be extremely alert tonight, and fighter pilots must be ready for interceptors tomorrow morning. It's vital that the P-38 pilots keep away Zekes and Oscars if the Mitchells are to conduct another thorough job."

"Yes sir," Lieutenant Colonel Smith said.

Whitehead then looked at Hawthorne and Rogers. "I'd like your heavies off at the same time as last night, about 2200 hours. Your bombers are to aim for the same targets—the runways. The Nips could have a skyful of fighters waiting for the B-25 strafers in the morning if the runways at Wewak don't get a good working over. Any questions?"

"No sir," Colonel Hawthorne said.

"We understand," Colonel Rogers nodded.

Whitehead looked at Don Hall, the 3rd Attack Group commander. "How many aircraft can you get off tomorrow?"

"At least thirty, sir," Hall answered.

"Good," the ADVON commander nodded. He

then looked at Smith. "How about your P-38s?"

"Seventy-five to eighty, sir," the Satans Angels CO said.

"Fine," Whitehead gestured. "Your take off will be at the same time tomorrow as it was today, and you'll meet the Port Moresby aircraft elements at the same rendezvous point as today."

"Will do, sir," Hall said.

"Okay," Whitehead sighed, "I guess this meeting is over. The FO sheets are pretty clear and quite detailed. Read them over carefully and then brief your own air leaders. Let's hope we can do as well tomorrow as we did today. Colonel," he looked at Don Hall again, "I suggest that you and Lieutenant Colonel Smith fly back to Buna at once and prepare your men and planes."

"Yes sir," Hall said.

Less than a half hour later, after the conference ended at ADVON 5th Air Force headquarters, Colonel Hall and Lieutenant Colonel Smith were on their way back to Buna, while the other air commanders returned to their own squadrons and groups at Port Moresby. Almost at once, ground crews at Ward and Jackson Dromes began preparing the 90th and 43rd Heavy Bomb Group planes for this evening's mission. Once more they loaded lead planes with incendiaries to light up the target, while other planes carried 2,000 pound bombs to dig deep holes in runways.

By 2000 hours on the evening of 17 August, the heavy bombers began taking off. Col. Harry Hawthorne led 11 B-17s and 13 B-24s from his Ken's Men 43rd Group off the Jackson Drome runway. At the same time, Col. Arthur Rogers led 25 B-24s from his Jolly Rogers 90th Group off the Ward's Drome runway. By 2300 hours, the 49 heavy bombers were winging over New Guinea's Owen Stanley range on the way to Wewak.

However, as the two US Bomber groups flew northward, the fickle SWPA weather suddenly acted against the Americans. Dense rain clouds swiftly closed over the mountains and the heavy bomber pilots needed to climb to 24,000 feet. The rain clouds thickened and then, booms of thunder and flashes of lightning erupted in the skies over New Guinea. In the darkness, and despite radar, many B-17s and B-24s lost their direction or separated from their four plane formations.

By the time the heavies had reached the Vitiaz Strait, shortly before midnight, both Colonel Hawthorne and Colonel Rogers learned to their dismay that over 20 planes had turned back because of the inclement weather. And, in fact, some of the squadron leaders had urged both Hawthorne and Rogers to abort the mission, lest they lose planes and crews in these horrible night time thunder storms.

"Nobody aborts unless he absolutely must," an angry Hawthorne cried into his radio. "We've got to chop up those Wewak runways or those B-25s will be sitting ducks tomorrow morning."

"Yes sir," Maj. Ken McCullar answered.

Hawthorne then called Colonel Rogers of the 90th Group. "Art, how many planes do you have left?"

"Fourteen," Rogers answered.

"We've got to keep them going," Hawthorne said. "It's vital that we knock out the Wewak runways."

"I'm with you, Harry," Rogers said.

The B-17 and B-24 formations continued on during this stormy night. Two or three more US planes had also aborted as the Americans flew up the New Guinea coast. Finally, at about 0100 hours, 18 August, Colonel Hawthorne scowled in irritation. Only 26 of the 49 heavy bombers had made it to IP. And worse, the dense rain clouds had obscured Wewak as had the same thick cloud cover plagued the US heavy bomber crews all the way from Port Moresby. Hawthorne picked up his radio mike and spoke soberly to his men.

"Looks like we'll need to bomb by radar."

"Radar?" Major McCullar cried. "Our radar is not that good, sir. We can't pinpoint those runways."

"We'll do the best we can," Hawthorne answered.

By 0130 hours, the first element of B-17s from the 43rd Group droned over Wewak at 8,000 feet. Once more searchlights pierced the darkness and ack ack shells burst about the sky. The thick cloud cover had stopped the searchlight operators from getting any B-17s or B-24s in their beams. Similarly, the Japanese AA gunners fired blindly, and they did little damage to the Fortresses or Liberators. Conversely, however, the Americans could see nothing through the dense clouds and heavy rain squalls. They really bombed almost blindly or not at all. The entire nine planes from the 43rd Group's 64th Squadron, for example, only dropped one bomb among them. The 63rd Squadron from the same Ken's Men Group dropped all bombs, but they exploded in a wide, erratic area, causing little damage and hitting no vital targets.

The other squadrons of the 43rd Group and the 11 planes of the 90th Bomb Group, the only Jolly Roger B-24s to reach target, had fared just as badly. Among all of the 2,000 pounders dropped by the 90th Group aircraft, they punched less than a dozen holes in the runways, and the Japanese could fill these quickly. As the 26 heavy bombers from the Ken's Men and Jolly Rogers left Wewak, crews could see nothing through the overcast. They had no idea what kind of damage they might have caused.

At Wewak itself, Gen. Yamusi Arisue expressed delight after the American heavy bomber raid. The US planes had caused only minimal damage to runways compared to the night before. Further, Arisue had learned that over 100 undamaged fighter planes in his 7th Air Division were available at Wewak to protect the base against any second Mitchell strafer attack at daylight.

"They will be back in the morning as they came this morning," Arisue said, "but this time we will not be asleep as before. We will be waiting for them and we will destroy these B-25s."

"Yes, Honorable Arisue," an aide answered.

And in fact, on the morning of 18 August 1943, the biggest air battle ever seen in the SWPA would erupt in the skies over Wewak.

CHAPTER TWELVE

The weather that plagued the heavy bombers during the night of 17-18 August had begun to clear by daylight, raising the morale of P-38 pilots and B-25 crews from the 5th Air Force. For this second Wewak mission, the 38th Bomb Group, the 9th Fighter Squadron, and the 80th Fighter Squadron would bring the bulk of its Mitchell strafers and Lightning fighters over the Owen Stanley Mountains without difficulty from Port Moresby.

By 0600 hours, the 38th Group had amassed 23 planes at Durand Drome. Although Lt. Col. Larry Tanberg had briefed the Sunsetters on the morning mission, he had remained behind while Maj. Ralph Celli of the group's 405th Squadron led the mission. Twelve planes from this squadron soon took off, while Maj. Howard Paquin's 71st Squadron left the same Durand Field with 11 Mitchells. As the 23 B-25s droned over the Owen Stanleys, the Sunsetter crews felt a mixture of anticipation and fear. The weather to the northwest appeared good, so Celli was sure he and his crews would have good visual observation over target. Yet all of these airmen knew they were not likely to catch the Japanese by surprise again.

In the 38th Group's lead plane, Maj. Ralph Celli looked at the open skies ahead and then called his crews. "We're on schedule; weather looks good. Escorts should be joining us within a few minutes. Gunners stay alert; pilots keep your formations tight."

"Yes sir," Lt. Bob Crooks of the 405th's 2nd Flight answered. The "½ Half Pound Mary" pilot then looked at copilot Ken Deltz. "Instruments?"

"All okay, Bob," Deltz answered. "Altitude and speed steady, pressure okay."

Crooks nodded and then called his other crew members. "All report."

"On course," Lt. Howie McKay answered from the navigator station.

"Cameras okay," Lt. Don Buttock answered from his section.

"Waist guns in good order, sir," Sgt. Bob Hancock replied from his waist position.

"Bubble guns swinging free," Turret gunner Sgt. Will Skinner said.

"Stay alert, especially gunners," Lieutenant Crooks said. "There's always a chance for Nip interceptors out of Lae."

"Yes sir," Sgt. Will Skinner answered.

In Aircraft #192, "Pacific Prowler," pilot Lt. Bill Travers stared at the other planes in the 405th Squadron formation and he then looked at the empty skies above. He glanced at his watch and half frowned. The escort had not yet arrived. He turned to his copilot, Lt. Ralph Robertson. "Where the hell are those P-38s? We're getting close to Lae and those Nips could have a CAP out of there."

"They should be along soon," Robertson answered.

In his navigator compartment, Lt. Ed Gervais checked his charts and squares. They were now only 100 miles southwest of Lae and they'd be passing the Japanese base within the next half hour. Where the hell were the P-38s? In the waist section, both Australian observer F/O William Lane and radio gunner Sgt. Ed Piper continually peered out of the port and starboard windows respectively, searching the skies and hoping to see those Lightnings before any Zekes or Oscars jumped their Mitchell medium bombers.

From his top turret gun position, Sgt. George Koch also scanned the skies. The weather looked clear up ahead, but he did not like waiting for the P-38s that should have been here by now. He swung his guns and lightly pressed the triggers. At least his weapons worked.

In the trailing 71st Squadron, Maj. Howard Paquin studied his formation of planes. Then he looked at his watch: 0700. They had taken off a half hour ago, but still had an hour and a half before reaching target, and he was already growing impatient. His squadron would hit But Drome that the 38th Group had failed to hit yesterday. Paquin turned to his co-pilot.

"Everything okay?"

"Yes sir, everything in proper order."

Paquin nodded.

In the top turret of Paquin's "Pissed Off" B-25,

Sgt. Jim Reese swung his bubble to the right and left, 90 degrees both ways. The turret moved smoothly. Reese checked the guns that also swung freely on their fulcrums. His weapons would be okay in case bandits jumped him.

In Aircraft #179, Capt. Bob Blair, pilot, and Lt. Jim Orr, copilot, studied the instrument panel in the cabin of their B-25. All systems registered normal. The two men had already flown 21 combat missions, but they felt uneasy today. Wewak was a long way off and they expected the Japanese to mount a swarm of fighters to avoid a second holocaust.

From his top turret, gunner Sgt. Ken Gilen checked the other B-25s around him and he then squinted into the clearing sky to study the other B-25s in his formation. The gunner felt anxious since the fighters had not yet arrived. In the waist, both navigator Lt. Frank Drees and radio gunner Sgt. Ed Courtney tinkered with their instruments to keep their minds off this dangerous mission. Drees worked over his charts, while Courtney fumbled with the radio dials.

In the Tail End Charlie flight from the 71st Squadron aboard B-25 "Happy Angels," pilot Jim Armor peered from his port cabin window, hoping for a sign of the escorts. Copilot Lt. Don Clark stared with equal anxiety out of the starboard window of "Angels." Both men had checked all instruments and found them in good order. In his navigator compartment, Lt. Bill Foster peered from a small port window at the empty sky to the left. He had been working with his tee, but he continually glanced outside, hoping to see the P-38s.

In the starboard section of the fuselage, waist gunner Sgt. Mike Ranner also looked into the empty sky and frowned. All he saw from his 8,000 feet altitude was an emptiness beyond his plane and the tips of the Owen Stanley Mountains below him. In the top bubble seat, turret gunner Sgt. Al Beall had quit waiting for the fighter escort. He sat calmly in the bubble, his fingers tapping the triggers of his guns. Beall suspected they were close to Lae and he would simply do what he could if he got jumped by bandits.

The 23 medium bombers of the 38th Bomb Group droned on for another fifteen minutes, until they were only fifty miles from Lae. But then, from his turret position in Tail End Charlie "Happy Angels," Sgt. Al Beall saw the dots in the sky behind him. He stiffened, wondering if the approaching planes were Japanese or American. As the shapes became more distinct, he recognized the twin fuselages and grinned. Beall quickly called his pilot.

"Sir, escorts coming toward us from six o'clock high."

Both Armor and copilot Don Clark craned their necks to get a look and when they saw the twin fuselages, Armor called the 71st Squadron CO, Maj. Howard Paquin to report the approaching planes. Within moments, the major relayed the news to other aircraft pilots and the Sunsetter crews stirred with excitement. Finally, the P-38s loomed big and clear about the 38th Group bombers. Capt. George Welch of the 80th Squadron, OTC for the fighters, called Major Celli.

"We're a little late, Major; sorry. We took more time than expected to refuel at Tsili Tsili."

"Glad to see you," Ralph Celli answered.

"I'm taking my squadron topside," Welch said. "The 9th Squadron will fly close cover."

"We read you, Captain," Celli answered.

The P-38s swarmed about the 23 B-25s from the 38th Group. Capt. George Welch took his 17 fighters from the 80th Squadron to a position from one to two thousand feet above the bombers before sending three Lightnings to the van as scouts. Maj. Jerry Johnson of the 9th Squadron sent nine of his P-38s to the starboard of the bomber formation, while he settled the other nine Lightnings on the port side.

The 35 fighters and 23 bombers roared northwest toward the Vitiaz Strait where they would rendezvous with the fighters and bombers out of Buna.

About 45 minutes earlier, at 0615 hours, 39 B-25s from the 3rd Attack Group had taken off from Dobodura in Buna. Only moments later, Lt. Col. Meryl Smith and 58 other pilots from the 475th Fighter Group had also taken off, zooming in pairs from Horanda Drome. Soon the 39 bombers and 59 fighters out of Buna were cruising northwest over the Solomon Sea toward Wewak as they had yesterday. The pilots from the 475th would refuel at Tsili Tsili on the way back.

As usual, the Grim Reaper Mitchells carried three man crews. In his lead B-25, Col. Don Hall and copilot Lt. Miles Green had completed instrument checks before Hall called his gunner, Frank Timberlane. "Sergeant, I know we've got a swarm of escorts around us, but we could still get jumped out of Lae, Madang, or Gasmata. Keep a sharp watch."

"Yes sir."

"Are the guns okay?"

"All checked out, sir; they're fine."

"If you see any bandits, let me know."

"I'll stay alert," Timberlane promised.

Sgt. Frank Timberlane, from his turret position, stared at the other B-25s around him as well as the P-38 escorts that hung above and astride the bombers. Timberlane was now on his forty-first mission. He had come to the SWPA over a year ago, fighting during the full six month Papuan campaign and then well into 1943. He had been the gunner aboard Maj. Ed Larner's B-25 during the famed Battle of the Bismarck Sea and he had won a DFC in that action. However, only a month after the battle, Timberlane had felt grief when Larner, on a routine flight without the gunner, had crashed and died.

Timberlane remembered vividly the wide damage they had caused yesterday at Wewak, and he had been astonished when the 3rd Attack Group had caught the Japanese totally off guard. However, the gunner had too much combat experience in the SWPA to believe they could catch the Japanese asleep again. Timberlane hoped the Lightnings could handle any bandits. Nonetheless, the gunner checked his guns, making certain the turret weapons were in good order.

As the formation of US bombers and fighters from Buna flew on, Col. Don Hall called Meryl Smith. "Colonel, any signs of bandits?"

"No sir," the 475th Fighter Group commander answered. "All clear ahead and on the flanks. I've got scouts out ahead and on the laterals."

"Good," Hall said. Then he called his bomber

crews. "Keep formation tight; nobody knows what kind of CAP the Nips may have over the Solomon Sea. We'll be rendezvousing with the Moresby formation in about a half hour."

"Yes sir," Maj. Jim Downs of the 13th Squadron answered. He had already made clear to his squadron pilots that A and B Flight would join the 8th Squadron in attacking Wewak Drome, while his C and D Flights would join the 90th Squadron in hitting Boram Field.

Behind Downs, in the next 13th Squadron B-25, Capt. Don McClellan stared at the P-38s that hung alongside of his formation. He felt relaxed, for he knew that American fighter pilots were good and the P-38s were more than a match for Japanese Zeros and Oscars. He looked at the instrument panel in the cabin of his Mitchell and then turned to his copilot, F/O Jack Harrington.

"Everything okay?"

"Pressure good, speed steady, fuel okay," Harrington answered. "I guess we're in good shape."

McClellan nodded and called his gunner. "Sergeant, everything back there in good order?"

"Yes sir," Sgt. Woodrow Butler answered. "Guns and turret okay."

"If you see any bandits, let me know."

"Roger," the gunner answered.

Sgt. Woodrow Butler had been in the SWPA war for over a year, and he was now on his 37th mission. He had downed three enemy planes with his turret guns and he had already earned an Air Medal and Bronze Star. Butler recalled those early days in 1942 when they invariably ran into swarms of Zeros.

214

Things were different now; the bombers had plenty of fighter escorts and the Lightning fighter had proven itself superior to any Japanese fighter. Butler was sure they would not catch the Japanese asleep again. He hoped the accompanying P-38s around the Mitchells could handle any Nippon interceptors.

In the 90th Squadron formation, Capt. Phil Hawkins, the squadron CO, studied a map in his lap, making certain he had pinpointed his target, the Boram Drome. When they got to IP, he would swing away from the formation with his squadron and the C and D Flights of the 13th Squadron. He would have nearly 20 planes, more than enough to finish off that airdrome. Hawkins took another look at the B-25s and P-38s around him and he then called his pilots.

"Rendezvous in twenty-five minutes; IP in seventy minutes. Pilots, keep formation tight; gunners, stay alert."

"Yes sir," Lt. Phil Patton answered. Patton had also checked his instruments to make sure his plane was in good order. He then turned to his copilot, Lt. Bob Wilkes. "Did you see anything, Robbie?"

"Not a thing, except for P-38s. I don't think we'll see any Nip fighters all the way to Wewak." The co-pilot grinned. "Those Jap pilots don't want to tangle with those Lightnings."

"I hope you're right," Patton said. "Still, I can't believe they'd let us waltz over Boram Field today like they did yesterday. I think they'll be waiting for us with plenty of fighters."

Wilkes again stared at the P-38s before he answered. "We've got plenty of fighters of our own."

Patton did not answer. Instead he called his gunner. "Sergeant, is everything all right back there?"

"Yes sir," gunner Harry Kiser said.

"If you spot any bandits, let me know."

"Will do." The turret gunner felt nervous despite the swarms of P-38s around him. This was only his fourth mission and he had heard plenty about powerful Wewak. Even though they had caught the Japanese by surprise yesterday, he expected no such luck today. Further, Wewak was a long way from home, over 400 miles beyond Buna. If their plane got shot up, Lieutenant Patton would have a hard time getting the Mitchell back to Dobodura. Kiser licked his lips and then tapped his fingers on the triggers of his twin fifties.

High above the bombers, Capt. Tom McGuire flew in the lead Lightning of the 475th Group's 431st Squadron. He had been looking about him constantly for any signs of bandits, but none so far. He called wingman Lt. Francis Lent.

"Frank, do you see anything?"

"Nothing, Tom, not a damn thing."

"Stay alert; we're passing Huon Gulf and Nip fighters might come out of Lae, Madang, or Finchhaven."

"I'll be awake," Lent promised.

On the starboard side of the formation, Lt. Col. Meryl Smith occasionally glanced at the open sea to his right. The Satans Angels CO had expected to see bandits emerge in the sky at any moment, Japanese Zeros or Oscars that came out of Gasmata on the north side of the Solomons Sea in New Britain. Smith had seen nothing. He called Capt. William

Weldon, whose 432nd Squadron P-38s hung on the port side of the Mitchells as close cover.

"Any sign of interceptors?"

"Not a thing, sir," Weldon answered. "The Nips are either ignoring us or they don't know we're here."

"They're probably all up in Wewak waiting for us. Stay alert."

"Yes sir."

Smith then called Maj. Daniel Roberts whose squadron maintained a close cover on the top of the Grim Reaper Mitchells. "See anything, Dan?"

"Nothing, Colonel, but we're keeping a sharp eye."

"We'll be passing Lae and Madang. The Nips could send fighters from there."

"We'll be ready," Roberts promised.

The formation roared on and finally, at 0815 hours, Major Roberts saw the dots in the sky to the south. He could tell that some of the aircraft were larger than others so he knew the planes were the Moresby element from the 5th Air Force and not Japanese fighters. He called Lieutenant Colonel Smith. "Looks like the P-38s and B-25s from Moresby are on the way to rendezvous."

"Right on time," Smith answered.

Within five minutes, the 23 Mitchells from the 38th Group fell into formation behind the B-25s from the 3rd Group. Capt. George Welch kept his 17 fighters above the Sunsetter Mitchells, while Maj. Jerry Johnson kept his Lightnings on close cover for the 38th Group bombers. By 0830 hours, the huge American air formation came within 30 miles of the Wewak Peninsula. Col. Don Hall cried into his radio.

"IP in ten minutes; ten minutes."

The American airmen stiffened and then looked straight ahead. None of them knew what to expect over target this morning.

High over Wewak, Comdr. Hideo Shoji of the 751st Kokutai's 26th Squadron maintained a CAP with 23 Oscars. He had been on CAP for the past half hour, relieving Lt. Comdr. Joyotara Iwami of the 27th Squadron at about 0830 hours. On the ground at the 751st Kokutai's But Drome, Lieutenant Iwami had sent his pilots from the 27th Squadron to their huts for a rest, but with notice to be available if called.

At Wewak Drome, Lt. Suzuki Yonai had mustered 17 Oscars and 10 Zeros from the 253rd Kokutai's 70th and 71st Squadrons. He would take off on the first alert. At Dagua Drome, Capt. Kusuma Sakai had readied 11 Oscars, all that remained from his 147th Squadron of the 17th Sentai. And finally, ten miles to the south, at Boram Field, Lt. Tadashi Shizizui was also on CAP, but with only 14 Zeros, all that he had salvaged from the American attack yesterday. Unfortunately, the promised fighters from Hollandia and Rabaul had not yet reached Wewak. Still, 98 fighters were a considerable force against 85 P-38s that had reached the target area from the 475th Fighter Group, 9th Fighter Squadron, and 80th Fighter Squadron.

At 0842 hours, the American 5th Air Force formations reached IP and Don Hall cried into his radio. "Okay, break off for attacks."

The B-25s then split into four separate formations. The 8th Squadron and half of the 13th Squadron from the 3rd Group headed for Wewak, with the 431st Squadron of the 475th Fighter Group as escorts. The 3rd's 90th Squadron and the other half of the 13th Squadron headed for Boram Field under escort of the Satans Angeles 432nd Squadron. The 38th Bomb Group's 71st Squadron, under Maj. Howard Paquin droned to But Drome with fighters of the 80th Squadron, while Maj. Ralph Celli led the 405th Squadron to Dagua with the 9th Fighter Squadron Lightnings furnishing cover. The 433rd Squadron from the 475th Group remained upstairs to engage the first formation of Japanese fighter planes that attempted to interfere with the Mitchell bombers.

Soon enough, both Lt. Tadashi Shizizui over Boram and Comdr. Hideo Shoji over the Wewak Peninsula saw the American planes crossing the coast. Both squadron leaders prepared to attack before radioing an alarm to Wewak. However, these two squadrons of Japanese fighters on CAP would be the only Nippon fighters from the 7th Air Division to engage the American air formations.

Unfortunately for the Japanese, the other four squadrons still on the ground at But, Dagua, and Wewak would not get off before B-25s came skimming over the three airdromes in numbing strafing and parafrag attacks. Capt. Phil Hawkins and wingman Lt. Phil Patton opened the assault on Boram Field, with blistering fire that destroyed three parked planes. They then dropped parafrags that ignited two of the 18th Sentai's 152nd Squadron fighters that were taking off to join Lieutenant Shizizui who was already airborne. The Zeros exploded and blocked the runway. Following planes from the 3rd's 90th and 13th Squadrons zoomed over the airdrome to destroy or damage scores of other planes that were scattered about the runway.

To the north, Col. Don Hall and wingman Lt. William Beck zoomed their B-25s over the Wewak runway to ignite more than a dozen Japanese Bettys, Oscars and Zeros that were scattered in areas beyond the airstrip. The Grim Reapers left four Zeros burning on the runway, so that other 253rd Kokutai fighters and bombers could not take off. Hall and his pilots carried out their raid unmolested because Lt. Col. Meryl Smith and his Satans Angels pilots had effectively kept away Japanese interceptors, while the Grim Reapers carried out their devastating assault. 3rd Attack Group B-25s left Wewak Drome in smoking shambles.

At But Drome, Maj. Howard Paquin swept over the runway with his wingman, Capt. Bob Blair, to open the 38th Bomb Group attack on this target. Paquin and his fellow 71st Squadron pilots caught four Zeros from Lieutenant Commander Iwami's 27th Squadron that were just taking off. The planes exploded in a glob of fiery wrecks, completely blocking the runway. Following Sunsetter pilots then caused more damage with impunity as B-25 nose strafing guns and descending parafrag bombs pelted scattered Japanese aircraft. Lt. Comdr. Joyotara Iwami never got off fighter planes.

By the time the Sunsetters from the 71st Squadron arced away from target, this airdrome on the Wewak coast looked like a raging shoreline fire. Few planes from Captain Saito's 751st Kokutai survived the assault.

These first three B-25 assaults went well, but as Maj. Ralph Celli of the Sunsetter's 405th Squadron came down at Dagua Drome with his squadron, his unit got jumped by Comdr. Hideo Shoji and his pilots of the 26th Oscar Squadron that had been on CAP. One Oscar pilot riddled Capt. Mark Donovan's B-25, damaging the left engine nacelle, the fuselage, and the left wing. But Donovan not only made his run, but he brought the crippled plane home.

Maj. Ralph Celli's plane caught solid cannon shell hits and riddling machine gun hits from two more Oscars. Flames quickly burst out of the smashed right engine and shattered right wing. However, Celli wobbled over the drome, leading his squadron, so that following pilots successfully found the target. Celli ordered his wingman, Lt. Robert Crooks, to take over as the major's own plane arced downward beyond the target and crashed into Wewak Bay. The major survived the crash, was taken prisoner, and sent to Rabaul, where he died of maltreatment at the hands of the Japanese. For his leadership, despite his heavily damaged plane, Maj. Ralph Celli was awarded the Congressional Medal of Honor.

While the B-25s raked the four airdromes at Wewak, the two CAP squadrons of Japanese fighters engaged the US escorting P-38s. But 23 Oscars from Commander Shoji's 26th Squadron and 14 Zeros under Lieutenant Shizizui from the 152nd Squadron were no match for the 85 P-38s that had accompanied the B-25s.

The Japanese fared badly in the heavy dogfights that raged over Wewak as Oscars and Zeros tangled with Lightnings. Chattering machine gun fire, thumping shells, and screaming aircraft engines echoed across the sky. A few of the Japanese on the ground defied possible injury from bomb shrapnel to watch the aerial battles, but they hardly liked what they saw. Both the P-38 fighters and the US pilots were much better than Japanese planes and pilots. The US airmen from the 80th and 9th Squadrons, especially, had wide combat experience while most of the Japanese pilots were raw and hastily trained.

The American pilots made short work of the 37 intercepting Japanese planes. The Satans Angels of the 475th Group alone shot down 15 of the Nippon fighters. Both Tom McGuire and his wingman, Lt. Francis Lent, got two planes each. McGuire downed a Zero with blistering fire that tore off the Zero's wing, and he got his second kill with 20mm shells that hit the Zero cockpit and exploded. Lieutenant Lent tailed one Oscar and ripped the fuselage apart with bursts of machine gun fire. He scored his second kill with exploding 20mm shells that blew away the engine of the Oscar.

The eight surviving Oscars from Shoji's 26th Squadron then scattered, unwilling to tangle further with the aggressive Satans Angels pilots.

In the 80th Squadron, Capt. George Welch got two kills when he shattered one 152nd Squadron Zero with telling 37mm shell hits. He downed his second plane when he ignited the fuel tank of the Zero with incendiary machine gun tracers. From the

9th Squadron, Maj. Jerry Johnson also scored two kills by sending one plane into an uncontrolled spin after shooting off the tail. He chopped off the left wing of his second victim with .50 caliber fire and this second Japanese plane cartwheeled into the jungle.

Totally, the 80th Headhunter Squadron pilots shot down five Zeros, while the 9th Forty-niner Squadron shot down six. The Americans knocked 11 of Lieutenant Shizizui's 14 planes out of the sky and three surviving pilots scooted off to safety.

By 1015 hours on this 18 August morning, the assault on Wewak was over. The American escort pilots had knocked 26 of 37 Japanese planes out of the air. However, the three Mitchell squadrons from the Grim Reaper Group and the two squadrons of B-25s from the Sunsetter Group had taken a much heavier toll on the ground.

In this second assault on Wewak in two days, the 3rd Attack Group destroyed at least 20 planes in their attacks on Wewak and Boram Dromes. One 3rd Group pilot, Capt. John Henebry from the 13th Squadron, had even attacked a tanker in Wewak Harbor with strafing fire and parafrag bombs to leave the oiler listing and smoking.

"I'm sure we sank her," Henebry said later.

For the 38th Bomb Group, the 18 August assaults on But and Dagua represented their finest hour thus far during their ten months of combat in the SWPA. The Sunsetter crews had destroyed at least 25 planes on the ground at But and Dagua while Sunsetter gunners shot three Japanese planes out of the air. For the first time in the Pacific war, the 38th Bomb

Group had topped the efforts of their friendly rivals, the 3rd Attack Group.

The Americans, in turn, had lost three B-25s, two from the 38th Group and one from the 3rd Group. The Americans had also lost five P-38s, three from the 475th Fighter Group and one each from the 80th and 9th Squadrons.

As the American formations headed for home, they had left another holocaust at Wewak, destroying about 80 7th Division planes. When the Japanese took stock again, they would discover that at least another 80 planes had also been severely damaged and they would find only ten serviceable planes on the entire sprawling base. Without doubt, in the two raids on two successive days, the US 5th Air Force had caused the near destruction of the Japanese 7th Air Division.

CHAPTER THIRTEEN

Elation prevailed at Moresby and Buna on the evening of 18 August as US airmen celebrated their victories at Wewak. Conversely, a gloom prevailed at the Japanese base. However, Gen. Yamusi Arisue was determined to carry out the MO II air operation. He again ordered every available man at Wewak to clear away wreckage from the four airdromes and to fill in bomb craters. He also sent an urgent plea to 8th Area Forces headquarters in Rabaul.

"We must have aircraft replacement."

"They are on the way," Adm. Junichi Kusaka of the 25th Air Flotilla answered. "The Wewak resupply convoy is also on the way and should be there in two or three days."

"Good, good," Arisue answered.

Poor weather closed the Bismarck Archipelago on August 19th and 20th, but on the afternoon of the 20th, US recon pilots spotted the Wewak resupply convoy approaching Wewak. The American observers immediately relayed this information to ADVON 5th Air Force headquarters in Port Moresby, and aides here quickly sent the information to Gen. Ennis Whitehead.

"The bastards aren't giving up," Whitehead said to an aide. "Okay, we'll send out the B-25 strafers tomorrow."

"Yes sir."

"I want the same complement that went out on the 18th. The 3rd Group will hit the airfields and the 38th Group will hit the convoy. I want five squadrons of P-38s to escort again. Make up an FO immediately and make sure that all squadron and group commanders get copies."

"Yes sir," the aide said again.

By dark, copies of FO 230 had reached all unit commanders: Col. Don Hall of the 3rd Attack Group, Lt. Col. Meryl Smith of the 475th Fighter Group, Lt. Col. Larry Tanberg of the 38th Bomb Group, Capt. George Welch of the 80th Fighter Squadron, and Maj. Jerry Johnson of the 9th Fighter Squadron. In turn, all five air commanders held briefings on the evening of 20 August for the mission the next day.

By 0600 hours, 21 August, the weather had cleared and the five 5th Air Force units took off: the 38th Bomb Group, 80th Fighter Squadron, and 9th Fighter Squadron from Moresby; the 3rd Attack Group and 475th Fighter Group from Buna. By 0700 hours, the air units had again rendezvoused off the coast of New Guinea over the Vitiaz Strait and then continued on to Wewak. Fifty-one Lightnings from the 475th Group escorted 33 Mitchells from the 3rd Group, while 34 Lightnings from the 80th and 9th Squadrons escorted 21 Mitchells from the 38th

Group.

At 0900 hours, Col. Donald Hall, again the OTC for the attack formations, cried into his radio. "IP in ten minutes. 8th Squadron will hit But, 13th Squadron will hit Wewak, and 90th Squadron will hit Dagua. 38th Group will hit the convoy."

"I read you, Colonel," Lt. Col. Larry Tanberg said. "We'll break off as soon as we reach IP."

The crews aboard the B-25s again rode with a sense of uneasiness. Most of them remembered that Oscars and Zeros had jumped the Americans on the 18th. True, the enemy fighter pilots had not caused excessive losses. However, the Japanese had damaged at least a dozen Mitchells from the 38th and 3rd Groups, while killing or wounding close to a hundred airmen from the two bomber units.

On this 21 August morning, aboard "Pacific Prowler" from the 38th Group's 405th Squadron, waist gunner Sgt. Ed Piper felt nervous. In his experience during combat against the Japanese, he had learned that the enemy usually responded with harsh aggressiveness after a devastating air raid by the Americans. Despite the P-38 escorts, Piper feared that scores of Nippon fighters might jump them as they had on 18 August when the Sunsetters lost Major Celli and one other B-25.

In the top turret of the same "Pacific Prowler," Sgt. George Koch also worried. He remembered the last raid when he saw Major Celli's plane catch fire and then waver precariously over target before crashing into Wewak Bay. "Pacific Prowler" had been lucky to escape hits from Japanese planes that day, but today might be different. He jerked from his musings when he heard the voice of Lt. Bill Travers on the intercom.

"Gunners, stay alert. We've got rumors that the Nips have a skyful of Zeros and Oscars over Wewak."

Koch tightened his face and gripped the triggers of his twin fifties.

Aboard the B-25 "½ Pound Mary," Sgt. Bob Hancock played with his radio dials, trying to pick up something from the Japanese in Wewak. But he heard nothing. Then, he almost laughed, despite his fears. Even if he did hear Japanese garble, he would have not understood it. The waist gunner then turned to his guns and swung his weapons. He could at least fire back if Japanese fighter planes came at him from the starboard side.

In the turret of "½ Pound Mary," Sgt. Will Skinner swung his bubble back and forth, 90 degrees in both directions. All about him he saw other B-25s and the swarms of P-38 fighters. Still, the Lightnings did not leave him relaxed. He too recalled that a dozen Japanese fighter planes had laced them on 18 August, despite the American fighter cover. The Nips could do the same thing today. Skinner also jerked when he got a call from pilot Lt. Bob Crooks.

"Sergeant, is everything okay? Any sign of bandits?"

"No sir, no Japanese planes. All okay here."

"Stay alert."

"Yes sir."

In the 3rd Attack Group, Sgt. Frank Timberlane sat stiffly in the bubble of the Grim Reapers lead plane. He had not seen any Zeros on the 18th as had crewmen from the Sunsetter group. Still, Timberlane also knew that the Japanese tended to respond violently when they got mauled from an American bomber attack. The brass had told them after the 18 August raid that the Japanese air forces at Wewak had been destroyed. Still, the Grim Reaper sergeant realized that the Japanese had plenty of planes in Hollandia and Rabaul, and they could bring them to Wewak quickly if they so desired.

Timberlane again was aboard Colonel Hall's plane that would lead the attack on the Wewak airfields, and this aircraft could be the first B-25 to get jumped by enemy fighters. He checked his guns. They were in good order so he would be as ready as possible.

Aboard the 13th Squadron aircraft of Capt. Don McClellan, Sgt. Woodrow Butler also stared from his bubble, studying the formations of P-38s above him and the hanging B-25s next to him. Wewak Drome was the principal field of the Japanese complex and most of the Nip fighters would probably come out of there. Although Butler had not met any Japanese fighters on the 17th or 18th, he doubted that he would be as fortunate today. The young gunner checked his weapons and tried to settle back in his turret seat.

Aboard Lt. Phil Patton's B-25 in the 90th Squadron, Sgt. Harry Kiser also wore a worried look on his face as his Mitchell roared toward Wewak. He recalled the 18 August raid quite vividly because a dozen Japanese planes had jumped his 90th Squadron formation after they left target. Kiser had seen one B-25 burst into flames and then arc into the jungle. He had also seen several other planes of his squadron suffer damage: punctured fuselages, shot up wings, riddled tails, or disabled engines.

Kiser himself had not fired his guns on that mission for he had not seen a Zero or Oscar. But he knew one thing: if his plane was fatally damaged, he would be dead, for at treetop level he could never escape the aircraft.

Two thousand feet above the B-25s, Capt. Tom McGuire maintained top cover with 16 fellow P-38 pilots from his 475th Group's 431st Squadron. He continually scanned the sky around him, especially upstairs. But thus far, he had seen nothing. McGuire had sent Lt. Francis Lent ahead in a four plane formation to keep an eye out for bandits. But Lent too had yet to see anything.

In the rear top cover formation of P-38s, above the 38th Bomb Group bombers, Capt. George Welch of the 80th Fighter Squadron also kept a steady watch in the skies around him. However, Welch had not seen enemy fighters. He looked at his watch: 0910 hours; ten minutes to IP.

On the right flank of the bombers, Capt. Bill Weldon of the 475th Group's 432nd Squadron had sent three of his P-38s to the north to patrol the starboard section of the 5th Air Force formation. These pilots needed to be alert because the Japanese had major airbases at Gasmata and Arawe on the southern coast of New Britain. Enemy fighter planes could easily come out of there and into the Vitiaz Strait. The starboard scouts had not seen a thing. Apparently the Japanese had no intention of attacking the Americans from the right flank.

On the port side of the droning B-25s, Maj. Daniel

Roberts of the 475th's 433rd Squadron had sent a quartet of P-38s to hug the New Guinea coast. The scouts had been keeping a close watch for any Japanese fighters that might come out of Finchhaven or Madang. Almost every five minutes, Roberts called his scout leader, Capt. William Henning, to ask the same question:

"Any activity along the coast?"

"Nothing, Major," Henning had always replied.

As the Americans continued northwest through the Vitiaz Strait they met no opposition. The US airmen did not know if the Japanese were asleep again, if they had simply run out of planes to challenge, or whether they were waiting for the Americans over Wewak.

Unfortunately for the US airmen, the Japanese *were* waiting for them over Wewak. Gen. Yamusi Arisue had gone for broke. Almost all the planes that had come into Wewak after the 18 August raid were fighters. The 7th Air Division commander believed rightly that the Americans would attack Wewak again, and his first concern was to destroy the American interlopers, especially the B-25s. He had set a priority for fighters in air reinforcements.

By 0900 hours, the Japanese had mounted an astonishing 70 Zeros and Oscars because Arisue had expected a new American attack on this 21 August morning, when the first good weather in three days had come over the Bismarck Archipelago. Further, Arisue had assigned these new fighters to his best air units; Lieutenant Commander Iwami of the 751st Kokutai's 27th Squadron, Lt. Suzuki Yonai of the 253rd Kokutai's 70th Squadron, and Lt. Tadashi Shizizui of the 18th Sentai's 152nd Squadron.

The 3rd Attack Group would find few planes on the ground at the Wewak dromes, but the 38th Bomb Group would reach the target just as the Wewak resupply convoy came into Hansa Bay. The Grim Reapers thus devoted most of their efforts to Wewak installations, while the Sunsetters attacked ships in the bay.

At 0920 hours, A Japanese observation plane radioed 7th Air Division headquarters: "Enemy aircraft approaching Wewak; formation includes both bombers and fighters."

General Arisue acted immediately. "You will notify all squadron leaders to attack at once," he told an aide. "They must destroy the B-25 strafers before these enemy bombers even reach Wewak."

"Yes, Honorable Arisue."

Within five minutes 71 Zeros and Oscars zoomed out to sea to meet the Americans. Another shattering dogfight erupted in the skies over the Bismarck Archipelago. The American escort units included 80 P-38s from the 475th Satans Angels Group, the 80th Headhunter Squadron, and the 9th Forty-niner Squadron. The Americans performed aggressively and capably with the US fighter pilots stopping most of the Japanese pilots from attacking the low flying B-25s.

Gunners aboard the Grim Reaper and Sunsetter Mitchells watched the fighters high above them: zooming, darting, and arcing about the sky. They winced from the echo of screaming engines, chattering machine gun fire, and thumping shells. All gunners were awake and they nervously held the triggers of their guns to shoot at Zeros or Oscars that reached the bombers.

"Keep your formations tight," Col. Don Hall cried into his radio. "Gunners, prepare to defend against interceptors."

Still, despite the dogfights raging above them, both Col. Donald Hall of the 3rd Group and Lt. Col. Larry Tanberg of the 38th Group kept their formations in order and soon broke off to attack their targets.

Colonel Hall expressed disappointment when he saw few planes about the three Wewak Peninsula airdromes. He called his squadron leaders. "If you can't find worthwhile targets about the runways, hit secondary targets."

"Yes sir," Maj. Jim Downs of the 13th Squadron answered.

The three 3rd Group squadrons broke off. Hall took the 8th Squadron over But. However, he only saw a half dozen planes about the airdrome. Within minutes, the Reapers had disposed of these parked aircraft. Then the 8th Squadron pilots zoomed their Mitchells at low level over the area, strafing campsites, dock facilities, buildings, and supply dumps. By the time the 12 planes from this squadron left the area, they had left a mass of fire and smoke in their wake: four buildings destroyed, two wharves flattened, three supply dumps enveloped in flames, and a dozen campsite huts set afire. In the assault nearly 100 Japanese airmen and shoreline sailors had been killed or wounded.

About the Wewak Drome, Maj. Jim Downs of the Grim Reapers' 13th Squadron caused the same kind of damage. After finishing off a mere four planes they saw about the Wewak runway, Downs and his fellow pilots swept over the treetops, looking for targets. They found plenty: several repair shops, campsites, a motor pool, and two large ammunition dumps. At these the Grim Reapers unleashed heavy machine gun fire and parafrag bombs from an altitude of only 50 feet above the ground. By the time the 13th Squadron Mitchells left, more raging fires and dense smoke rose in their wake.

Downs and his pilots had destroyed all of the repair shops, half of the campsites, the entire line of vehicles in the motor pool, and both ammo dumps. Here too the Americans killed or wounded nearly 100 Japanese airmen and soldiers.

Capt. Phil Hawkins swept over Dagua Drome with 13 fellow pilots from the Grim Reapers' 90th Squadron. They did not see a single Japanese plane on the ground. So these airmen also searched for secondary targets. They walloped campsites, supply and warehouses, lines of motor vehicles, AA gun pits, and two fuel dumps. Like the airmen from the other 3rd Group squadrons, Hawkins and his men left a debacle of fire and smoke behind him.

By the time the 3rd Attack Group left the area, little was left at Wewak, only a few parked planes and no important installations.

Over Hansa Bay, Lt. Col. Larry Tanberg of the 38th Bomb Group soon enough saw the array of Sugar Charlie cargo ships zigzagging about the water to avoid the American bombers. Tanberg split his formation, sending his 71st Squadron after transports while he led the 405th Squadron after cargo marus.

The low level strafing and parafrag attacks by the Sunsetters proved as accurate as the Grim Reaper attacks on land targets. Incendiary strafing fire ignited ships, while descending parafrag bombs blew apart superstructures on the small 500 and 1,000 ton marus. The Sunsetter pilots came back again and again to lace the vessels in Hansa Bay. By the time the 21 Mitchells from the 38th Bomb Group arced away from target, they had left four ships listing and sinking and three more marus burning furiously.

The Sunsetter pilots also swept over the shoreline with more strafing fire and parafrags, destroying docks, warehouses and several small craft. The attacks enveloped the entire Hansa Bay shoreline in a ribbon of smoke and fire.

The B-25s had caused widespread damage because they had met little opposition from the scores of Japanese fighters—thanks to US P-38 fighter pilots.

Capt. Tom McGuire of the Satans Angels 431st Squadron, furnishing top cover for the 3rd Group, led 17 pilots in the first clash against the Japanese, 30 planes under Lt. Comdr. Joyotara Iwami of the 751st Kokutai's 27th Squadron. In the darting, zooming dogfight that lasted about ten minutes, McGuire and his pilots shot 14 enemy fighters out of the air for a loss of three P-38s. McGuire himself shot down two planes, ripping away the tail of one aircraft and shattering the fuselage of another. Lt. Francis Lent of the same 431st Squadron also downed a pair of fighters, killing one Japanese pilot with machine gun fire and chopping off the wing of a second Oscar with telling shell hits.

Lieutenant Commander Iwami got two P-38s to run his kill score to sixteen US planes. He downed one Lightning with 20mm shell hits that knocked off the twin tails, and he downed the second with solid hits that ignited both P-38 engines. However, Iwami's scores were small consolation for the serious losses in his squadron and he broke off the fight.

The other Japanese fighter squadrons fared no better. Pilots from the US 9th Squadron, 80th Squadron and the other squadrons from the 475th Group waded into the Zero pilots of the 70th and 152nd Japanese Squadrons with blazing guns and booming cannons. The harsh aerial battles lasted about fifteen minutes with the Japanese losing 21 planes and an equal number damaged. The 9th Squadron lost one P-38 and the 475th Group lost two P-38s, while the 80th Squadron lost no planes.

In this fight on August 21st, the American pilots from the five P-38 squadrons downed 35 Japanese planes. Nearly half of the Japanese Oscars and Zeros had been lost with nearly half of the surviving Nippon fighters damaged.

As the American planes headed home, about a dozen Zeros jumped the B-25s, but the Mitchell gunners destroyed three of them, damaged a few more, and drove off the rest. Sgt. Harry Kiser of the 3rd Attack Group, Sgt. Will Skinner of the 38th Bomb Group, and Sgt. George Koch of the 38th Group had scored the kills.

After the 21 August raid, the Americans had completed the Wewak wipe out. The three attacks by the US 5th Air Force on 17, 18, and 21 August had destroyed 221 Japanese planes on the ground. US fighter pilots had shot an additional 71 planes out of the air, and B-25 gunners had downed 16 planes—a total of 308 Japanese aircraft. Further, the US airmen had wrecked the four Wewak airdromes, along with supply and storage facilities, four ammo dumps, four fuel dumps, several campsites, dock installations, repair shops, and four ships. The formidable Wewak complex lay in shambles.

Although several bomber and fighter units from the 5th Air Force had participated in the Wewak wipe out, only the 3rd Attack Group and the 475th Fighter Group received DUCs for the Wewak aerial campaign. The 90th and 43rd Heavy Bomb Groups, the 38th Bomb Group, the 35th Fighter Group, the 9th Fighter Squadron, and the 8th Fighter Squadron had also made major contributions to the destruction of Wewak that had ended any Japanese threat of a counteroffensive in Papuan New Guinea. However, the Grim Reaper reputation for excellence had no doubt influenced the DUC award; or, perhaps the USAAF believed that the 3rd Attack Group strike on 17 August had been the major blow in reducing Wewak to impotence. Since the 475th Fighter Group pilots had downed most of the Japanese interceptors over and about Wewak, perhaps the USAAF considered the Satans Angels' efforts exceptionally worthwhile.

With the destruction of Wewak, Gen. Douglas MacArthur could now carry out his Eckton II offensive for the occupation of Lae and the Nadzab Valley. Since Australian ground forces from Wau had occasionally made forays within short distances of Salamaua, MacArthur used a ploy by sending a diversionary Aussie force down the trail from Wau toward the Japanese base. The Japanese thus sent the bulk of their 51st Infantry Division, 5,000 men, to Salamaua. The ruse worked, for General Adachi, CinC of the 18th Army, had left only 2500 soldiers and 1,000 naval men at Lae, and many of these were service troops rather than combat troops.

For two days, US 5th Air Force aircraft, including Australian air units, carried out a series of attacks on Lae dock areas, supply areas, ammo dumps, and troop concentrations. On the morning of 4 September 1943, the Allied amphibious force, 7800 men from the Australian 9 Division, landed on the Lae shoreline. A sky full of American and Australian fighter planes kept Japanese air interference to a minimum during the invasion. Only three Japanese bombers reached the landing site, hitting an LCI and killing three American sailors.

The Australians pushed rapidly inland from the beaches, but at 1400 hours, radar men picked up bogies. A squadron of Japanese bombers was approaching the invasion site. However, the 9th Fighter Squadron with 20 P-38s and the US 348th Fighter Group with 23 P-47s intercepted the Japanese formation and shot down 20 of the enemy planes. Still, the Japanese damaged a US destroyer with torpedo hits and destroyed an LST with the loss of 42 men.

Meanwhile, on the same morning of 4 September, the US 54th Troop Carrier Wing dropped the 503rd Parachute Regiment into the Nadzab Valley, 15 miles inland from Lae Harbor. Ironically, the 3rd Attack

Group's 89th Squadron that had not participated in the Wewak strikes, used its A-20 light bombers to furnish an excellent smoke screen for the American paratroopers. Meanwhile, B-25s from the 3rd and 38th Groups strafed and bombed Japanese positions around Nadzab to alleviate any possible resistance against the US airborne troops.

Within 24 hours, Australian ground troops and American airborne troops had overrun Lae, killing most of the 2500 Japanese defenders and driving off the few survivors. The Allies quickly set up strong positions on all trails leading into the Lae-Nadzab area. By the morning of 6 September, both an aviation engineer battalion from the Aussie 7 Division and the US 871st Aviation Battalion had come into Nadzab to begin construction of airstrips. Within two weeks, engineer units had completed two runways that paralleled each other.

By 11 September, the Allied troops had completed occupying the area and they then began an assault on Salamaua. Most of the 6,000 Japanese here, cut off from reinforcements and supplies, had been evacuating at night via submarines and barges, while many more fled into the Owen Stanley jungle hills in the hope of making their way to Madang or Wewak. By 16 September 1943, the Allied troops had occupied Salamaua.

The Capture of Lae had given the Allies an excellent port facility some 200 miles up the coast from Buna, while the occupation of the Nadzab Valley had enabled the US 5th Air Force to construct major airbases within easy striking distance of Japanese bases up the New Guinea coast, including Wewak. Gen.

Douglas MacArthur now had an advanced staging base to assail other Japanese bases in New Guinea and even Gasmata and Arawe on the south coast of New Britain. Further, the successful offensive had given MacArthur control of the Solomon Sea, Huon Gulf, and the Vitiaz Strait.

Gen. Hatazo Adachi, the CinC of the Japanese 18th Army, now realized that any counteroffensives in New Guinea were out of the question. His 50,000 man army could only be used in defensive positions to stop the Allies from coming any further up the New Guinea coast.

"We suffered a serious disaster at Wewak from the August air attacks," Adachi told his Australian captors after the war. "Once more we failed to consider the cunning and ingenuity of the Americans which enabled them to destroy our air force at Wewak at a most opportune moment for them. We had no air power to challenge the invasions of Lae and Salamaua and so we lost these vital bases."

Said Gen. George Kenney, CinC of the 5th Air Force, after the Eckton II successful operation: "I've got the best damn airmen who ever flew in combat. We asked them to fly missions against distant Wewak targets that could have ended in disaster for our bomber crews. However, my boys responded with aggressiveness and determination. With these kinds of combat flyers in my air force, we simply could not lose."

The Wewak wipe out by the U.S. 5th Air Force had broken the stalemate in the New Guinea war. Not only had the victory wiped out the Japanese Air Division, but the air operation had enabled ground forces to occupy Lae and Salamaua, a campaign that had opened the way for further offensives in the SWPA.

"Once the air force knocked out Wewak and the Japanese air force," General MacArthur said, "I knew that we had reached a turning point in the Southwest Pacific, and I knew I was then on the way back to the Philippines."

PARTICIPANTS

Americans

Gen. Douglas MacArthur, CinC, SWPA Forces

Gen. Richard Sutherland, SWPA Forces Chief of Staff

Gen. Sir Thomas Blamey, CinC, New Guinea Force, Port Moresby

Gen. George Lasey, 7 Australian Division

Col. Kenneth Kinsler, 503rd Parachute Regiment

Gen. George Kenney, CinC, Fifth Air Force

Gen. Ennis Whitehead, commander, ADVON 5th Air Force, Port Moresby

Gen. Donald Hutchinson, commander, 1st Air Task Force, New Guinea

871st Airborne Engineer Battalion — Lt. Col. Murray Woodbury

470th Automatic Weapons Battery — Maj. Jim Coburn

3rd Attack Group, Dobodura — Col. Donald Hall

38th Bomb Group, Port Moresby, Lt. Col. Lawrence Tanberg

43rd Bomb Group, Port Moresby, Col. Harry Hawthorne

90th Bomb Group, Port Moresby, Col. Arthur Rogers

35th Fighter Group, Port Moresby, Lt. Col. Malcolm Moore

475th Fighter Group, Buna, Lt. Col. Meryl Smith

9th Fighter Squadron, Maj. Gerald Johnson

80th Fighter Squadron, Capt. George Welch

Australian 60 Battalion, Bulolo, Lt. Col. Robert Marston

Japanese

Gen. Hitoshi Imamura, CinC, 8th Area Forces, Rabaul

Capt. Toshikaze Ohmae, 8th Air Forces Chief of Staff (IJN)

Adm. Junichi Kusaka, CinC, 25th Air Flotilla, Rabaul

Gen. Hatazo Adachi, CinC, 18th Army, Wewak, New Guinea

Gen. Yamusi Arisue, commander, 7th Air Division, Wewak

751st Kokutai (IJN), Capt. Masahisa Saito, But Drome, Wewak

253rd Kokutai (IJN), Comdr. Shuichi Watakazi, Wewak Drome, Wewak

17th Sentai (IJA), Col. Koji Tanaka, Dagua Drome, Wewak

18th Sentai (IJA), Maj. Shinichi Kapaya, Boram Field, Wewak

4th Lae Base Force, Col. Takashi Miyazaki

9th Transportation Fleet, Adm. Takeo Takagi

9th Escort Fleet, Adm. Raizo Tanaka

9th Battle Fleet, Adm. Kuso Morita

BIBLIOGRAPHY

Books

Alcorn, John, *The Jolly Rogers*, Historical Aviation Album publishers, Temple City, Calif. 1981

Birdsall, Steven, *Flying Buccaneers—History of the 5th Air Force*, Doubleday & Co., Garden City, L.I., 1977

Constable, Trevor, and Toliver, Raymond, *Fighter Aces of the USA*, Aero Publishers, Fallbrook, Calif., 1979

Craven, W.F., and Cate, J.L., *The Pacific: Guadalcanal to Saipan*, Univ. of Chicago Press, Chicago, 1950

Dexter, David, *The New Guinea Offensive*, Australian War Memorial, Canberra, 1961

Haugland, Vernon, *The AAF Against Japan*, Chapter 7, "Wewak: the Big Take Out," Harper Bros. Publishers, New York City, 1948

Hess, William, *Pacific Sweep*, Zebra Books, New York City, 1974

Jablonski, Edward, *Air War: Wings of Fire*, Doubleday, New York City, 1971

Jablonski, Edward, *Flying Fortress*, Doubleday & Co., Garden City, L.I., 1965

Johnson, George, *Pacific Partner*, World Book Co., Australia, reprinted by Duell, Sloan, & Pierce, New York City, 1944

Kenney, George, *Kenney Reports*, Chapter 6, "June-August 1943," Duell, Sloan, & Pierce, New York City, 1949

Maurer, Maurer, *Air Force Combat Units of World War II*, USAF History Division, Washington, DC, 1953

Odgers, George, *Air War Against Japan*, Australian War Memorial, Canberra, 1958

Russ, Kenn C., *5th Air Force History*, Historical Aviation Album Publishers, Temple City, Calif., 1973

Sunderman, Major James, *World War II in the Air: The Pacific*, Franklin Watts, New York City, 1962

Toland, John, *The Rising Sun*, Random House, New York City, 1970

Archive Records

All archive records from the U.S. Air Force Historical Library, Maxwell Field, Alabama.

AMERICAN

Action Reports:
ADVON 5th Air Force, August 1943
Allied 5th Air Force Narrative Report, July–August 1943
ADVON 5th Air Force FO 70, 4 September 1943
V AF Service Command (Fraser narrative)
CinC, SWPA, Lae Operation, dated 23 October 1943
Report by 7 Australian Division, Operation Outlook, Lae
Report by Major A.J. Beck, "Paratroop Drop at Nadzab," 5 September 1943

Mission Reports:
38th Bomb Group
#228, 17 August 1943
#229, 18 August 1943
#234, 21 August 1943
Combat Chart #6, Wewak
3rd Attack Group
#624, 17 August 1943
#625, 18 August 1943
#627, 21 August 1943

Histories:
  3rd Attack Group—August 1943
  38th Bomb Group—August 1943
  43rd Bomb Group—August 1943
  90th Bomb Group—August 1943
  35th Fighter Group—July–August 1943
  475th Fighter Group—12–26 August 1943
  9th Fighter Squadron—August 1943
  80th Fighter Squadron—August 1943

Narratives: Report of Wewak mission by Capt. Tom
  McGuire, Capt. William Weldon, and Capt.
  William Henning, 475th Fighter Group

Biographic Sketches:
  Gen. Ennis Whitehead
  Col. Harry Hawthorne
  Maj. Don McCullar

JAPANESE

Diary of Operational Statistics — 7th Air Division, July–August 1943, by Col. Rinsuka Keneko

USSBS (US Strategic Bombing Survey postwar interviews)

Capt. Takashi Mino — 25th Air Flotilla chief of staff

Capt. Toshikaze Ohmae — 8th Area Forces chief of staff

#194, Comdr. Shuichi Watakazi, 14 Oct. 1945

#440, Col. Kinsuka Keneko, 21 Nov. 1945

#445, Gen. Hatazo Adachi, 26 Nov. 1945

#451, Col. Koji Tanaka, 26 Nov. 1945

#461, Gen. Hitoshi Imamura, 28 Nov. 1945

#497, Capt. Takashi Miyazaki, 2 Dec. 1945

Interviews

Retired Gen. Lawrence Tanberg, former commander, 38th Bomb Group

Retired Gen. Donald Hutchinson, former Air Task Force commander, 5th Air Force

James Gallager, 49th Fighter Group Association

Magazine articles

Fraser, Everett, *Impact Magazine*, October 1943, "A Tribute to Aviation Engineers"

Dawes, Allen, *Yank Magazine*, 24 Aug. 1943, "Jap Wewak Base No Longer a Target"

Maps: US Air Force Historical Center Library, Maxwell Field, Alabama

Photos: US Air Force Historical Center Library, Maxwell Field Alabama

National Archives (Izawa collection of Japanese) Washington, DC

38th Bomb Group Association

Mr. Matthew Gac, Rochester, NY

ACKNOWLEDGEMENT

I would like to extend my appreciation to Retired Generals Lawrence Tanberg and Donald Hutchinson, Mr. Matthew Gac, Mr. Ken Darrow (all formerly of 5th Air Force), as well as the 49th Fighter Group Association and 38th Bomb Group Association. I would also like to thank Mr. Cargill Hall and his staff at the USAF Historical Center at Maxwell Field.

And finally, I would like to thank my wife Frances who helped me to study reams of archive records in researching for this book.

THE BEST IN ADVENTURE FROM ZEBRA

WAR DOGS   (1474, $3.50)
by Nik-Uhernik

Lt. Justin Ross molded his men into a fearsome fighting unit, but it was their own instincts that kept them out of body bags. Their secret orders would change the destiny of the Vietnam War, and it didn't matter that an entire army stood between them and their objective!

WAR DOGS #2: M-16 JURY   (1539, $2.75)
by Nik-Uhernik

The War Dogs, the most cutthroat band of Vietnam warriors ever, face their greatest test yet—from an unlikely source. The traitorous actions of a famous American could lead to the death of thousands of GIs—and the shattering end of the . . . WAR DOGS.

GUNSHIPS #1: THE KILLING ZONE   (1130, $2.50)
by Jack Hamilton Teed

Colonel John Hardin of the U.S. Special Forces knew too much about the dirty side of the Vietnam War—he had to be silenced. And a hand-picked squad of mongrels and misfits were destined to die with him in the rotting swamps of . . . THE KILLING ZONE.

GUNSHIPS #2: FIRE FORCE   (1159, $2.50)
by Jack Hamilton Teed

A few G.I.s, driven crazy by the war-torn hell of Vietnam, had banded into brutal killing squads who didn't care whom they shot at. Colonel John Hardin, tapped for the job of wiping out these squads, had to first forge his own command of misfits into a fighting FIRE FORCE!

GUNSHIPS #3: COBRA KILL   (1462, $2.50)
by Jack Hamilton Teed

Having taken something from the wreckage of the downed Cobra gunship, the Cong force melted back into the jungle. Colonel John Hardin was going to find out what the Cong had taken—even if it killed him!

Available wherever paperbacks are sold, or order direct from the Publisher. Send cover price plus 50¢ per copy for mailing and handling to Zebra Books, 475 Park Avenue South, New York, N.Y. 10016. DO NOT SEND CASH.

NEW ADVENTURES FROM ZEBRA

THE BLACK EAGLES:
HANOI HELLGROUND   (1249, $2.95)
by John Lansing

They're the best jungle fighters the United States has to offer, and no matter where Charlie is hiding, they'll find him. They're the greatest unsung heroes of the dirtiest, most challenging war of all time. They're THE BLACK EAGLES.

THE BLACK EAGLES #2:
MEKONG MASSACRE   (1294, $2.50)
by John Lansing

Falconi and his Black Eagle combat team are about to stake a claim on Colonel Nguyen Chi Roi—and give the Commie his due. But American intelligence wants the colonel alive, making this the Black Eagles' toughest assignment ever!

THE BLACK EAGLES #3:
NIGHTMARE IN LAOS   (1341, $2.50)
by John Lansing

There's a hot rumor that Russians in Laos are secretly building a nuclear reactor. And the American command isn't overreacting when they order it knocked out—quietly—and fast!

MCLEANE'S RANGER #2:
TARGET RABAUL   (1271, $2.50)
by John Darby

Rabaul—it was one of the keys to the control of the Pacific and the Japanese had a lock on it. When nothing else worked, the Allies called on their most formidable weapon—McLeane's Rangers, the jungle fighters who don't know the meaning of the word quit!

SWEET VIETNAM   (1423, $3.50)
by Richard Parque

Every American flier hoped to blast "The Dragonman," the ace North Vietnamese pilot, to pieces. Major Vic Benedetti was no different. Sending "The Dragonman" down in a spiral of smoke and flames was what he lived for, worked for, prayed for—and might die for . . .

Available wherever paperbacks are sold, or order direct from the Publisher. Send cover price plus 50¢ per copy for mailing and handling to Zebra Books, 475 Park Avenue South, New York, N.Y. 10016. DO NOT SEND CASH.

McLEANE'S RANGERS
by John Darby

#1: BOUGAINVILLE BREAKOUT   **(1207, $2.50)**
Even the Marines call on McLeane's Rangers, the toughest, meanest, and best fighting unit in the Pacific. Their first adventure pits the Rangers against the entire Japanese garrison in Bougainville. The target—an ammo depot invulnerable to American air attack . . . and the release of a spy.

#2: TARGET RABAUL   **(1271, $2.50)**
Rabaul—it was one of the keys to the control of the Pacific, and the Japanese had a lock on it. When nothing else worked, the Allies called on their most formidable weapon—McLeane's Rangers, the fearless jungle fighters who didn't know the meaning of the word quit!

#3: HELL ON HILL 457   **(1343, $2.50)**
McLeane and his men make a daring parachute drop in the middle of a heavily fortified Jap position. And the Japs are dug in so deep in a mountain pass fortress that McLeane may have to blow the entire pass to rubble—and his men in the bargain!

#4: SAIPAN SLAUGHTER   **(1510, $2.50)**
Only McLeane's elite commando team had the skill—and the nerve—to go in before the invasion of Saipan and take on that key Jap stronghold. But the Japs have set a trap—which will test the jungle fighters' will to live!

NEW ADVENTURES FROM ZEBRA

DEPTH FORCE   (1355, $2.95)
by Irving A. Greenfield

Built in secrecy and manned by a phantom crew, the *Shark* is America's unique high technology submarine whose mission is to stop the Russians from dominating the seas. If in danger of capture the *Shark* must self-destruct—meaning there's only victory or death!

DEPTH FORCE #2: DEATH DIVE   (1472, $2.50)
by Irving A. Greenfield

The *Shark*, racing toward an incalculable fortune in gold from an ancient wreck, has a bloody confrontation with a Soviet killer sub. Just when victory seems assured, a traitor threatens the survival of every man aboard—and endangers national security!

THE WARLORD   (1189, $3.50)
by Jason Frost

The world's gone mad with disruption. Isolated from help, the survivors face a state in which law is a memory and violence is the rule. Only one man is fit to lead the people, a man raised among the Indians and trained by the Marines. He is Erik Ravensmith, THE WARLORD—a deadly adversary and a hero of our times.

THE WARLORD #2: THE CUTTHROAT   (1308, $2.50)
by Jason Frost

Though death sails the Sea of Los Angeles, there is only one man who will fight to save what is left of California's ravaged paradise. His name is THE WARLORD—and he won't stop until the job is done!

THE WARLORD #3: BADLAND   (1437, $2.50)
by Jason Frost

His son has been kidnapped by his worst enemy and THE WARLORD must fight a pack of killers to free him. Getting close enough to grab the boy will be nearly impossible—but then so is living in this tortured world!

Available wherever paperbacks are sold, or order direct from the Publisher. Send cover price plus 50¢ per copy for mailing and handling to Zebra Books, 475 Park Avenue South, New York, N.Y. 10016. DO NOT SEND CASH.